I'M
WATCHING
YOU

An unputdownable psychological thriller
with a breathtaking twist

AMANDA BRITTANY

Joffe Books, London
www.joffebooks.com

First published in Great Britain in 2022

Cover art by Nick Castle

ISBN: 978-1-80405-552-6

For Noah and Erin — the magic in my life.

PART ONE: 2009

CHAPTER ONE

Charlotte

Friday, 12 June 2009

Rain hammers against the grubby window, as the train rumbles its way towards Ensley. My body is still, but my mind whirrs — darting through my life as though I'm drowning.

I bring my thoughts back to the moment, my gaze turning to Ryan and Mia sitting opposite. My heart aches at everything I've got so wrong. How we've travelled together on an eighteen-year journey through hell.

They are next to each other, the gap between them four, maybe five inches, but they are miles apart.

I think of their birth. Perhaps it's the sight of a mother several seats away, a contented baby snuggled in her arms, that's provoked this thought. Ryan catapulted into the world first, eyes too big for his face. He grew into those eyes later — my handsome boy. Mia was dragged free with forceps, the midwife panicking that my daughter may be starved of oxygen, though insisting, once the bald bundle with the wrinkled face was plopped into my arms, that she was fine, absolutely fine — totally fine. I wonder now if she was. If the damage was done before she even left my body.

Mia's vivid blue eyes are pinned to her phone. She's slumped low in her seat, the collar of her green coat turned up like a protective barrier, as she twiddles a strand of dark hair around her index finger, so tight it turns her flesh creamy white.

Ryan is tense, fists clenched, the scar on the back of his hand stretched, shiny across his young flesh. His hatred for his twin sister is tangible, and I don't blame him in some ways — his anger is justified. But she's still my girl.

Mia glances up, meets my eye, and I turn away from her intrusion, fix my eyes on the bubbles of rain sliding sideways across the window.

A train storms down the track in the opposite direction, and my body leaps, a pain shooting down my thigh. Gordon threw me against the wall six months ago, broke my leg in three places. I've been told I may have a permanent limp. I thank God every day that he's gone.

'She won't want us.' Mia's voice is low and even. 'You know that, yet you make us come.' She doesn't want to live in Ensley with her gran. She was happy with Gordon. They had a strange sort of bond I could never quite understand.

I pull my eyes reluctantly back to my daughter — pale, her hair long, the ends split. She's right. Mother won't want us sharing her space for long. But we've nowhere else to go. Gordon's farm went to his brother, an equally cruel man, who threw us out before Gordon's body was scooped off the rocks below Ridley Point.

Mia and Ryan should be old enough now to find their own way in life — I did at their age — but mentally neither is equipped. My fault, I know. In fairness, Ryan has got himself a job lined up on a construction site near Ensley. That's something, I suppose. At least he's trying, which is more than Mia will ever do.

'Staying with gran will be temporary,' I say, not for the first time, always aware of the northern accent that we all picked up from Gordon. 'Until we can find somewhere better.'

My mind flashes to Willow Nook Cottage where I grew up — the stunning view of Quarry Lake from my childhood bedroom window. We won't stay long. Mother won't allow it. And anyway, I don't want to be with her any longer than we have to.

Mia shoves her phone in her pocket. Anyone looking on would think she's a normal teenage girl, but she's far from it. I knew she was wired wrong from a very young age. Watched on through the years as those wires kept on crossing. I should have done more.

My eyes drift once more to Ryan's scar. At the age of seven, Mia sliced his hand with a knife. She said Ryan had taken her sweets.

'Good for Mia, fighting her corner,' Gordon said, as Ryan screamed and clung to me, petrified, his blood covering my pale-blue dress. 'He's such a little wimp. Needs a firm hand. You're ruining him, Charlotte.' We lied at the hospital. Told them Ryan had cut himself on one of Gordon's tools. Swore the confused, crying boy to secrecy, said he would lose his sister if anyone knew the truth. I regret that now.

Six months after that I saw smoke billowing from Mia's bedroom. I found her sitting cross-legged on the floor, her dolls melting in a heap in front of her, their hair on fire. I was frozen for a moment, the fumes catching in my throat, the smell of burning rubber acrid. 'I'm too old for dolls,' she said, so calm, as she looked up at me with a twisted smile. Only a porcelain doll with long dark hair survived that day. She still takes it everywhere, as though it's her only friend.

I should have got help for my daughter years ago, but then, in my defence, she would go for months, sometimes years without doing anything to worry me, and Gordon would insist she was fine, that he admired her because she knew exactly what she wanted and took it. *Much like him*. The school, apart from saying she was a quiet girl without many friends, never picked up on that side of Mia. So I locked my fears away and threw away the key, believing that despite her inability to make friends, and the way she spent hours in her room alone, that all was well. That Gordon's abuse and his cruel ridicule of Ryan were enough to contend with. It was only a few weeks back that my husband told my boy he was a nerd because his favourite film was *Iron Man*, and then smacked him around the head with his large, rough hand, telling him there's no such thing as superheroes — that nobody is ever going to save him.

Ryan sees where my eyes have landed. Shoves his scarred hand into his pocket. I give an involuntary shake of my head. It's all too late now.

'We're here,' I say, as the train screeches to a halt at Ensley Station and the familiarity of my childhood village washes over me. The echo of Mother's voice nineteen years ago bounces into my head uninvited: *You must have an abortion, Charlotte.*

The twins rise to their feet at the same moment, tall and slim, grabbing their cases from the overhead compartments. Ryan handing me mine.

We disembark and, walking in single file, rain hammering our hooded jackets, drag our bags over the metal bridge and into the pretty, quaint village of Ensley in Hertfordshire. I'm at the rear, smaller, limping, trying to keep up with my children's long strides, feeling so much older than my thirty-seven years.

I stop and take a breath, scanning the High Street: Lola's café, the micro-supermarket, the Fox. Not much has changed here, but I'm a completely different person now.

It's a five-minute walk to Willow Nook Cottage. A new beginning, but with the same old hurdles that have made me stumble all my life.

I wonder sometimes, in this skin I've been given, if it will ever be possible to be happy.

CHAPTER TWO

Riona

Friday, 19 June 2009

The young woman hovering outside Lola's as I reach the High Street follows me into the café.

It's 7.30 a.m. My boss likes me to open up early to catch trade from commuters on their way to the station. I don't mind. It makes me feel important, grown up, and it won't be for much longer. I'll soon be leaving boring Ensley for university, and I can't wait.

I reach the counter and pick up my yellow-spotted apron, conscious of the young woman now hovering behind me, far too close. I turn. Her long dark hair is unruly, the ends split, her skin chalk white, like a porcelain doll. A grubby canvas bag dangles over her shoulder, hanging against her hip. Her stare makes me uneasy, though I can't explain why.

I fake smile and tie my apron. The tick of the clock echoes loud. The café feels claustrophobic. *What's up with you, Riona?*

'There's something going on up near the gates that lead to Quarry Lake,' she says, as I switch on the coffee machine and it hisses to life. 'People are gathering.'

My eyes flash towards the window, unsure what I expect to see. The sun is bright, the road empty, as it often is when I first arrive.

She glances over her shoulder, curls a tendril of hair around her finger. 'Women are gossiping,' she says, and I detect an accent. 'Huddled together like clucking hens.' She bites down on her lip, pauses for a moment, as though savouring her words. 'Coffee, please.'

'Of course, yes.' I take a mug from the rack.

She unbuttons her coat to reveal a shabby grey tracksuit before turning and heading for a seat by the window. She sits, drops her bag at her feet. I pour a mug of coffee and take it over, looking towards the door, hoping for another customer to appear. 'I haven't seen you in here before, have I?'

She shakes her head. 'We arrived in Ensley a week ago. I hate it here. I was happy in Yorkshire with Gordon.' She takes the coffee from me, sips, her eyes back on the window, seeming to see past the swirling gold lettering spelling out Lola's name.

'Gordon?'

Her gaze returns to me. 'My stepfather. He's dead now.' She sounds calm, but there's something in her tone, sadness perhaps, though I can't be sure — her staring blue eyes give nothing away. 'I'm Mia Carter.'

'Riona Foley.'

'I don't normally get up this early. It was the scream that woke me.'

'Scream?'

'Mmm, around six thirty. A woman with a dog by the lake — I saw her from the bedroom window of Gran's cottage, fumbling with her phone, looking quite distraught.'

My heart rate picks up speed. 'What's happened, do you know?'

She raises an eyebrow, her stare challenging. 'Maybe she found a dead body.'

Sirens pierce the air, getting closer. Two police cars race past the café window, and my curiosity gets the better of me.

'I need to close up,' I say, removing my apron, and throwing it over the back of a chair.

Mia takes a gulp of her coffee. 'You want to investigate, Riona?'

Truth is, my adrenaline is fizzing, and I don't much want to stick around here if there's been a murder. 'I want to know what's happened, is all.'

She picks up her bag, stares at me for a moment, a tightness about her jaw, before putting the mug down. 'This is real life, Riona, not a TV drama.' She rises, heads for the door, opens it and steps into the bright morning without another word.

As the door closes behind her, I pull out my phone and message my friend Stacey, knowing she'll want to know if something exciting is happening in boring Ensley. She thrives on drama.

* * *

As I approach the gathered crowd, I see my aunt. Short, plump, her cropped dark hair standing on end, her phone pinned to her ear. She's a detective sergeant, and I doubt I'll get close enough to ask her what's going on.

Two police cars block off the entrance to Quarry Lake, and uniformed detectives are busy cordoning off the area with tape. I imagine it's the same at the other end of the lake. Whatever's happened, it's serious.

I recognise a few villagers and glimpse Mia standing alone some distance away, her arms folded across her body. I move behind a tall man, hoping, for a reason I can't fathom, that she won't see me.

'Yikes! What the hell's going on?'

I spin round to see Stacey, free of make-up for a change — the sprinkling of freckles she normally attempts to hide, visible across her perfect nose, her red hair pulled up in a high ponytail.

'I think someone's been murdered,' I whisper, putting two and two together and making five. My tone is upbeat, the words I'm saying not registering.

'Go ask your aunt, she'll know.' Stacey gives my back a push, and I stumble forwards into the man I was hiding behind, apologising quickly when he turns and glares at me.

'She's busy,' I say to Stacey, once the man has released me from his stare. 'I can't.' I love my aunt, who took my sister and me in when we were eight, but there's a lot of difference between Aunt Bernie and her alter ego Detective Sergeant Foley.

We move closer, and I notice Mia has been joined by a woman in her late thirties with tight blonde curls. She takes Mia's hand and they turn and head away, the older woman limping. 'She told me she heard a scream by the lake,' I say to Stacey, pointing at Mia. 'She saw someone with a dog. On her phone, apparently, probably calling the police.'

'She looks a bit of a weirdo, don't you think?'

'Mia?' I shrug. 'She's OK.' But I'm not sure I believe my words. I hadn't felt comfortable around her in the café.

'Riona!' My aunt is heading towards us with a snippy look on her face, her stride quick and confident. 'Riona, aren't you meant to be at work?'

'I just—'

'Trust me, Riona, you don't want to be here. Get back to the café, please.'

'Fine,' I say, in my best sulky voice. 'But what's—?'

'Go. Now.' Bernie turns and strides towards the gates leading to the lake, disappearing through them and out of view.

I turn to leave, but Stacey grabs my arm. 'You're not going, are you? Stay. She won't know.'

'Lola's coming to the café at nine thirty.' I shake free from her grip. 'She'll be annoyed if she finds me bunking off.'

'You're a total wimp, Riona,' she calls after me as I walk away, ignoring her. *Breaking rules and sod the consequences* might be Stacey's motto, but it isn't mine.

CHAPTER THREE

Bernie

Tuesday, 28 July 2009

Inspector Blake goes through everything we have on the case once more, but there's nothing new. The meeting is a complete waste of time, and he knows it. The Ensley Killer is still free, and we are no closer to catching him than we were a month ago.

I stare up at the photos of the three young women pinned to the whiteboard, remove my glasses and rub my tired eyes. This case is consuming my every waking hour.

The first victim, eighteen-year-old Kerry Ann White, was found dead by Quarry Lake on the nineteenth of June by a dog walker. It was a frenzied attack. She was bludgeoned over the head repeatedly with what forensics are sure was a hammer. We suspect the weapon is at the bottom of the lake, though divers have yet to find it. It seems Kerry Ann was knocked unconscious with the first blow. She wouldn't have suffered after that, thank God. There was no sign of sexual assault.

Breaking the awful news to her father at his house near Tring had been right up there with the worst experiences of my life. I saw my father cry when my brother died ten years ago in a car accident, saw his pale grey eyes shimmer with tears, his chin crinkle, but I'd never seen a man sob the way Colin White had when we told him his daughter had been murdered. The news had broken him.

Now, from where I'm perched on the edge of a desk, I scan the photos. All three women were in their late teens, dark haired. Whoever this person is, they seem to have a type. One of the women is still in a coma, the other escaped unscathed physically. Both luckier than Kerry Ann White, some might say. Although I'm sure they don't feel lucky.

'So we know the assailant wore a yellow hi-vis jacket on two occasions,' the inspector reminds us, tapping a whiteboard pen against his mouth. The lid is off and black spots of ink appear on his lips and unshaven chin. Nobody laughs. 'A witness to the second attack and the third victim both agree on that.'

Inspector Blake is a strong man in his mid-thirties, but he's slipping. His eyes, cradled with dark cushions, are bloodshot, his shirt grubby around the collar, crinkled as though it hasn't seen an iron in months. This case is getting to him. It's getting to us all.

'So, the second attack,' Blake goes on, pointing at a picture of the young woman who is still in a coma. She looks carefree, happy, and I fight down a surge of sadness. *'It was taken in Greece last summer,'* her mother told me through painful tears, when she handed me the photo, making me promise to return it.

'As we know,' Blake continues, 'the assault took place just inside the entrance of Quarry Lake at 8 p.m. on the fifteenth of July. Two passers-by saw our survivor lying on the ground, someone in a yellow hi-vis standing over her, with what looked like a hammer in their hand. The perpetrator ran towards the lake as the couple approached. They called the police. Stayed until an ambulance arrived.'

'Anything on her laptop yet?' I ask.

'The tech team has said she'd been on a free website called *Let Love Find You.*' He rolls his eyes, clearly unimpressed, rubbing his forehead with so much force his fingertips turn white. 'But whoever she'd been talking to, their account's been deleted. Foley, can you get onto the dating site as soon as? They may still have data on this person, whoever they are.'

'On it,' I say, jotting the info in my notepad.

He pauses for a moment, his gaze moving to the photograph of Clare Marsden, the third victim. It shows her snuggling with a ginger cat, her eyes bright, her smile wide. 'We know Clare arranged to meet someone calling himself Oliver Jones on the twenty-fourth of July,' he says. 'She met him on the same free dating site, though we suspect the name is fake. Clare's been in a state of trauma since it happened, can't remember much about the night she was assaulted, other than waiting at the entrance of Quarry Lake for this so-called Oliver Jones. She recalls someone approaching in a yellow hi-vis, but didn't connect whoever it was with the guy she'd planned to meet. She was on her phone, barely looked up. Didn't see their face, and was grabbed and dragged a few yards, but thankfully, being good at martial arts, she got away and ran. Once home, she joined the dots, realising it was similar to the other attacks in Ensley she'd read about.

I nod. It's seems likely to me, and probably everyone in the meeting room, that some bloke has paraded as a fictitious man to lure women to Quarry Lake.

'So, I'm guessing if the dating profile of this Oliver Jones, whoever he is, is deleted we've got nothing much to go on?' a young DC says.

'Clare took a screenshot of the bloke she was going to meet—'

'And?' I say, hopeful.

Blake shakes his head, pins a photo of a blond, handsome man with a neat beard to the board. 'Stock image, I'm afraid. This phantom bloke has gone all out to disguise his identity. However, Clare does recall a bit about his profile — though how true it is, we don't know. Apparently he liked heavy metal music, and his favourite film is *Iron Man*.'

'Sounds like a good percentage of young men,' I say, hearing the defeat in my voice.

'Indeed. And, as I say, it's probably fiction if the photo is anything to go by. Hopefully we'll get some data from the site. Maybe an IP address for our offender.'

'Any leads with Kerry Ann White?'

'Nothing,' he says, shaking his head. 'She doesn't really fit with the idea of online dating, if we're to believe her father.'

My mind drifts once more to Colin White. I caught up with him again last week at Luton Airport, where he works as a member of the ground crew.

'My Kerry Ann would never be foolish enough to meet up with a stranger she met online,' he said through more tears, fidgeting with his chunky gold bracelet with trembling fingers. 'She didn't even own a computer or phone.'

He told me how his wife had died three years ago from cancer, that the two of them — he and *his Kerry Ann* — were closer than they had ever been. The loss of Kerry Ann's mother had bonded them. *Kerry Ann always told me everything. She's a good girl.* I felt for him. Though I couldn't help thinking it's unusual for a young woman not to have a phone or computer. Had there been things Kerry Ann kept from her father?

Inspector Blake ends the meeting, pressing his hands over his face as officers drift from the room.

I approach my desk, flop down into the swivel chair and stare at the photo of Riona and Alene when they were children that I really should update. I can't help worrying about them, and I doubt they tell me everything, just as Kerry Ann White probably didn't tell her father things he might not want to hear. But I know, despite wanting to, I can't wrap them up in cotton wool. They must live their lives, be strong and confident. But at eighteen, I'm aware they haven't got the same kind of self-preservation that they'll get as they grow older. It's Riona I worry about the most. She hangs about with Stacey Roberts, who has no limits to what she might do for thrills — not surprising with her upbringing. Truth is, I'll be glad when Riona goes off to university and gets away from Stacey's influence. But until then it's my job to protect my nieces. It's my job to protect my girls. Then again, Colin White undoubtedly thought the same about his daughter.

It's around 7.30 p.m., when I leave the station. It's still warm out, the sun low in the sky. I'm exhausted, my white blouse crumpled, and I detect a tang of body odour I'm not proud of. I need a shower and a good night's sleep if I hope to be on the ball tomorrow. I head towards my car, press the fob to release the central locking.

'Sergeant Foley.'

I recognise the voice and turn to see Colin White climbing out of a red Fiesta. He heads towards me.

'Mr White,' I say.

He's average height, bland-looking, I suppose, with the kind of face you would struggle to remember. The most distinctive thing about it is the heavy bags that cradle his eyes. As he approaches he loosens his tie as though it's choking him and undoes the top button on his short-sleeved shirt, which stretches across his rotund stomach. It looks new, sharp creases from its packaging visible. 'I've been waiting for you,' he says. 'Is there any news?'

I so want to give him hope, but we have nothing yet. I slowly shake my head. 'I'm sorry. We've got a few leads we're following up, but—'

'You have nieces,' he says. 'How would you feel if it was one of them?'

I'm not sure how he knows about Riona and Alene, but I'm acutely aware of how I would feel. 'I know how painful this is for you, Mr White. And we're doing everything in our power to catch whoever did it.'

His grey eyes fill with tears, and I find myself floundering, ashamed by the relief I feel when he turns and walks away, heading back to his car, his shoulders rounded, slumped under the pain he's carrying.

14

CHAPTER FOUR

Riona

Friday, 14 August 2009

Erika's voice is pretty and tuneful, my own vocals lower, folky, as we sit cross-legged in the darkness, singing my father's Irish ballad.

'Enough, already!' Stacey hates us singing together, can't bear being left out of anything. 'You sound like a couple of strangled cats.'

We stop mid-chorus, exchanging brief glances and raising our eyebrows. Stacey always wants to be the centre of everything. I suppose we tolerate her green-eyed monster in the name of friendship, but sometimes, like now, she grinds on me.

I stretch my arms above my head, yawning, wanting the evening to end. It's gone eleven and there's a chill in the air, after what's been a beautiful summer's day. I don't want to be here, sitting in the dark by Quarry Lake where Kerry Ann White was murdered and two other young women were attacked. I blame Stacey for encouraging us, for playing on our morbid curiosity — perhaps I'm too easily led. My aunt seems to think so.

'Oh come on,' Stacey had said after our night out, buying a two-litre bottle of cider from the off-licence and dragging us through the iron gates that lead here. 'I don't want this evening to end.'

Apart from a snag of crime scene tape caught on the branch of a tree, fluttering in the light breeze, and several bunches of long-dead flowers, there are no other reminders of the terrible tragedy that occurred here in June.

Stacey picks up the cheap cider, tilts her head back as she takes a long swig.

'Do you think he'll attack again?' I say, my eyes flicking around the area.

Erika draws her mouth into a thin straight line, bites her lip, the thought clearly making her uneasy. 'Maybe. Or hopefully he's taken off, realised your aunt was moving in on him.'

She isn't though. Aunt Bernie and the team of officers on the case have no new leads. I know because she sits downstairs in the early hours, her head in her hands, a tumbler of gin by her side, as though she can't cope with the burden. By morning, she appears strong once more, determined she'll 'catch the bastard', but her skin is blotchy, her eyes saggy. She's not herself at all.

A sudden movement behind us in the surrounding trees makes my heart thump. Twigs crack. I swing round. 'Christ, what was that?' Trees sway, their branches creaking. *What the hell am I doing here?* If Aunt Bernie knew, she would go ballistic. She'd insisted I shouldn't hang out anywhere isolated long before the murder, and I'm beginning to realise there's a big difference between being a rebellious teenager and a complete idiot.

'Did you hear that?' I whisper, when more twigs crack. Whoever is out there, they are moving further away from us.

'A deer maybe.' Stacey's pupils shrink to pinpoints as she flashes zigzag beams across the dense trees with her torch.

'Or a ghost?' Erika's face pales. She's always had an irrational fear of the supernatural. Stacey and I saw *Twilight* at the cinema, and we've read all the books — it's our thing — but Erika refuses to watch or read anything remotely creepy.

'I'm more worried about a real-life predator,' I say, my voice shaky. 'Maybe we should make a move.'

'You think it could be the killer?' Erika's eyes widen.

'I don't know, but we shouldn't stick around to find out.'

'You're both being ridiculous,' Stacey says. 'It's like I said, an animal or something. Or perhaps it *is* a ghost.' She wiggles her fingers, making ghost-like noises, moving towards Erika.

'Shut up.' Erika pushes her away.

The area definitely feels creepy, though I don't believe in ghosts. I've never believed the stories, even as a child, that Ensley Wood is haunted by those who have lost their lives in Quarry Lake over the years.

I look at my friends. This really isn't what I want from life. We've finished our A levels, about to embark on an adult world. Sitting by Quarry Lake sharing secrets and cider really doesn't appeal anymore.

I rise, pull my jacket around me and move towards the lake's edge, shining my torch towards the black water. The stillness is mesmerising. The bleeps of a thousand crickets and an owl hooting in the distance make my spine tingle. I stand for some time, looking across the water at the unused boathouse. A light flickers in the window, a candle perhaps.

The full moon appears from behind a cloud, highlighting the white cliffs opposite. It's a sheer five-metre drop into the water from the clifftop. It's over there that the lake is at its deepest. I jumped in when I was fifteen, egged on by Stacey, regretting the difficulty I got into once I hit the surprisingly freezing water. I survived Quarry Lake. I was one of the lucky ones. Not everyone has. It's lethal below the surface.

I return my gaze to the boathouse, where a light still flickers, as clouds move across the moon once more, wondering who lit the candle and why.

* * *

'Where's Ryan?'

I look up from the book I'm reading to see Mother standing in the bedroom doorway, her dressing gown tied tight, her greying hair loose to her shoulders. She hates that we're here, invading her space.

'No idea,' I say.

'You should be watching him, Charlotte.' She tilts her head like a bird, wraps her arms around her skinny body, giving the appearance she's in a straitjacket. 'Don't you think it's odd that there have been three attacks in Ensley since you arrived?'

I slam my book closed, acting horrified by her suggestion, yet my own niggles of doubt have crept in. Ryan works on a construction site. His yellow hi-vis jacket hangs in the cupboard in the hall — the kind the killer wore. And he acts so closed off, mysterious, disappearing, not saying where he's been. I push down my fears, but still they bubble up, spilling over. I move to the edge of the bed.

Mother shrugs. 'Well, I obviously don't know the twins like you do, but—'

'You don't know them at all.'

'Because you left, Charlotte — moved in with that man.'

'You threw me out.' Is her memory of events so different to mine? 'I had no choice but to accept Gordon's offer. He promised to take care of me and the babies.' His name burns on my tongue. I should never have trusted him. A man in his early forties — never married — happy to take on an eighteen-year-old girl pregnant with another man's twins. 'You said I had to have an abortion or I was out.'

She huffs. 'Well, I don't remember it like that at all,' she says, shaking her head. 'I may have suggested it would make sense to have an abortion, because the father didn't want anything to do with you or the babies, that having children so young would ruin your life.'

'Like it did yours?'

She scowls. I've hit a nerve. She brought me up on her own after my father walked out. I only vaguely remember him, but from what she's told me, we were better off without him anyway.

I take a deep breath in an attempt to stop myself from saying more, pushing down the urge to scream at her. The woman is delusional.

Behind Mother, a blur of green moves across the landing as Mia creeps from her bedroom. Before I can call out to her, she races down the stairs.

Within moments the back door slams, and I wonder where she's heading, if she overheard our conversation.

'And she's a strange fish too,' Mother says. 'You really have made a pig's ear of raising those kids, Charlotte.'

'And you did so much better at raising me?' I get up, heading towards her, and she steps backwards as though she's afraid of me. It's odd what over eighteen years apart has done to the dynamics between us. I feared her once. Though never cruel physically, her tongue was like a knife throughout my young years, cutting away my confidence. But now Mother is small fry compared to how Gordon treated me. I've been through so much worse. She's almost an angel in comparison.

She huffs again, turns and walks away, her footfalls muffled by her slippers on the stairs.

I move towards the window. Mia is at the foot of the back garden now, opening the gate that leads to Quarry Lake. I lift my eyes, as the moon moves from behind a cloud to see a young woman hurrying into the trees in the distance. A young man stands near the water's edge, by the white cliffs — Ryan?

A surge of fear rushes through me I can't quite explain, but I know I need to go out there. I race down the stairs, grab a torch from the drawer in the hall, and head into the dated kitchen, glancing at the filthy sides, the plates mounted up. I push past Mother who is making a milky drink — something she always does before bed — and out through the back door, into the night, the door slamming on her weak plea to know where I'm going.

As I stumble down the garden, cursing my useless leg, my heart hammers against my ribs. I don't know why I feel the need to follow my daughter. But what I do know is that Mother is right, the attacks in Ensley happened soon after we arrived, and the fear that my son had something to do with them keeps me awake at night.

CHAPTER FIVE

Riona

'So, will you sleep with him?' Erika's Swedish accent is as charming as ever, though there's a slight slur as she encourages Stacey to talk about some bloke she's planning to meet later.

Stacey has slept with most of the young men and teenage boys in the village. It's who she is. Her upbringing churned her up and spat her out, like a cat with a hairball. Sleeping with anyone who half gives her attention seems to be the only way she can feel needed. Beneath a thick layer of arrogance, she has no self-worth. She tilts her head, her auburn hair like fire in the torchlight, and takes a long swig from the bottle of cider.

'Well?' Erika persists.

'Stupid question.' She bursts into laughter, dimples forming in her cheeks.

'Why are you meeting him so late?' I say, heading back to them and sitting down once more.

'Because I can.' It's true her mother wouldn't notice if she didn't return at all, and her father is long dead. Aunt Bernie drives me mad at times, but at least I have someone who cares about me — someone who's looking out for me.

She leans forward. 'And he's married,' she whispers, as though the trees have ears. 'He's got to wait until his wife's asleep.'

'You need to be careful, Stacey,' Erika says. 'One of these days some wounded wife is going to kill you in your sleep.'

She laughs, takes another gulp of cider, before passing it to Erika.

'Don't be ridiculous.'

'Your funeral,' I say.

'Let's hope not.' Erika snorts. Sprays cider through her nose. Wipes it away with plump fingers.

Attempting to tune out on my friends, I hone in on the darkness, unpicking my thoughts. I'll be glad to get away from Ensley, away from Stacey. I can't wait to start university in September, make new friends — the beginnings of a new life. I'll miss my aunt and sister, of course, but I won't miss *this*.

'I need a wee,' Erika says, bringing me out of my thoughts. 'Ooh, did I share too much?'

'Yep,' I say with a smile.

She rises and disappears into the trees, the night swallowing her, and my eyes return to the water.

Six lives have been lost in Quarry Lake over the years, but tonight the 'Danger! No Swimming' sign is the only clue to the deep water's hidden secrets, the still, glistening surface giving nothing away. Nobody would know it had once been a clay quarry that flooded in the 1930s. That drowned vehicles — old quarry buggies and a crane — are still down there, creaking metal hands under the inky black, reaching up, just out of sight, waiting to catch out unsuspecting swimmers. It has always been called Quarry Lake. In the seventies, the boathouse was erected by an entrepreneur with a dream that people would come here at weekends with picnics, take boats out, but it never took off. Now it's abandoned.

Stacey has stopped talking, her audience of one crouched behind a tree somewhere. 'Sit down, Riona,' she calls over to me, and I turn to see her patting the dry, cracked earth beside her. 'You're making the place look untidy.'

I want the evening to end. It's half past eleven. My bed is calling. But although I'm tempted to take off, Aunt Bernie has drummed into me to never walk home alone. *We haven't caught the Ensley Killer, Riona.* I know I have to wait for my so-called friends and walk back with them.

I flop down and cross my legs. 'Hand that over.' I reach for the cider, though I don't want any more, not really. It's just something to do. And as the flat, warm liquid slides down my throat, I think I might throw up.

'Who was that?' Stacey looks towards the trees, her voice unusually jittery. She jumps up and pulls her denim jacket round her. 'Hello! Is anyone there?'

I'm not sure if she's really nervous. Pretending is the kind of thing she does, but when something moves in the darkness — a figure, head down, pushing through the trees — my stomach leaps into my mouth. 'Erika?' I call, flashing my torch and rising to my feet too.

Stacey grips my arm, moves in close. 'Who's there?'

The next few moments seem to last forever, as thoughts of the Ensley Killer bounce around my head. *He hasn't been found. What if he kills us all?*

Suddenly Erika bursts through the trees, making Stacey and I scream. 'Got ya!' She laughs hard, bending over double and hitching at her underwear.

'Bitch.' Stacey rubs the back of her neck. 'I knew it was you all along.'

As fear peters away, I notice Erika's holding a cellophane-wrapped bunch of fresh flowers.

'Where did you get those?' I move towards her, run my hand over the beautiful white roses.

Erika looks over her shoulder. 'Back there, I think someone left them for that girl who died.'

'Is there a label?'

Erika fumbles with the bunch of flowers, the cellophane crackling. 'Yep.' She pulls out a card and reads it. 'It just says "For Kerry Ann".'

'Sweet,' Stacey says with a sickly smile.

'You need to put them back,' I say. 'Out of respect, you need to put them back exactly where you found them.'

* * *

Charlotte

I push through brambles, the hazy beam of my weak torch my only guide. The sound of mumbled voices some distance away spurs me on as I push through brambles, getting closer to the water.

'I know what you're up to, Ryan.' It's Mia, her voice ripping through the air, and I see my daughter frantically pointing towards where the girl disappeared into the trees.

'It's none of your business, Mia. Just leave me alone, for God's sake.' Ryan comes into view, marching away from Mia, heading towards me. I flick off my torch, crouch behind a tree as though I'm some sort of spy.

My mind flashes to Jenny Philpot. Ryan met her when he was delivering eggs to a local garden centre six months ago. He started seeing her just before Gordon died. He seemed the happiest I'd ever seen him. But Mia didn't like it. It wasn't that she wanted Ryan for herself. She didn't. It was more that she couldn't bear him to be happy. She thrives on other people's misery, much like Gordon did.

I wish now that I'd told Ryan he couldn't bring Jenny to the farm. But he begged, said she wanted to see the animals. *It will give me Brownie points, Mum.*

I watched from the window the day he brought her there. Saw Mia following them around. Hiding just out of sight as Jenny cooed over the animals and the happy young couple kissed. I should have gone out there, made Mia come inside.

There was so much blood that afternoon. It soaked into Jenny's dark hair. I covered my ears as the girl screamed and cried. I'd seen Mia throw the jagged stone, saw it skim through the air, unable to do anything. Perhaps she hadn't meant for it to slice open the girl's temple — perhaps she only meant to scare her.

I saw the girl fall to the floor, called an ambulance.

Jenny never came near Ryan again. She told him it was over by text. He cried in his room for days. Said Mia was ruining his life. I should have done something. I should have done more. I'm a useless mother.

Now Mia grabs Ryan's arm. 'I know what you did. I saw you. You're a killer, Ryan, and you'll pay for it. You'll go to prison.'

I rise from my crouched position, wanting to move closer, to hear what Mia is saying. But I want to turn away too, to run, cover my ears, and bury my head as I always do. As I've done all my life.

'I've got your laptop, Ryan, and I'll take it to the police. Show them how it was you who met those young women. They'll arrest you for murder, Ryan. They will.'

Their voices become whispers on the air, heated but inaudible. I will myself to move closer, to try to hear what they are saying, but I'm frozen, unable to move.

'I hate you, Mia. I wish you were dead.' It's Ryan, louder now, his voice broken. I flick my torch back on. Move towards my children. She's thumping him; my daughter's hammering her fists against my son's chest. She's as tall as he is, just as strong, but he pushes her away with force. She stumbles. Topples backwards. He reaches out a hand to catch her, but she flounders, her arms flailing in the air before she suddenly disappears from view.

She screams.

A splash.

I run to Ryan's side.

He stares down at my daughter thrashing about in the dangerous water below.

I can't swim, and neither can Mia.

Then there is silence. She stares up at us, her dark hair spreading around her like a cape, her coat heavy, weighing her down, pulling her under.

Ryan finally kicks off his shoes and goes to jump in after her, but I grab his arm. 'You'd never survive,' I cry, knowing how treacherous it is.

He doesn't argue, and together we look down, my whole body shaking, tears streaming down my face, as my daughter disappears, as though dragged beneath the water by the metal claws below, and I curse this sudden feeling of relief.

CHAPTER SIX

Riona

A cry from far across the water, near the white cliffs, has stunned us into silence. A splash followed. I hold my chest as we stare across the lake. 'You heard that, right?'

'A fox's mating call,' Stacey says. 'I've heard them on YouTube.'

My eyes skitter across the darkness towards the run-down boathouse, where the flickering light still burns.

'I don't know. It sounded like a woman to me,' Erika says, crunching the flowers against her. 'And there was a splash. I'm sure I heard a splash.'

'What if someone's fallen in?' Stacey says. 'We should go check it out.'

'You've got to be kidding me.' I bite my lip, my anxiety in overdrive 'What if it's the killer?'

'We can't just ignore it.' Stacey sounds excited. 'There are three of us. Come on, we'd never forgive ourselves if someone's in trouble over there.' And with that, she picks up a large stick, turns, her torch on full beam, and marches away from us, trees swallowing her small frame.

'Hang on,' I call after her. 'We should call the police.'

'And say what?' Erika says. 'That we heard a splash?'

'And a scream.'

Erika drops the flowers to the ground disrespectfully and chases after Stacey, leaving me alone.

'Wait,' I call after them, racing to catch up.

Stacey is some distance ahead of us, her torchlight visible in the darkness, as she moves closer to the white cliffs. We follow, Erika linking her arm through my elbow, so close I can feel her heart racing.

The walk from where we'd been sitting takes five minutes. I see Stacey up ahead, near the cliff edge looking down into the water below. I shine my torch in her face, and she turns and carries on down the incline towards the boathouse, her torch beam lighting the area.

We follow, glancing down at the still water below as we go. If someone fell in, there is no sign of them now.

We reach the boathouse, and Stacey appears from inside, unoiled hinges squeaking into the dark night, as the door swings closed behind her. 'There's nobody in there.' She gives a dismissive shrug. 'Someone's been here though, lit a candle, and there's a blanket on the ground. But whoever they were, they've gone.'

I shiver, and cast my eyes across the trees. 'Let's go home,' I say. 'Something doesn't feel right. I'm getting pretty creeped out.'

'We should put the candle out, don't you think?' Erika nods towards the boathouse. 'We wouldn't want it to catch fire.'

I look at the flickering flame in the window, unsure if I want to go inside. From where we are, it's a long walk back to the entrance. Anything could happen to us, and nobody would come running.

'Who do you think lit it?' Erika asks, easing open the door, and together we step inside. The smell of damp hits us, and the wooden floor creaks under our feet as we enter. Two old, battered rowing boats, under a roofed area, clang rhythmically against their moorings, barely seaworthy. I move my torch around me, the beam falling on a far wall, where rusty tools hang.

'Christ, what's that?' Erika says, and I turn, lighting her startled face with my torch. On a wooden, battered table is a coil of thick rope.

'Left from years ago, I should imagine,' Stacey says. 'Stop being so dramatic.'

A *thud, thud, thud* comes from where the boats are moored, and I gasp, clasping my chest. 'What the hell was that?'

'Christ, you two are such wimps.' Stacey rolls her eyes. 'It's only the boats banging against their moorings, Riona. Get a grip.'

But I'm not sure. The noise seems to be getting louder, and a strong spicy odour, like aftershave, wafts on the air.

I head towards the candle, blow it out with one puff. 'Let's go home,' I say, dashing towards the door. 'Stacey, Erika, come on, please, this is way too freaky.'

* * *

Charlotte

The house is in darkness as I hurry up the garden — trying to keep up with Ryan — and in through the back door. My heart is thumping and the pulse in my neck is out of control. Tears stream down my cheeks.

My daughter drowned. My daughter drowned. My daughter drowned.

Ryan is silent. He hasn't reacted. It's as though he's numb. But I'm alert. I have to be. We need to leave. Now.

I have so many questions I need to ask my son: *What did Mia know about you? Who was the girl running into the trees? Why was Mia threatening to go to the police?* And the question that threatens to choke me. *Are you a killer?*

But for now I am silent, my mind processing, percolating what to do and how to protect my son.

29

I close the kitchen door behind us. The only light is from the moon shining through the window, making the world inside Willow Nook Cottage a dusky grey, highlighting the dust particles floating in the air.

'Pack your bag,' I whisper, wanting to take my son in my arms, tell him everything will be OK. But I stop myself. I don't know that it will be. 'I'll pack mine and Mia's, and write your gran a note. I'll tell her the three of us have found somewhere to live, that we won't be back, OK?'

He nods, runs a hand across his mouth, his eyes so big, so sad.

'We can take my dad's old truck.' I never did understand why he didn't take it when he left. 'He won't be needing it, wherever he is.'

I lift a set of keys from a row of hooks near the battered cooker, a brief memory of the last time I saw my father smashing into my mind. I'd come down the stairs, woken by loud, angry voices. Listened in the darkness as my parents argued. 'Go to bed!' my mother yelled, spotting me huddled by the wall. 'This has nothing to do with you, Charlotte.' I was only six.

I clench the keys in my fist. The truck hasn't been driven in years. Mother rarely leaves the cottage, and if she does, she tends to walk. She won't even notice it's gone.

We make our way into the hallway, where I trip over a pile of magazines. 'Shit,' I whisper, a pain soaring up my leg. This house is far too cluttered.

Upstairs, we creep across the landing, Ryan disappearing into his room, trance-like. First, we need money. Mother doesn't use a bank, has always kept her cash in the airing cupboard, in several shoeboxes. I find it easily. Grab a handful of notes. I doubt she'll even miss them.

I step into the box room — almost a cupboard — where Mia spent most of her time after we arrived. I see the photo of Mia and Gordon pinned to the wall, their faces serious, their closeness tangible, and my stomach clenches.

Tears sting my eyes as I take in the paperback on the bedside cabinet, a bookmark slipped in halfway through. I stare at the porcelain doll resting against the skinny, crisp-like pillow. Registering how much like Mia it is, with its straggly black hair, its dark eyes, its pale face.

'I'm sorry,' I whisper, perching on the edge of the single bed. 'I'm so sorry I let you down.'

Mother coughs, throaty, in the room next door, and I know I haven't got time to grieve, not right now. I rise, and yank Mia's case onto the bed, unzip it and lift the lid. I throw in the books and her clothes — not many, we didn't bring much when we left the farm. I place my hand over the doll's face. I should take that too, Mia would have if she was here, but I shudder. This thing has always given me the creeps — not helped by Mia talking to it, moving it around the farm, saying it moved by itself. Unable to bring myself to put it in the case, I shove it in the small bedside cabinet, along with the photo of her and Gordon, and close the door.

Mia's case packed, I creep across the landing, enter my room and throw everything I possess into mine. Once downstairs, almost robotically I take Ryan's yellow hi-vis jacket from the cupboard and lay it over my case, picking up on a vague smell of bleach. I bash down rising dark thoughts that I will need to destroy it.

I write a note for Mother, and meet Ryan by the front door several minutes later.

'I can't find my laptop,' he says, and Mia's words by the lake bounce into my head. *'I've got your laptop, Ryan, and I'll take it to the police. Show them how it was you who met those young women. They'll arrest you for murder, Ryan. They will.'*

'We haven't got time to look for it,' I say, praying wherever Mia put it, nobody will ever find it.

'I can't leave it, Mum.' His voice is raised, anxious.

'Shh, you'll wake your gran.' I lift the truck keys to show purpose — to show we need to get going. 'We'll head down south, Cornwall perhaps. Somewhere quiet where nobody knows us.'

He nods, and I realise he's said very little since we watched Mia disappear under the water. I know he's hiding something, that inside his head swirl secrets he may never reveal. But I know too, whatever it is, whatever he's done, I will be here for him. Protect him. Always.

As he opens the front door, I place the note I've written on the hall cabinet, propped up against the cluttered ornaments, and glance one last time up the stairs to make sure Mother hasn't heard us.

We've found somewhere to stay. We won't be back. I'll email you once we're settled. Charlotte, Ryan and Mia.

CHAPTER SEVEN

Riona

Sunday, 27 September 2009

Alene stands in my bedroom doorway. 'So you're really going, then?' She scoops her dark, bobbed hair behind her ears, her skin pallid.

'Yep, and I can't wait to get away from Ensley.' I throw a pair of jeans and my favourite jumper into my overfull case and squeeze the lid closed. 'George is meeting me at the station when I get there.'

'George?'

'Some bloke I met at induction. He's pretty cute.'

'I'll miss you.' She folds her arms around herself.

'Will you?' I wasn't sure she would. We've drifted apart over the last few years, no longer the inseparable sisters we were when we arrived in Ensley ten years ago after our parents died. I zip my case, staring up at her as I do so. 'Are you OK? You look a bit . . .'

She steps into my bedroom, her eyes flicking over the posters of Lady Gaga and Katy Perry, landing on my cluttered dressing table, photos of Stacey and Erika pinned to the mirror. 'I think I'm pregnant.'

'What?' I drop down onto the edge of the bed. 'Oh God, Alene. How? Who?'

'Well the "how" is pretty obvious,' she says, half smiling, although it doesn't reach her eyes. 'And the "who" doesn't matter anymore.'

'Of course it matters.' I rise, move close to her and take hold of her hands.

'What will you do?'

She pulls her hands free. 'I'll have the baby, if that's what you mean. I just need to break the news to Aunt Bernie, is all.'

'She'll be fine with it, Alene. She'll understand.'

'I know.' She rubs the back of her neck, paces a few steps towards the window. 'I just wish you weren't going. If there was ever a time I needed you, it's now.'

I turn away from her, and an inner demon I'm not proud of yells that this is her problem not mine. 'I'll visit,' is all I can think to say. 'Often. I promise. And you can come to Bristol to see me whenever you want.'

'To university lodgings, with a baby?'

'I mean while you're pregnant.'

'Even worse.'

'You've got Bernie, Alene. She'll take care of you, I know she will.'

'Bernie works all the time, Riona, climbing the ranks. You know that — and she's preoccupied with the Ensley Killer . . .' She peters out as though defeated, and I feel a surge of guilt. I could take a gap year, perhaps. That would be the right thing to do. I could support my sister through this. But then what happens in a year? She'll have a tiny baby, and she'd need me even more. I need to start my new life. Get away from here. I can't sacrifice my own life for hers.

I look at my sister. See the tears in her eyes. 'You'll be OK,' I say, dragging my case from the bed and thumping it to the floor. 'I'm on the end of a phone always. And when the baby's born, I'll be the best auntie ever.' I go to hug her, but she steps away from me, and a lump wedges in my throat. *Am I an awful person?*

'Ready, Riona?' It's Bernie in the doorway, her complexion pale too, eyes dark from worrying that the Ensley Killer hasn't been caught, despite there being no more attacks since July.

I overheard her talking on the phone with her inspector back in August. She was out on the patio, pacing, didn't know my bedroom window was open — that I was listening. They'd traced an IP address from an online dating profile. Someone called Oliver Jones, who all three women had spoken to via the site. 'So much for Kerry Ann not having a computer or phone,' she was saying. 'Colin White clearly doesn't know his daughter as well as he thought he did.' The IP had been traced to a backstreet internet café in Stevenage. But despite questioning the owner and staff, they'd come up with nothing. Bernie sounded so deflated that day, desperate to catch whoever had destroyed three women's lives.

Bernie jiggles her car keys, all set to give me a lift to the station. She looks at my sister, must see the tears in her eyes. 'What's wrong, sweetheart?'

'Nothing, I'm fine.' Alene turns and walks towards the door. 'I guess I'll miss Riona, that's all,' she adds without looking back.

PART TWO: 2021

CHAPTER EIGHT

Charlotte

Friday, 3 December 2021

It has been over twelve years since I left Ensley to live in an isolated area of Cornwall with Ryan. For so long life has moved along at a slow pace, with so few people in our lives, that being out in the world today, seeing so many people rushing around, living life to the full, feels daunting.

I head across the petrol station forecourt, my limp as pronounced as ever. The doctor was right, I have been left with a limp — a limp that constantly reminds me of those wasted years with Gordon.

I pull out my purse as I join the queue to pay, a surge of fear rising inside me. What if they discover the truth about what happened to Mia? *What if my son is a killer?*

Memories of my daughter force their way in, as they always do. Often in the early hours I wake with a start, seeing her face disappearing under the water.

I could never reach her when she was alive. Never quite knew what was going on behind the girl's vivid blue eyes. It hurt that Gordon seemed to have a connection with her, was painful to see her respond to him and not me. They would sit for hours snuggled up on the sofa watching TV or head out for long walks in the countryside. He made such a fuss of her, and she never once suffered Gordon's wrath the way Ryan and I did. Sudden tears burn, squeezing their way through my lashes. I dash them away with the back of my hand as I pay for the petrol, recalling how Mia was the only one who cried at his funeral. Even his brother didn't shed a tear.

Once back behind the wheel, I think about the rented, run-down house where Ryan and I have lived for what feels like forever. Where life has stood still for so long. Where we've hidden in the shadows, stagnating like a garden pond, always worrying, watching from the window, waiting for someone to arrive and say, *We've found your daughter.* Or worse, *We know you're son's a killer.*

I pull my phone from my bag and send a brief message to Ryan, despite the 'no phones' sign on the forecourt:

> *Full tank. Just setting off. Should take about five hours. I'll be with your gran by around three o'clock. Everything will be OK, lovely boy, I promise. I will keep you updated. Mum x*

I start the engine and pull off the forecourt. Our dark secret kills me a little more every day, the years chipping away at my sanity, my well-being, but never my resolve to protect my son.

Once I'm on the A30, the radio is blaring out a song I remember from the eighties. I try to clear my head, so I can plan what I'm going to say to my mother, the thought of seeing her again after all these years stirring my stomach.

My mother's email — the one that triggered this visit to Ensley — was vague. She could have told me so much more, but instead she dangled the words I couldn't ignore:

> *They're draining Quarry Lake, building houses on the land.*

I tried to call her several times, but she didn't pick up. Had she always known the truth about what happened that night? Surely not. How could she?

'Hi, Mum,' I practise now from inside the cocoon of the car. 'Surprise!'

I move the car into the slow lane, where traffic is steady, with long gaps between vehicles, the way I like it. There's no risk of an accident here, no chance of bumping into someone. I flick the rear-view mirror towards me. Glimpse my reflection. I had pretty white-blonde curls as a child, and I wore my hair long in my late teens, attracted the boys. But now those curls are tight, bleached and dry, and my once-bright eyes are heavy, puffy, lined behind my steel-rimmed glasses. I'm almost fifty, but I know I look older. But then, what does that matter now?

I sigh. The turmoil of my life shows in the mirror.

But is that a devil or an angel looking back at me?

I can never be quite sure.

CHAPTER NINE

Riona

'You OK?' Erika appears from her office, catching me about to leave for my lunchtime run around Quarry Lake. She always senses when something is wrong, is perceptive of other people's feelings, so different from the teenager she once was. Losing her father when she was in her twenties has played a part in that.

'I just need to get rid of some of this built-up angst.' I strap my phone to my upper arm. There's no point in trying to fool Erika. 'My sister came round last night.'

'Ah, I see.' She narrows her blue eyes and shoves her hands in the pockets of her brightly coloured patchwork trousers. Her blonde hair, streaked with purple, is pulled back in a stubby ponytail. 'Well, you know where I am if you need to talk.' Her Swedish accent has weakened over the years, but it's still there.

'To be honest, things didn't go too bad, considering. It's just . . .' *Things will never be right between Alene and me. I wasn't there for her when she needed me most, and I'm not sure she will ever fully forgive me for that.*

Erika tilts her head, as though waiting for me to finish.

'She's messaging some bloke.' It's easier to veer away from the past problems between my sister and me, and focus on the now. Erika's a great friend, but sometimes she blurs the line between friendship and counselling, and I don't want to be counselled, not today. 'I think she must have met him on a dating app.'

'Again? After what happened last time?'

Her last relationship ended in disaster. I shrug. 'I can't be sure, she's being very vague,' I say, recalling how cagy she'd been with the details. 'But she seems to like him.'

Erika smiles. 'Well, I hope he treats her better than Vince did.'

'Me too.' And I do. Alene deserves happiness. 'Anyway, I'd better go or I won't fit my run in before my afternoon clients.' I go to put in my earphones, when Erika raises her hand to stop me.

'One more thing before you go,' she says, twisting her mouth and furrowing her forehead so she looks rather peculiar. 'Stacey Roberts called.'

'Stacey? I thought—'

'Apparently she's not getting on too well with the counsellor I recommended two months ago and wants to know if I have any spaces on my books.'

'And?'

'Well . . . I told her, again, that my books are full, and it's not such a good idea for me to take her on as we know each other.'

'Good.'

'Except—'

'Except?' It comes out sharp. Erika knows if she takes on Stacey I'll flip.

'I feel a bit sorry for her, that's all. She has lost her mum.' She raises her shoulders in a shrug.

'Her mum treated her dreadfully. Why would she even care?' I know it sounds awful, but I have no time for Stacey.

'It doesn't always work like that, Riona. And apparently they were close at the end.'

'Really?' I roll my eyes.

'I know what she did, Ri, but she seems to have changed. And it was a long time ago. I just thought . . .'

I don't reply. Instead I shove my earphones into my ears, and the power of Kelly Clarkson's 'Stronger' hitting my eardrums goes some way to relieving my desire to pick up the phone to tell Stacey to keep away from our clinic. To keep away from me. I lift my hand in a wave, not wanting to take my anger out on Erika, and leave the building, letting the door slam closed behind me.

It's cold out. The morning frost hasn't thawed, covering cars and rooftops. I'm decked out in a woolly hat and gloves, but once I'm heading down the road, the thump of my trainers against the pavement and the power of the music relieving my tension, my body temperature rises.

I glance over my shoulder. The winter sky is pale behind the white Victorian detached house where Erika and I set up our business together two years ago. We lease the ground floor, while the upstairs apartment is mine. From outside, the building still looks like a beautiful old house, but now the front door leads to the clinic's reception area, rather than the original hallway. Erika offers clients grief counselling, and I offer what she calls 'a bag of happy allsorts'.

I love my job.

It's my vocation.

I'm a qualified reiki practitioner, with diplomas in chakra healing, mindfulness and crystal healing, and my degree in psychology always comes in handy. The fact I can help people to heal mentally, or to simply maintain a healthy mind, makes me feel valuable as a person. I wish, more than anything, I could help my sister, but have accepted it's unlikely I ever will.

I reach the entrance to Quarry Lake as memories of Stacey flood in. I had thought, despite her desire to sleep with anyone who half looked her way — married or single — she would never go after someone I was seeing. I was wrong. It happened twelve years ago, just after I moved to

Bristol to study. It was early days in my relationship with George, when I invited her to visit. We went out for drinks and a meal, and I batted down that she was blatantly flirting with my boyfriend, telling myself it was just what she was like, that she meant nothing by it. When I caught her kissing him later that evening I ordered her to leave. George insisted she came onto him, that she took him by surprise when she leaned in and placed her lips against his. I believed him then, but I know now it wasn't all one sided. *It takes two.*

I'm aware Stacey still lives in Ensley, but I've managed to avoid her since I returned three years ago, and I aim to keep it that way. I'm not that great at forgiving friends who let me down.

It's quiet at Quarry Lake. Always is around lunchtime. I make a point of running around this time each day. Avoiding busy times when the place bustles with chatting parents and noisy children, making their way from one side of the village to the other for school or playgroup.

Ensley is a village in two halves, divided by the stunning yet formidable lake and the dense wooded area. The pathway that curves round the three-acre expanse of water is the only way to reach the other half of Ensley, unless you go via the main road, which takes five minutes by car.

I step onto the path, the cool air making my breath visible — a puff of smoky air in front of my lips — as I head through the canopy of trees. I slow down, cut off my music and remove my earphones, wanting to hear the call of winter birds, the ripples on the water, the rustle of wildlife. I want to sit on a bench in the clearing next to the lake for a few minutes and push away negative thoughts. George hurt me three years ago, and I still struggle to control the pain that twists my stomach. He shattered my heart, and I'm still trying to glue it together, unsure it will ever go back the same as it once was. I know he shouldn't still have a place in my head. Shouldn't still have the power to bring me down, but he does, and I wonder if I will ever be able to think of him without tears burning the backs of my eyes.

CHAPTER TEN

Charlotte

I stand on the doorstep of the house I grew up in, taking long, deep breaths, shivering in my flimsy jacket.

It's time to face my mother. I have no choice. However much I want to turn back, return to Cornwall, I need to know exactly what she meant in her email. Find out what company are going to dredge the lake and build houses on the land — if it's even true — and how much she really knows about the night we left Ensley.

For a brief moment I wish Ryan was here, standing beside me. But it's better that he's in Cornwall, out of harm's way.

I press the doorbell, and a chime rings out within the walls.

The outside of Willow Nook Cottage looks more unkempt than it had when we left, the frost unable to cover an abundance of weeds that fill the borders. The jostling pansies that once looked so pretty are long gone. I run my gloved fingers over the flaking white paint on the front door. It crumbles, falls to the ground like snow. The dead twigs that twist around the door frame look almost sinister — skinny fingers that might move in a moment and grab my throat.

I wait a few seconds more before pressing the doorbell again. Nothing. The silence that seems to move about me makes me shiver. Am I afraid? Or is it simply the cold?

I crouch, groan, my limbs are tired. My whole body is tired. I feel so much older than I am. I open the letterbox. 'Mum! Mum, are you in there? It's Charlotte.' *Surprise!*

I rise and move towards the window. Cup a hand over my eyes and peer in through the glass. Through the nets I make out stacks of newspapers covering the floor, ornaments, magazines, mugs, plates, books on every surface. Has my mother become a hoarder?

I return to the door, and with a clenched fist thud hard against the wood. 'Mum!' I push back my hair. 'For goodness' sake, open up. It's Charlotte.'

I wait. Nothing. But the woman can't be out, surely. She never goes out. Not even to the local shop anymore. She has her groceries delivered. That's what she told me in one of her brief emails.

A van passes slowly in the lonely lane, and I imagine the driver watching me. I close my eyes. I haven't come all this way for my mother to play games. I head through the side gate and into the back garden, where I try the kitchen door, the French doors and peer in through the window. 'Mum!'

I remember when I was young, Mother kept a back-door key behind the shed, in a plant pot. I head down the long garden, where I played as a girl, and through the haphazard nettles that sting through the cheap cloth of my trousers. Memories of my childhood flood in. I hated it here. Not that life was any better in Yorkshire, or Cornwall for that matter. My life has been a rollercoaster of disasters. I don't feel sorry for myself, only for my children.

The key is still in the plant pot, rusty now. Though something I can't quite put my finger on tells me it's been moved recently. I pick it up and retrace my steps, looking up at the bedroom windows of Willow Nook Cottage as I go. They seem to stare back at me like dark, evil eyes.

With a deep breath, I shove the key into the lock and turn it. Opening the back door, I call out, 'Mum. Mum, it's me, Charlotte.'

I look about me. The kitchen hasn't changed, still dirty and even more dated. The smell of decaying food hits my nostrils. Though it doesn't take long to realise the smell is more than that. It's pungent, sickening. Acid rises in my throat.

I leave the kitchen and head into the hall, fear rising. Something's wrong.

The sight of Mother's skinny body crumpled at the foot of the stairs, her head at a strange angle to her shoulders, dried blood caked on her forehead, sends mixed messages to my psyche. I stand, frozen in the doorway — numb, void of emotion. Mother never cared about the twins or me. And now I will have to find out the facts about the development on Quarry Lake for myself. It won't be easy, not without rousing suspicion.

I pull out my phone, and, shaking, dial 999. 'Police,' I say, my voice cracking, my body beginning to tremble. 'It's probably too late for an ambulance.'

CHAPTER ELEVEN

Riona

Saturday, 4 December 2021

'Janet Grayson was found dead at Willow Nook Cottage yesterday,' one of my clients — nice woman, though a bit of a gossip — says. 'Janet's daughter, Charlotte Carter, found her at the bottom of the stairs in a crumpled heap.' *Been lying in the hallway for a couple of weeks, apparently. Found maggots, apparently. Fallen down the stairs, apparently.*

I'm caught between morbid curiosity and an overwhelming sadness. I can't begin to imagine how awful it must have been to find her. How I would feel if it was Aunt Bernie.

My mind drifts to yesterday, seeing Charlotte walking towards the front door of Willow Nook Cottage, dragging her case behind her. Had she been about to find her mother dead? And where are Ryan and Mia? I've never met Ryan and only vaguely recall Mia, but something draws me in. Are they here in Ensley too?

I suppress my interest in the family. I'm not about to gossip, it's hardly professional. I'm meant to be aligning this woman's chakras.

'Definitely consider gardening,' I say, once we've finished. 'It will help no end with your root chakra. And red foods like pomegranates and beetroot in your diet will help too.'

I'm relieved when she leaves around seven o'clock. It's Saturday, and I'm looking forward to a night out at the Fox with Erika and my sister. I lock the main door, even though Erika is still with a client, and step through the door that leads into my tiny hallway. I take the stairs towards my flat, greeting my cat, Wanda, at the top. Tickling her ears as she purrs.

After a quick shower, I spray on Dior J'Adore, put on my favourite green tunic and drag a pair of black leggings off the dryer. A quick whiz of the hairdryer makes my hair look a little too curly, but with no time to straighten it, I bunch it into a pretty slide, hoping for the best. I pick up my jacket, and make my way back downstairs, applying pale pink lipstick as I go.

Back in reception, Erika's door is still closed, and I wonder why I've rushed about, I should have known she would go over her time. Her final client is an eighty-two-year-old man who recently lost his wife of sixty years. His granddaughter encouraged him to have bereavement counselling, and Erika, always kind-hearted, has gone over the man's allocated hour.

I flop down onto one of the squishy chairs that we recently bought to make the place more welcoming and pull my phone from my bag. I flick through my Instagram feed, noticing likes on my photo of a robin from Kieran, Aunt Bernie and Erika. I scroll on, liking almost every photo of Mr Spoon and Eggbert, Erika's Sphynx cats, and the wonderfully eerie, arty pictures Kieran has put up of Quarry Lake. I'm not sure he should have an Instagram account at eleven, but guess it's harmless enough. He doesn't post photos of himself, and his profile picture is of a woodpecker. A memory pushes in of the two of us: Kieran aged seven, me explaining how my camera worked, his eyes bright with interest. I imagine how proud my dad, the grandfather he never knew, would have been to see us both following in his footsteps, two generations with a keen interest in photography, even if I've lapsed a little over the last three years.

Movement outside the window draws my attention. I drop my phone into my bag and rise. I move slowly towards the bay window and peer out at the quiet road, an odd tingling sensation in my spine. I look over my shoulder at Erika's closed door and up at the oversized clock on the wall. It's quarter past seven. *I said we'd meet my sister at seven-thirty — hurry up, Erika.*

I step closer to the front door, noticing an envelope dangling out of the letterbox. I pull it free, feeling my forehead furrow as I study my name scrawled across it in an uneven hand.

I go to open the front door, but something stops me. Instead I return to the window and look out once more, but can't see anyone.

I rip open the envelope with anxious fingers and pull out a sheet of paper, scan the words.

I'm watching you.

Erika's door swings open, and I turn, fumbling the letter into my jacket pocket, my heart bouncing against my ribs.

'Everything OK, Ri?' Her hair is loose around her shoulders. 'You look as though you've seen a ghost.' The old chap Erika has been counselling appears behind her, pale eyes bewildered under bushy, grey eyebrows, shoulders rounded in his misshapen cardigan.

I look towards the door. 'I'm fine,' I say, hearing a slight quiver in my voice.

* * *

'Are you sure you're OK?' Erika looks at me with concern as we make our way past the church. A twelve-foot, lit-up Christmas

52

tree in the grounds reminds us it's just over three weeks until the big day. Her hands are stuffed deep in her jacket pockets against the chilly evening. 'You seem a bit on edge.'

She's right. I am. I don't like this feeling. Those three little words in the letter are swimming round in my head like piranha fish waiting to bite, but I can't bring myself to tell Erika about it. I don't want to worry her when she's looking forward to a relaxing night out.

As we turn the corner by the graveyard, I see movement in the shadows of the alleyway opposite. I slow my pace, dart my eyes across a hedgerow where someone could be crouched hiding. I'm jittery, being paranoid, and need to get a grip.

Erika glances back at me. 'What's up with you, Riona? You're acting pretty odd.'

'Nothing.' I dash to catch her up. But as I look back I feel sure someone is there in the darkness, watching. 'I guess I just want tonight to go well with Alene.'

Erika looks up at me as we continue onwards. She's not small — around five foot three — but I'm five foot nine, and always feel tall next to her. 'It will,' she says, pulling her hand from her pocket, and slipping it through my elbow. She's affectionate — a hugging, hands-on kind of friend, so different from my sister.

I do need tonight to go well with Alene, as much for Kieran as for me. He's always been precious to me, and I know he wishes his mum and I saw more of each other. I adored him from the moment he appeared in the world, and like to think of myself as a super-aunt, who spoils him rotten any chance I get. Despite my relationship with Alene being rocky, she's never kept Kieran away from me, and would often drop him off in Bristol to spend the weekend with George and me before I moved back to Ensley.

Alene is standing outside the Fox when we arrive. She's wearing heels, a black dress that flutters around her calves in the breeze and a droplet pearl pendant at her neck, her jacket draped over her arm. She raises her hand in a wave as we approach, and Erika moves in for a hug, seemingly unaware of the way my sister stiffens at her touch. I don't attempt to hug her. I gave up trying years ago.

'You look freezing,' I say, noticing goose pimples on her lower arms.

'I am a bit.'

'It's good to see you again,' I say, opening the outer bar door for her.

She smiles, loops her dark bobbed hair behind her ears. 'Twice in one week.'

Erika pushes open the second door, and the sound of laughter and chatter reaches our ears. Cheap Christmas decorations seem to have been randomly thrown at the walls and ceiling to see if they stick, but the ambience is great.

The place is already rammed. It's the only semi-decent place for villagers to go on a Saturday night.

'Grab that,' I say to Erika and Alene, spotting an empty table.

'Where are we taking it once I've grabbed it?' Erika smiles. 'Won't the landlord object?'

'I'll get the drinks,' I say, rolling my eyes. 'What are you both having?'

'Orange juice for me,' Alene says, as she follows Erika towards the table. 'I'm driving.'

'The usual, please,' Erika calls, as I push through the throng towards the bar.

* * *

'It's manic in here tonight,' I say, after wrestling my way back through the crowd, surprised the drinks got here in one piece, considering the amount of times I bumped into someone. I place the tray on the table and sit down, blowing a straying curl from my forehead.

'Cheers.' Erika picks up her drink and takes a long gulp.

I take off my jacket and throw it over the back of the chair before picking up my wine, my eyes fixed on my sister.

'So how are things going with . . . ?' I realise she hasn't told me the name of the man she's been messaging.

'I really like him,' she says, running her hand over her neck, and I feel Erika glance my way. 'And he seems to like me.'

'That's great.' I want to ask his name, but there's a stiffness about her that stops me. 'So, are you going to meet up with him?'

She nods. 'Hopefully. I'll see how it goes.' She avoids meeting my eye and begins cracking her knuckles — a nervous habit she started when our parents died. I find myself staring, trying to work her out, noticing she's had more collagen filler injected into her lower lip that she really didn't need.

We've never talked much about how she got pregnant with Kieran. I moved away, and she never did tell Bernie and me who his father was. One careless night with someone who meant nothing to her, was all she's ever told us. When she fell pregnant with Kieran it put paid to her plans to become an engineer, and she's never attempted to go down that route since, now working part-time on the construction site just outside Ensley where she worked before Kieran was born.

I still feel guilty that I took off to Bristol and spent three years studying psychology, leaving her to cope. I could have been there for my sister. But instead I couldn't wait to get away from Ensley.

Apart from the odd visit, and the times Kieran stayed over with George and me, I never saw much of Alene until I returned here three years ago. So it's not surprising we've struggled to get to know each other again. Aunt Bernie had kept a roof over her and Kieran's head, but her life was taken up with the police force for much of her time. I think both Bernie and I would do things differently given our time again.

Alene's phone buzzes across the table, and she looks at the screen. 'I'd better take this,' she says, turning her chair as though she wants privacy, and apart from a couple of 'OK, darlings', I can't pick up on what she's saying.

'You OK now, Riona?' Erika says, taking a sip of her drink, and I bring my attention to my friend.

'I'm fine, honestly.' I think about the odd letter in my pocket, wanting to say something to her, knowing I have to. I go to retrieve it. 'The thing is—'

'I'm going to have to love you and leave you, I'm afraid,' Alene says, turning as she ends the call. She drops the phone into her bag. 'Kieran's having a bit of a moment. Getting himself all agitated. I probably shouldn't have left him alone, but he insisted he's grown up enough to not need a babysitter.'

I can't help thinking that it wasn't Kieran's call to make, but keep quiet. 'Is he OK?'

'Yes. Yes, he'll be fine,' Alene goes on. 'I just need to get back to him.' She rises, gulps back her orange. 'Sorry,' she says.

'Don't be.' I go to touch her arm, but think better of it. 'You must go. Kieran comes first. And keep me updated about your new man.'

She smiles. 'I just hope it works out, that's all, and I'm not making another mistake.' She raises her hand, turns and dashes across the bar and out through the door. I worry for my sister, and hope she's not pinning too much on this man she barely knows.

'Kieran still running rings around Alene, then?' Erika says.

I nod. 'He can be quite a handful.' He can be, sometimes getting himself in quite a state.

'I noticed she's had more work done.' Erika runs her finger across her bottom lip, raises one eyebrow.

'Collagen filler, I think. I can't get my head round why she does it. She really doesn't need it. She's beautiful.'

Erika shakes her head. 'Clearly doesn't see what we see when she looks in the mirror.'

'Another drink,' I say, as Erika drains her glass.

'Why not? But it's my round.'

I rise. 'It's fine, you can get the next two.' I smile and head towards the bar, knowing, by the amount of punters clamouring for drinks, I will be a while.

I'm just about to be served when a man zips in front of me. 'Hey,' I say, tapping him on the back. He turns and smiles.

'Sorry,' he says, raising his hands in surrender. 'My bad.' He moves so I can step in front of him, my body brushing against his as I move closer to the bar. 'Tom Evans,' he says close to my ear.

I glance back. 'Sorry?'

'I'm Tom Evans.'

I feel an instant attraction, a weird flutter inside. It's the first time I've felt anything like it since I met George twelve years ago. 'Riona Foley,' I say with a smile. 'I haven't seen you in here before, have I?'

CHAPTER TWELVE

Riona

'A girl could die of thirst around here, Riona.' Erika looks up at Tom as he hovers behind me holding her Aperol Spritz cocktail in one hand, a glass of red wine in the other. 'And who is this?'

'This is Tom Evans.' I sense my cheeks flush that I'm bringing a complete stranger to the table. But he looked a bit lost at the bar, said he didn't know anyone, and while I waited to be served we got talking about the senior school in Hitchin we'd both attended, old teachers we'd both had, despite our five-year age difference. 'He used to live in Hitchin. He's down visiting, staying with his uncle and aunt on the Oakfield Estate.' I'm giving Erika far too much detail, but my mouth seems to have a mind of its own.

'Well, hello there, Tom Evans. I'm Erika.' She raises her hand in a quaint wave before taking the cocktail from him. 'Nice to meet you.'

'You too, Erika.' He pulls over a stray chair and sits down.

'So, what brings you back to Hitchin, to Ensley?' she says.

He lowers his head, and a slight worry Erika's touched some sort of nerve causes my heart to pick up speed. He lifts his head, his haunting blue gaze back on Erika. 'I'm here reminiscing, I suppose.' He dashes his hand across his stubbled chin. 'My sister died recently.'

'I'm so sorry to hear that,' Erika says. 'Sorry for your loss.'

'She'd been ill for a while.' He shrugs again, dismissive, but I see the pain in his eyes. 'I thought coming back would stir happy memories of when we were kids, but it's not really working. It's so much harder than I thought it would be.' He picks up his wine, takes a long gulp. 'Sorry, I didn't mean to—'

'No, no worries, it must be so hard to lose a sibling,' I say, thinking of Alene, how I've lost her already, yet she's still right here.

He takes another gulp of his wine. Then another. 'I don't suppose we could change the subject?' He coughs, as though his throat has tightened. 'I really shouldn't have mentioned her.'

'Of course, yes,' I say, struggling to find something to talk about.

'So, what do you do, Tom?' Erika says, obliging.

He throws her a grateful smile — a nice smile. He's back. 'Well, I live in Norfolk, and I'm a full-time dog walker.' He takes out his phone, taps the screen a couple of times. 'This is my Facebook page,' he says, showing us a photo of three cute dogs looking up at the camera.

'What an amazing job,' I say. 'I'd love to do that.'

'I've set up my own business near Cromer,' he says, shoving the phone back into his pocket. 'Tom's Dog Walking — not very original, I know.' He smiles, his enthusiasm for his work shining through. 'So many people work full-time, so I'm paid to take their precious fur-babies for long walks in the countryside.'

'Living the dream, then.' I smile.

'Unless it's pissing it down.' He laughs. 'I love dogs — have two of my own, and the job keeps me pretty fit.' He pauses, stares into my eyes. 'Anyway, enough about me, tell me about you guys. What do you do?'

We tell him about the clinic, and I mention I live above it, and Erika and I go on to talk about how we've been friends for years, and as the subject changes to films we've seen, the latest psychological thriller on Netflix, Tom suddenly rises. He tucks a finger in the collar of his polo shirt and pulls the fabric away from his skin, as though it itches.

'Actually, sorry to cut you off, but I think I need a bit of air. It's warm in here, don't you think?' And before we can answer, he makes his way across the bar towards the exit.

I pull my eyes from the door swinging closed behind him and spin round, meeting Erika's stare. 'Was it something I said?'

'Probably,' she says with a laugh. 'Actually, I need the loo.' She laughs, gets to her feet and disappears into the throng of people around the bar.

'Bloody hell.' I sniff my armpits, making myself chuckle.

* * *

Five minutes later Erika reappears, her face flushed. She plonks herself down on the chair next to me. 'Jeez, that was weird.'

'What was weird? You OK?'

'Not great, I've just had an odd thing happen to me in the loos.'

I furrow my forehead. 'What sort of thing?'

'Well, while I was in there, this was pushed under the door.' She hands me an envelope and looks about her. 'I'm a bit freaked out by it, if I'm honest.'

The envelope looks the same as the one that was posted through the letterbox at the clinic, except Erika's name is on the front written in the same scrawling hand. Inside there's a piece of paper, with the words:

I'm watching you.

'Oh my God.' I pull the letter I received earlier from my jacket pocket and show it to her.

She scans the words, her forehead crinkling. 'Why didn't you tell me about this?'

'I would have. Was going to. It came just before we left. I didn't want to worry you.'

'So this is why you were acting odd on the way here?'

I nod. 'I don't like this, Erika.'

'Me neither, who could have sent them?'

She hands me back the letter, and I push it back into the envelope, shove it into my jacket pocket. 'I've no idea.' I haven't. I'm nowhere near perfect, but feel sure I haven't done anything that warrants a poisoned pen letter. George bounces into my head. He was upset when I walked out — promised he would change — but that was three years ago, and I haven't heard from him since. And the author of these letters is targeting both Erika and me. 'Could it be one of our clients?'

She presses her hand against her chest as though trying to slow her heartbeat. 'I can't imagine any of them being capable of this.'

I shake my head. 'I'm sure it's just someone being an idiot.' I look about me, suddenly suspicious of everyone. 'What I mean is . . .' I've got nothing. I don't even know what I mean. I try for a smile and Erika mirrors it.

'What you mean, Ri, is it's just some weirdo, and we should both ignore it.'

'Yes, exactly, it's definitely not bothering me.'

'Liar.'

'Well, I'm not going to let it spoil our night.' But I'm looking around the pub. Paranoid as I take in the faces of villagers and strangers, searching out who could have sent the letters.

Erika nods towards the landlady who's setting up a microphone in the corner. 'Open mic later,' she says. 'I may treat everyone to a rendition of "Waterloo".'

'Stereotypically Swedish, as always,' I say with a laugh.

She laughs too, but there's a tension in her tone. 'I'll get in some more drinks, shall I?'

I watch her go before rising. I desperately need air. Leaving our jackets on the chairs, so nobody pinches our table, I push through the punters and out into the deserted pub garden.

The night sky is starless, the only light a string of lanterns swinging in the cold breeze. I cross my arms, trying to keep warm, taking deep breaths as my eyes skitter around, passing the shadowy children's play area, a wooden hut for smokers. I spot Tom some distance away, sitting at a table under a faded parasol, his head in his hands.

'Are you OK?' I say, approaching, and he lifts his head.

Dark shadows cross his chiselled face. 'Yeah, it's just being back here, you know. Remembering Becky.'

'Your sister?'

He nods, runs his hand across his neck.

'I'm so sorry.' I sit down beside him, keeping my distance, not wanting to invade his space.

He fiddles with his fingers. 'We were so happy as kids. I sometimes wish for that time again.' He smiles. 'What about you, Riona? Did you have a happy childhood here in Ensley?'

I nod. 'I did, yes. Though I didn't arrive here until I was eight.' I shuffle closer. 'Spent my early childhood in Ireland.'

Tom doesn't seem to hear my words. His eyes focused on a cluster of trees.

'What's wrong?' I say, looking to where he's staring.

He shakes his head. 'I thought I saw something, a flash of yellow.' He rakes his fingers through his dark wavy hair before bringing his gaze back to me. 'I should have stayed away from here,' he says. 'But it's like when you know a certain song will evoke memories, emotions that will get you right here.' He touches his chest. 'You know you shouldn't play it, because you'll sob your heart out, but you go right ahead and play it anyway. It's like that being here.'

'Well, I'm glad you came to Ensley.'

'Thanks.' He smiles. 'I like talking to you, Riona.'

I have absolutely no idea what possesses me, but I lean in and kiss him softly on his cheek. He responds, his lips brushing against mine.

'Oh God, sorry,' he says, bringing me to my senses. He gets up. 'I don't know what I was thinking. That wasn't meant to happen.'

'It's fine.' *Nice.* I rise too.

'I'm going to head back to my aunt and uncle's place,' he says, moving away from me.

'Well, you know where I am if . . .' *Calm down, Riona, you're acting too desperate.*

With a wave, he turns and makes his way towards the car park.

'I hope we get to catch up again before you go back Norfolk,' I call after him, unable to keep my runaway mouth shut.

'Me too,' he says without looking back, disappearing into the darkness.

Back in the pub, Erika is gulping back another drink. I sit down beside her. 'I got you another wine,' she says, pointing to a large glass of red.

'Thanks.' I glance towards the door. 'Tom's left, by the way.' I take a sip of my wine.

'You fancy him, don't you?'

'No, of course not.' My cheeks sting with embarrassment.

'I can see it your eyes, Ri. You need to live a little. You spend all your time wrapped up in the clinic or running. It's been three years since that bastard cheated on you.'

'I know.' I look towards the door again, wishing Tom would return.

The tapping of the mic quietens the crowd. 'So, first up on open mic tonight we've got Erika Danielsson and Riona Foley singing an Irish ballad Riona's father wrote.' The landlady smiles over at us. 'Please give it up for Riona and Erika.'

'No way,' I hiss into Erika's ear, as everyone claps. 'What the hell? Did you organise this?'

'Oh come on, Riona. We haven't sung your father's ballad since we were teenagers. It'll be fun.'

I reluctantly get to my feet. 'A cappella?'

'Yep.'

Two minutes later, Erika and I are singing, and the pub crowd are swaying to our rendition of the tragic love story. Halfway through the song, a camera flashes and I feel for a moment as if I'm on the stage at Wembley Arena. We put our heart and soul into our performance, and as we do so, my mind drifts to my childhood, how happy Alene and I were in Ireland before our parents' tragic accident. We end the song on a high note, and the gathered crowd clap and cheer, and I must admit I feel good.

'Amazing,' the landlady says as we return to our seats. 'Have a drink on the house, ladies.' She follows us, places a hand on my arm. 'Oh did that bloke find you earlier, Riona?'

'What bloke?'

'Tall, good-looking, didn't say his name. He asked if I knew who you were, and I pointed you out.'

I'm puzzled. Does she mean Tom? 'Did he have dark hair? Wearing a blue polo shirt?'

But the landlady has moved on through the crowd, and I realise I've had enough for one night. 'I need my bed,' I say to Erika, taking my jacket from the back of my chair and shoving my arms into the sleeves.

Erika pulls a sad face. 'But it's only ten o'clock.'

'Sorry.' I sigh and kiss her cheek. 'I'm such a party pooper these days.'

'Well, I'm going to stay for a bit.' She looks about her. 'I know half the people here, I'm sure someone will talk to me.'

She's right, there are plenty of people here who she knows, so I feel no guilt as I flutter my fingers and head for the door.

CHAPTER THIRTEEN

Riona

Sunday, 5 December 2021

I wake to find Wanda asleep on my head, her stomach gurgling.

'Hello, sweetie,' I say, stretching my hand out from under the duvet to tickle her before picking my phone up from the bedside cabinet. I hover the screen above my tired eyes, squint. It's gone ten o'clock. I normally feed the cat at eight. I'm such a cruel cat mummy.

I sigh, thump the phone back down and snuggle further under my duvet, curling up like a foetus. The memory of singing my father's ballad in front of what felt like the whole village last night washes over me. It was a strange evening.

However much I love my job, I'm relieved it's Sunday, and the clinic is closed. Apart from a run by Quarry Lake later, I intend to cocoon myself in my apartment for the whole day and attempt to forget about the odd letters.

My sleepy mind drifts to Tom Evans. Had he asked the landlady who I was before he pushed in front of me at the bar? If so, why didn't he say he'd been looking for me?

I close my eyes. Maybe it wasn't Tom who spoke to her. Perhaps someone else was looking for me. In fact, it could have been anyone. I push down a sudden wave of paranoia that it has something to do with the letters, and try to focus on what a great guy Tom seemed to be. I know Erika would tell me I have every right to like someone. That George never deserved me anyway, and it's time I moved on. But then — I slip down further in the bed as though someone is watching my thoughts — I kissed a complete stranger.

Wanda pushes her paws on top of the duvet and mews. I really need to ban her from the bedroom, but know it's never going to happen.

'OK! OK!' I scramble up to a sitting position, glancing at my phone once more as I move to the edge of the bed. There's a text message from Erika sent late last night, telling me I missed her Abba routine. I smile, not surprised she took over the mic again after I left, and feel slightly disappointed I missed her performance. She has a great voice.

I take a deep breath and push my feet into my seal pup slippers, collecting my robe as I enter the bathroom.

Once showered and dressed, I head into my tiny, cluttered kitchen, my hungry cat on my heels, like a shadow. I feed Wanda and stream water into the kettle before flicking it on. Behind the closed blind, rain splatters the window. I stop for a moment, listening, loving the sound as it hammers against the glass, reminding me of a crackling fire.

As the kettle rumbles to a crescendo, I pull up the blind. Behind the raindrops clinging to the window, fields spread for miles. I move forward, closer to the outside world. Someone in a yellow hi-vis jacket stands motionless towards the back of the nearest field. Is it the same person I saw on the white cliffs by Quarry Lake? I grab my chest, feeling the thud of my heartbeat under my fingers. The figure looks out of place, wrong out there in the rain. I can't make out their features, they're too far away, though even from here I see they're deathly pale. It's as though they're looking right at me.

I shudder and yank down the blind, thoughts of the Ensley Killer catapulting into my head.

I'm being ridiculous. It's just somebody working in the field. Hundreds of people in all sorts of trades wear yellow hi-vis jackets. A postie, perhaps? No, they always wear orange jackets, and anyway, what would a postie be doing in the middle of a field?

My heart is racing. *For goodness' sake, pull yourself together, Riona.*

I take a mug of black coffee into the lounge, trying to put the odd sighting out of my head, and flick on the TV. I pull the throw from the back of the sofa, cover my feet, and drag it up around my neck, snuggling into it, and as I thunder through the TV channels, taking long deep breaths, my heartbeat slows to an even beat.

I love how cosy my lounge is. There's enough space for my orange two-seater sofa, a grey wing-backed chair and two occasional tables, though it's a tight squeeze. Aunt Bernie bought me most of the furniture when I first moved in. In fact, she's always spoilt Alene and me, from right back when she welcomed us to England after our parents died. She once said we were the daughters she never had, always adding with a laugh, 'and never thought I wanted!' She was a career woman before anything else, her job with the police always her priority, though we never went short, and I've always been grateful for that.

I watch an episode of *Friends* I've seen a million times, then an episode of the American *Office* — attempting to immerse fully into lazy Sunday morning mode. But I can't; my mind keeps drifting to Tom, to the figure in the field, to the letter that was posted through the door of the clinic yesterday, to the one Erika received while we were at the pub.

Focusing on the letters, I open up my laptop, intending to go through my list of recent clients, already knowing it's a waste of time as they are all so lovely, when I notice an email from a name I recognise instantly. Stacey Roberts. Anyone can find my work email address, it's on the clinic's website, so it wouldn't be difficult for her to get hold of. I think of the pressure she's putting on Erika to be one of her clients. Is she about to resort to pestering me?

I go to delete the message. I don't want to hear what's she got to say. But I'm aware of a slight tremble in my hand I can't control, and a burning curiosity getting the better of me. I open the email and scan her words:

Hi Riona,
I know I'm probably the last person you want to hear from, but have you seen it? I don't know who put the account up, but I don't like it — it's completely freaking me out. If you want to talk, please get in touch.
Stacey.

I slam closed my laptop. What the hell is she talking about? She's always liked excitement — drama. Is she trying to get to me that way?

After a long moment, I open my laptop once more. I need to answer her email, ask her what she's talking about. I'm about to write back when the doorbell rings.

CHAPTER FOURTEEN

Charlotte

Sunday, 5 December 2021

I Facetimed Ryan yesterday, told him his Gran is dead. He didn't seem to care. Said she wasn't a good person. He bases that on the fact she never protected me when I got pregnant with him and Mia. He said if she hadn't thrown me out, he wouldn't have had to witness and suffer Gordon's abuse.

I guess he's right to some degree.

'But it's more complicated than that,' I told him. 'Your gran had her own issues, your grandfather walking out when I was young being one of them. She didn't want me to struggle the way she had.' I wasn't sure why I was defending her memory. She could have done so much more. Perhaps I want to rewrite history, morph her memory into something more pleasant.

Ryan looked pale, dark-eyed on the screen. He's not been sleeping. But then neither have I. Lately I've had three cups of tea and my porridge before 4 a.m. It seems getting up and pacing the lounge, back and forth, back and forth, is the only way to stop demon thoughts from swirling.

'Why are you sitting in the dark?' I asked him, peering closer to the screen, struggling to pick out his surroundings.

'I've got a rotten migraine,' he said. I've never known him to suffer with bad heads. The pressure is clearly getting to him.

He asked me then if he could come to Ensley, be here for me, but I told him no. That he was to stay where he is — keep inside the house. We just need to get through this little problem and all will be well, I promised, but we both know it's not a little problem at all.

Now, I look over at Mother's PC on the edge of the dining table, piles of paper stacked either side of it. It's how we kept in touch over the last twelve years, by email, and the occasional phone call that normally consisted of more long silences than chatter. The emails we exchanged were kept brief. In fact, I hadn't heard from her in a while when her message came about Quarry Lake. Two lines, that's all. *They're draining Quarry Lake, building houses on the land.*

I did a search online before I left Cornwall, but found nothing about a building development at Quarry Lake. I need to ask around, talk to villagers, but I must be careful. I don't want to make people suspicious. I drag my fingers through my hair, wincing as I catch a tangle.

When we left Ensley twelve years ago, I asked Ryan, as we drove south through the night, my hands tight on the steering wheel, what Mia's final whispered words were, deciding, at that moment, not to tell him I'd overheard any of their conversation — that I knew she was about to go to the police, that she'd accused him of being a killer. If he wanted to confess, he would. Otherwise, we would bury it so deep it would be as though none of it ever happened.

'It doesn't matter now,' was all he said, his tone calm as he pushed in his earphones, the tinny sound of Slipknot escaping from them into the claustrophobic atmosphere in the car. 'She's gone.'

I left it at that. And as days turned to weeks, then months, there never seemed to be a right time to ask him again. Perhaps I didn't want to know. But sometimes, in my darkest hours, I wonder if my boy killed Kerry Ann White, if he attacked those other two girls, leaving one in a coma. I stare at him when he doesn't know I'm looking, trying to see inside his head. Mia had been so obviously damaged — was Ryan damaged too, but so much better at hiding it?

A tear rolls down my face. I'm not a bad person, I convince myself, but I wasn't a good mother as the twins grew up. I should have protected Ryan from Gordon. I should have got help for Mia.

I get up, and walk into the hall, climb the stairs, avoiding the stacks of magazines and newspapers. I've been through everything I'll say if they dredge the lake and find Mia's body, but despite reassuring my son it will all be OK, none of it sounds believable. We took off. We said Mia was with us. The Ensley Killer never struck again after we left. Things will unravel, and I know that however much I want to protect my son, he will become a suspect if the cold case is revisited, that we'll both be accused of killing Mia. I just have to pray Mother got it wrong and they don't intend to dredge Quarry Lake.

I hover on the bleak landing. The walls are musty, creeping with damp, the floral wallpaper curling, peeling, bulging. I've been over almost every inch of the cottage since I returned looking for Ryan's laptop. If things unravel we can't let the police find it. There's only one more place to look. I reach for the handle of Mia's room, push the door open. A stronger musty smell hits me as I enter, a chill settling across the back of my neck. I move across the creaking floorboards, ease open the sash window, taking in the view of the lake.

I take a deep breath and turn to face the tiny room. The wardrobe, the bedside cabinet, the single bed.

Mia's porcelain doll is propped up against the skinny, crisp-like pillow. Had my mother put it there? I feel sure I put it in the bedside cabinet before I closed the door and left for Cornwall.

CHAPTER FIFTEEN

Riona

'Hey, Aunt Riona.' Kieran moves from foot to foot on my doorstep, his Spiderman rucksack heavy on his back. He's pale, apart from a sprinkle of dark freckles across his nose and two pink blots from the cold on his cheeks. His hands are shoved deep into the pockets of blue jeans, the collar of his winter jacket turned up. 'Can I come in?' he says, dashing raindrops from his fringe.

'Of course, is your mum with you?' I step forward, glance out of the front door. The rain is heavy. There's nobody about.

'She just dropped me off at my mate Josh's house round the corner. She's gone now. Doesn't know I'm here.' He sniffs. 'Can I come in?' he repeats.

I move backwards, and he steps inside, closes the door behind him. Halfway up the stairs, I glance back over my shoulder and study him as he pulls his rucksack off his back and thuds it down. He takes off his wet jacket, throws it on the floor. 'Maybe I should call your mum,' I say, aware I don't want to upset her. 'Tell her where you are. We wouldn't want her to worry.'

He shakes his head, follows me up the stairs. 'It's fine. I'm going back to Josh's in a bit. Mum will never know I was here.'

I turn my ring around my finger, uncomfortable with the deceit, but let it go.

'So, are you OK?' I ask once we're in the lounge. I know he isn't. I know that look, the one that says he wants answers I haven't got. He will ask if I know who his father is, and I will see the pain in his young eyes, the need for me to fill the gaping hole that however much he shovels he will never fill. And I'll try to make the pain go away, like I did when he was a toddler, when he'd fallen and grazed his knees. But there's no magic kiss or strawberry ice cream that will solve the problems in his head, which all come back to who his father is and why his mum is often a mess.

He sinks down into the armchair. I perch on the edge of the sofa.

He sniffs. Gets up. Paces. Sits down.

'What is it, Kieran?'

He shoves his face into his hands, his knees spread apart — a lanky lad for eleven.

'Kieran?'

He looks up at me, blue eyes, puppy-like. 'I think my mum's seeing someone.'

I'm taken aback. This isn't what I expected at all.

He's right, but I can't tell him about the man Alene's been messaging. It's not my place. 'What makes you think that?' A question with a question. It means I'm not lying to my nephew.

'I dunno, Aunt Ri, it's just, well, she's on her phone all the time. Smiling at the screen with gooey eyes.'

'Smiling's good.'

He tugs at the cuffs of his jumper, brings them down over his hands. 'I think she might be on a dating app or something.' He shrugs. 'She's acting all weird, like she did when she first started seeing Vince.'

I get his concern. Vince had chucked in his job as soon as he moved in with my sister and Kieran. It turned out he preferred drinking and sitting around watching TV in his smelly, holey socks to spending time with Alene. He wasn't an evil man, just a lazy advantage-taker, who had no real interest in Kieran or my sister.

'Not every man is like Vince,' I say. 'And you never know, it may turn out well this time, be good for your mum.'

He frees his hands from their woollen prison. His nails are grubby, bitten short. 'I don't want her to get hurt again, is all. Vince really messed her up, you know — she thought he loved her.'

He sounds so grown up for his years. 'You mustn't worry, lovely boy.' I touch his cheek gently. 'Your mum is sensible. She's learned from her mistakes, and would never move so fast again.' I don't even know if that's true, but feel it's what Kieran needs to hear right now. 'If she is seeing someone, she'll be careful. She won't want you hurt, that's for sure.'

He crosses his arms over his head, as though holding in his anxiety. 'So, how did you two get on at the pub? Did you get to talk to her much?'

I want to say we didn't get a chance. *You called her, remember? Wanted her home.* 'We're getting there, Kieran,' I say instead, tapping his knee. 'Tell you what, I'll pop round to see her later. See how she is.'

His face brightens for a moment. 'Thanks. I'll hopefully be home by then.'

I give a little clap. 'Now, do you want a drink? I've got cola, juice, gin?' I expect him to laugh — we have the same kind of humour — but he's lost in his own thoughts, and as I rise to head into the kitchen, he gets up too.

'I better go round my mate's,' he says. 'Just in case Mum realises I'm not there and worries.'

I move closer. Give him a hug. He's trembling, so I squeeze tighter. 'Things will work themselves out, sweetie,' I say. 'I'll be over later, I promise.'

He throws me a twisted smile. 'I've put up some more photos on Instagram,' he says.

'Great, I'll have a look.'

'Thanks.'

I hear his footfalls on the stairs. The front door banging closed behind him. I've loved Kieran from the moment he came into the world — his shock of black hair as a tiny newborn, his intelligent questioning eyes staring up at me as a toddler. I wish I knew how to help the boy who is teetering on the edge of his teenage years.

I make my way into the kitchen and flick the kettle on once more. Gingerly, I pull up the blind. It's still raining, huge splatters against the window.

Whoever was standing in the field earlier in the yellow hi-vis has gone.

* * *

Later, I pull out my phone and open Instagram, ready to scroll through Kieran's latest photos. I see immediately that someone called watching_you_666 has tagged me. I clasp a shaking hand over my mouth, knowing I should have made my profile private. I click on the account. It has no followers, and nobody is being followed. My body fizzes, anxiety rising as I take in two photos that have been uploaded onto the profile. The one I've been tagged in is of me singing in the pub yesterday evening, my mouth open and my eyes wide. My skin crawls at the thought of someone, a stranger in the crowd, aiming their phone camera and snapping the picture, then uploading it here. To think I'd felt as though I was at Wembley Arena when I saw the flash last night. The other picture makes me equally uneasy. It's a picture of Stacey Roberts sitting on a bench, and she's been tagged too. I click on her account. It's mainly photos of a pug in various brightly coloured coats, and studies of different guitars. There are a couple of pictures of Stacey playing a red guitar, her hair falling about her face.

This must have been what Stacey had emailed me about.

After flicking backwards and forwards from the strange account to Stacey's I close down Instagram.

Watching_you_666? There was no doubt in my mind now. This was connected to the anonymous notes, and I would have to get in touch with Stacey, whether I liked it or not.

CHAPTER SIXTEEN

Riona

As a child, Stacey Roberts lived in an area of Ensley we kids called the Bermuda Triangle. It was said people went there to disappear. Most of us stayed away from the three roads that made up that triangle. Scary rumours circulated that drug barons lived there, and there were dead bodies in basements or buried in the back gardens of the 1930s semis. Looking back, I doubt there were any bodily remains under the patios and lilac trees, but we were young and imaginative. To us it was a dangerous place, and despite being Stacey's best friend at the time, I never ventured there.

It's OK now. The scary families moved away in the noughties, and the houses had makeovers by the housing corporation in 2009. Double-glazing and cute porches now hide the area's dark past, and new families have moved in.

Stacey spent most of her time at my house when we were kids and during our teens. We were inseparable, though very different. I was sporty, wore jeans and trainers most of the time. Still do. And she strutted down the road in heels too high for her skinny legs from about the age of thirteen. Sometimes I caught Alene watching Stacey and me playing in the garden from her bedroom window. She was envious of our closeness, and never understood why, when she came over from Sweden in 2008, we let Erika join our gang of two and not her. I wonder that myself now. Alene was younger, only by ten months, but I somehow saw her as too babyish, told her to go away when she tried to invade our space. I feel bad about that now.

Since arriving back in Ensley three years ago, apart from her attempts to get an appointment for bereavement counselling with Erika when her mother died, our paths haven't crossed. I felt no guilt that I was the reason Erika turned Stacey away from the clinic. Stacey attempted to seduce my boyfriend twelve years ago, and I will never forgive her for that. But my resolve to never let the woman back into my life has waned. I still don't trust her, but know I have to contact her about the odd Instagram account.

My mind drifts back to last night, when I saw the flash of a camera as I sang. I wish I had taken more notice. I pick up my phone, and fire off a quick message to Erika:

Good night, wasn't it? Hope you had a great time. ☺
Listen, did you notice someone taking a photo when we were singing? x

The reply is almost instant:

Nope! Head hurts. Can't think. Need water. Need sleep. Need pain killers. x ☺

* * *

Around 2 p.m., I keep my promise to Kieran and set off to my sister's house. I live on one side of the village, Alene on the other in Angel Drive, just around the corner from Aunt Bernie's, where we lived when we were young.

Outside my apartment I point my key fob towards my car, intending to drive. But the rain has stopped, and a cool sun squeezes through a pale sky, and there's only a skittering of what look to be harmless grey clouds. I shove the fob into my bag, deciding a walk may go some way to clearing my head.

The entrance to Quarry Lake is around the corner from my apartment, and I'm there within moments, stepping through the gates. Apart from the melodic sound of birdsong and the whisper of the breeze through the canopy of trees, it's quiet along the pathway leading to the water. The earlier downpour has washed the frost away, and the air feels fresh.

Quarry Lake was a clay pit in the early part of the twentieth century, a steam pump keeping the area dry. When the pump malfunctioned, and the expense of replacing it was too much, the pit closed and eventually flooded. It's a beautiful sight today, if you don't look beneath the water.

Avoiding puddles, I walk along the path, attempting to clear my head.

It's as I pass the first bench I hear a whisper, the words incomprehensible. I shudder. It's impossible to tell if it's male or female. I stop, a chill racing down my spine as my eyes flick over the dense trees, where anyone could be hiding, watching me. *Pull yourself together, Riona.* I'm being silly, the whisper was simply the rustle of the trees.

'Riona.' This time it's clearer. My name. I'm sure someone whispered my name.

'Hello?' I cry out, moving onwards, picking up speed. 'Hello?'

A rustle in the trees some distance away — a flash of yellow.

My breath coursing in and out, I veer away from the trees and start running, splashing through muddy puddles without a care for my trainers, throwing looks back over my shoulder every few moments.

Once I'm at the exit, I stop to catch my breath. I can't see anyone behind me. There's nobody here. And I wonder for a moment if I imagined it.

CHAPTER SEVENTEEN

Riona

I reach Angel Drive, my heart hammering, and stand some distance away from my sister's neat sixties semi, where she's lived for the last five years, needing to calm down before I ring the doorbell. Alene spent the money our parents left her on this house when Kieran was six, deciding it was time to move out of Aunt Bernie's. My inheritance went into buying a little terraced house in Bristol with George. When we sold up, I invested it in the clinic and bought the apartment above.

On the faded blocked-paved drive stands my sister's sparklingly clean mint-green Fiat 500, and propped at an angle against the wall of the open garage is Kieran's bike.

Once calmer, I head up the path, narrowing my eyes in an attempt to see through the nets at their bow-fronted window, feeling sure someone's standing behind them.

I take a moment, reluctant to alert them that I'm here, before I've worked out how to begin my conversation with Alene. It really is that difficult.

Shifting closer, I take a deep breath and ring the doorbell.

Alene opens up immediately, making me think she'd seen my approach. She's dressed in skinny black jeans and a cream crew-neck jumper. Her shiny, dark hair is pulled back in a tight bun. 'Riona. What are you doing here?' Her voice is clipped as she pokes her head out, her eyes flicking across the quiet road, as though checking nobody saw me. 'I wasn't expecting you.'

'It's lovely to see you too, sis.' I attempt a smile, taking in that her face looks red and sore. I know I'm pulling a bewildered face I can't take back.

She touches her cheek. 'Microneedling, if you're wondering,' she says. 'I had it done this morning. It generates new collagen. You wouldn't understand.'

She's right. I wouldn't. Why she needs to mess about with her face is beyond my understanding. 'I'm guessing the redness disappears after a while, and that's not part of your new look.'

She smiles, cracks her knuckles. 'Yes, of course it does. It will leave my skin firmer, smoother—'

'You'll need to slow up soon, or people will think you're my daughter, not my sister.'

She laughs, seeming to love the idea. 'Do you want to come in?'

'No, I'm here as your new garden gnome.'

She rolls her eyes and moves to one side. 'You're rather large to be a gnome, Riona.'

I enter the hall, a comforting aroma of baking greeting me, and slip off my jacket. My sister takes it from me, and hangs it on a hook by the door, as I lean against the floral Laura Ashley wallpaper tugging free my trainers.

She watches me, and I sense she's on edge. I expect she's worried the mud will get on her carpet.

'Something smells good,' I say. Alene has always baked, though she never eats cakes, always too conscious of her weight. Even Kieran isn't much of a fan of sweet things. Most of her creations end up being passed on to Aunt Bernie, who devours them without worrying about her weight at all.

'Red velvet cake,' Alene says, disappearing into the kitchen, and I follow. The units are dark and dated. Have been here since she bought the place, and for probably the thirty years before that. It's clean — so clean.

'Was Kieran OK when you got home last night?' I want to bite my tongue. Kicking off with something I already know isn't a good start. Maybe I should have come right out and said Kieran came round to see me earlier. But then I don't want to get the boy into trouble. I feel my thoughts tangle, and I almost want to cry.

'He was fine. You know how he gets sometimes. He insisted he was too old for a babysitter, but then started to get the creeps after I left. Thought someone was in the back garden, as the security lights came on. Of course, there was no sign of anyone when I got back here, and those lights turn on randomly all the time. I just wish I'd asked Aunt Bernie to be with him.'

'I guess eleven is quite young to be left on your own,' I say, knowing by the narrowing of Alene's eyes that I've said the wrong thing. But I feel sometimes Alene thinks the boy's so much older than he is.

'What would you know about bringing up a child, Riona?'

I say nothing. Her words sting, though I guess she isn't to know George and I were trying for a baby when he cheated. That I so want a child of my own. It's something I've never shared with anyone, not even Erika, and probably never will.

I watch as she fills the kettle and takes mugs from a mug tree.

'So how did the rest of your evening go?' she says, flicking on the kettle and turning her gaze my way. 'Did you and Erika have fun?'

'It was OK.'

'You don't sound too sure.'

'No, I enjoyed it.' I'm desperate to tell her more. I want to mention Tom, confide in her about the email from Stacey, the photos on Instagram, the letters Erika and I received. I would love to tell her everything, but I'm not sure we're close enough. It was different when we were children. In Ireland, we clung to each other like Velcro when our parents died. But as our teenage selves took over the children we once were, we lost that bond. I blame myself for that.

She continues to stare, as she leans against the work surface. 'Is everything OK, Riona?' She tucks a straying hair behind her ear. 'I mean, you don't normally just pop round to see me.' There's a subtext here that I can't work out. Would she have preferred I didn't come? Preferred I called first? Or is she glad I'm here — wishes we saw more of each other?

I'm not sure what to say. Should I bring up the man she has been messaging? Somehow work in that I think Kieran suspects? Suggest she tells him what's going on? Who he is. But then I get why she doesn't, after Vince. 'So, where's my lovely nephew?' I say instead.

'He's in his room uploading some photographs to Instagram that he took at Quarry Lake earlier. He went there with a mate and his mum.' A pause. 'He really takes after you and Dad with his eye for a brilliant shot, doesn't he?'

'He does, yes.'

'I missed out on that artistic gene.' She smiles. 'He'll be pleased to see you, Riona, always is. I'll text him that you're here, in a minute.'

Text him? When he's in his room?

As though reading my thoughts, she says, 'He doesn't like being disturbed when he's concentrating.'

But he's eleven. Eleven! A little boy! Stop treating him like he's so much older.

Once the coffee is made, Alene carries two steaming mugs into the lounge, and I follow balancing a slice of red velvet cake, I'm not sure I want, on a bone china plate She places the mugs on silver coasters on the polished wooden coffee table, and I put down my cake. The lounge is pristine. The old-fashioned, embroidered three-piece suite is positioned around the table, facing a heavy gas-effect fire. A small TV is nestled in the corner.

We sit down, one each end of the uncomfortable sofa, like bookends.

On a beech-wood unit there's a cluster of photos, and my eyes fall on the silver-framed photograph of our parents. Mary and Phillip Foley on their wedding day: my father, not handsome, but quirkily charming in a blue-and-yellow-checked suit; my mother, a picture of happiness in her white dress, her dark hair woven with flowers. I gulp back a sudden wave of tears. The grief still hits every now and then, often when I least expect it, and I wonder if it always will.

Aunt Bernie told me once that the moment she met my mother she loved her. That Mary and my father had been meant for each other, that soul mates didn't begin to cover it. I comforted myself as a child that because they died at the exact same moment, they would have travelled up to heaven holding hands, but I don't know what to believe anymore. I'm much more sceptical than I was back then.

I turn away from the photo, my eyes skimming several pictures of Kieran – baby, toddler, schoolboy. For a while there was a large photo of Alene and Vince, but that's been gone for a while now. There are no pictures of Alene and me, even as children, which makes me sad, but then I've no photos up of her in my apartment either.

We sip our drinks, and a silence stretches, tense and uncomfortable. My mind runs through ways of bringing up the subject of Kieran knowing she has met someone. It's better that she knows, surely.

'I'll text Kieran, shall I?' she says, picking up her phone.

I imagine him upstairs, his pleasure as he uploads photos of wildlife he's captured, oblivious that I'm here. I take another sip of my coffee.

'Something odd happened this morning,' I say, surprising myself. Am I so lost for words that I'm prepared to confide in my sister? Or is the inner me desperate to get closer to her?

'Really?' Her eyes brighten. 'What sort of thing?'

I pull my phone from my bag, open up Instagram, and shuffle along the sofa, closer to my sister, sensing her tense. 'I was tagged on Instagram.' I show her the strange account.

She peers at the small screen with narrowed eyes. 'That's Stacey Roberts, isn't it? And are you singing?' She looks up at me.

'The one of me was taken last night, after you left.'

'So, who took it?'

I shake my head. 'That's the point. I have no idea. I received an email from Stacey too, telling me about the account.'

'You don't know who set it up?'

'No, not a clue.'

'That's a bit odd, Riona. You need to report it.'

'Yes, yes I will. But first I need to talk to Stacey.'

'After what she did?' She blinks, drinks her coffee.

'I'm not going to renew our friendship or anything like that.'

'Well, good, she doesn't deserve it. She still lives in the village, did you know?'

'Yes, I've managed to avoid her since I got back.'

'I see her about sometimes. She's got a little pug. I don't think she knows who I am anymore.' Her voice tenses. 'I never had much to do with you and your friends.'

Guilt gnaws at my insides. 'And I've always felt bad about that.'

'Don't feel bad. We were kids. Water under the bridge, as they say.'

I'm not sure any water has flowed under that bridge. Truth is, the water is motionless. Never quite shifting so we can move on.

'Do you know where Stacey lives?' I ask, turning my phone over in my hands.

'Still in Bridge Court, in her mum's old house, I think.' Her eyes glaze over. 'I heard years ago that her mum came into some money — which was all a bit dodgy, if you ask me — and bought the place from the council. When she died it came to Stacey.' She pauses for a moment, as though thinking. 'Yes, Bridge Court,' she says with confidence. 'Not sure what number.'

'The Bermuda Triangle.'

She laughs, and I love that we are sharing a moment. 'It's a nice enough area now.'

I drop my phone back into my bag, and another silence falls. I'm relieved when Kieran appears in the doorway, hands deep in the pockets of his black joggers.

Alene jumps to her feet, pats his cheek gently. 'I'll make you a drink, sweetheart.'

'No. It's fine, Mum. I'm not thirsty. Sit down. Please.' There's a grown-up confidence in his tone, despite his voice being high, unbroken. 'I wanted Riona to come. We need to talk.'

'What?' My sister's cheeks flush. She folds her arms around herself and looks at me with a dagger-like stare. 'Why?'

My heart starts to gallop, as I wish now I'd told Alene the truth. That I had spoken to Kieran earlier.

'I know you're messaging someone, Mum. A bloke. And Riona has confirmed it.'

'I . . .' I want to scream that I haven't confirmed anything. I know Kieran's just a child and I should call him out, but he's trying to articulate in a grown-up world, and I can hear the anxiety in his voice. He needs to know I've got his back.

The flush in Alene's cheeks drains away

'Who is he, Mum? Why can't you tell me?' The mood in the room has plummeted. Alene's eyes flash angrily, and I don't blame her. Kieran hasn't handled this well, but then kids aren't meant to handle this kind of thing. I want to say something, but I can't find the right words, and a lump wedges in my throat.

'This is none of Riona's business, Kieran,' Alene cries.

'I know.' I look from her to her son, who suddenly looks like the toddler he once was. I'm desperate not to upset either one of them. 'But there's no need to get angry, Alene, please don't overreact.'

'Overreact? I'm not overreacting, Riona, and I'm not angry,' she cries. 'I just don't want you in my house right now. Conspiring with my son. I want you to leave. Please.'

I rise quickly, knowing this has damaged any progress we've been making, knowing at the root of this is the fact she'll never fully forgive me for not supporting her through our teenage years, and that any little incident like this is going to unleash her inner, angry teenager, every single time. 'I'm so sorry, Alene. I—'

'You need to leave, Riona. Please. You haven't exactly made a success of your own life, so who are you to interfere in mine?'

'I wasn't doing that, Alene. I just—'

'What? Just wanted to poke your nose in? I didn't want Kieran to know until I knew how I really felt. I've only just started talking to him again, it's such early days, and now you've messed it up.'

Again?

'Mum!' Kieran's voice is full of tears, and I want to take him in my arms and hug him close, but I know it will only make things worse. I leave the room, bashing away tears from my cheeks with the palms of my hands.

In the hall, I tug on my trainers, flakes of mud dropping onto the carpet. Why did I think I had the right to get involved? But I know why: I would do anything for my nephew, anything at all that he asked of me . . . and despite everything, I love my sister, and only want the best for her.

Outside, the puffs of grey cloud from earlier have mutated. The sky is dark, and slanting rain splatters my face as I race down the path and onto the pavement. I'm tempted to head round the corner to Aunt Bernie's, but I know I will only blurt out about Alene messaging someone and end up making things worse. Instead I drag up my hood, and, with my head down against the downpour, I make my way towards Quarry Lake.

Rain pounds against my back with force, pushing me along the path that curves round the lake. I splash in puddles, my socks soaked through, trainers squelching, the dark sky heavy on my shoulders, weighing me down. I glance to my right. Without the sun's rays to bring out the stunning royal blue, the expanse of water looks grey and eerie, rain thundering on its surface like a million bullets. I pick up speed, pushing the strange whispers of earlier from my thoughts, desperate to get home.

CHAPTER EIGHTEEN

Charlotte

I sit at the heavy oak table, the newspapers that covered it when I arrived now stacked outside the back door. I open up my laptop and google 'Hertfordshire Developers'. It's a futile search that I've done a thousand times before, always coming up with nothing. I've been through all the requests for planning permission. Everything. I need to return to Cornwall, to Ryan. Accept Mother got it wrong, or perhaps lured me here for reasons I will never know.

I turn to the window beside me. Rain blurs the view of the lonely country lane.

Someone is heading up the path, pushing through the rain, making his way up towards the front door. I go to duck out of view, but it's too late. The man raises his hand in a wave. He's seen me.

The doorbell chimes, the sound bouncing around the musty, dusty cottage. I rise, brush the creases from my cotton trousers, straighten my jumper and head for the door. I put on the chain and open up.

'Hi.' The man is handsome. Tall. Slim. 'Are you Charlotte Carter?'

'What of it?' I say.

'I was sorry to hear about your mother.'

'I don't need your sympathy.'

'But it must have been a shock.'

Agitation rises; I haven't got time for this. 'What exactly do you want?'

Rain rolls down the man's face, soaks his hair. 'The thing is, you need to leave Ensley. Go back to wherever you've been living all these years. It's not safe here.'

I go to push the door closed, but he moves forward, holds it open with force. 'You're making no sense,' I say.

'I can't explain in any more detail, Mrs Carter, but you need to leave. Now. You're not safe.' He releases the door, and it slams closed.

My stomach churns, uneasy feelings swirling around me.

I move into the dining room, watch the man hurry down the path, his head down, disappearing into the country lane. Who is he? Why does he think I'm not safe? And why can't I get it out of my head that his visit has something to do with my daughter's drowning?

CHAPTER NINETEEN

Riona

I reach home, drenched and unsettled, and pull off my muddy trainers and rain-soaked jacket, before taking the stairs to my apartment.

After a shower, I snuggle on the sofa with my Kindle, trying to lose myself in a murder mystery I downloaded a few days ago. Wanda, never one for missing a chance to cuddle up, jumps onto my lap. Purrs as I tickle her ears.

'Things are a bit weird right now, Wanda,' I say, convinced she understands, and she looks up at me with gleaming green eyes as though she does. I feel strange. In fact, I haven't felt right since I received the odd letter at the clinic. Things are off-centre, and my inner self is crying out to me to be careful.

Wanda continues to purr, kisses my chin.

'Thanks,' I say. 'I needed that.'

Later, just after six o'clock, I'm at an exciting place in the book — the killer is about to be caught — when Wanda meows.

'Dinner?' I say, and she jumps from my lap and dashes into the kitchen. I follow, and she continues to meow softly, twisting her slim, silky body around my legs. I decant a tin of far-too-expensive cat food and a few biscuits into her dish, and I'm about to make myself some crackers and cheese when the doorbell chimes.

I rarely get unannounced visitors; even Kieran earlier was a surprise. If anyone comes to my flat it's either a delivery or people trying to convince me to find their God. Even Erika and my aunt normally call first. I look a mess in my leggings and a long, misshapen jumper. My hair is frizzy after the shower. There's no way I'm letting anyone in — unless, of course, it's Kieran again.

I leave Wanda eating and, without turning on the landing light, tiptoe down the stairs like a cat burglar. The porch light highlights a tall figure behind the glass door panel. A man, I decide, and my heartbeat quickens, my mind springing to stalkers and serial killers. I'm being ridiculous. *What's the matter with me?* But then I know the answer to that. Weird things are happening.

'Hello,' I call out.

'Riona, hi, it's Tom Evans.'

'Tom? How did you know where I live?' I'm aware I sound distrusting.

'You mentioned you live in the flat above the clinic. Sorry, maybe I shouldn't have come.'

'No, it's fine.' I look down at myself, spotting my massive seal pup slippers. Part of me wants to say, *Now is not a good time*, but I have to admit I'd like to see him again. 'I've just got out of the shower.'

His shape moves closer to the glass. 'I just wanted to say it was great meeting you, that I would have messaged or called, but don't have your number.' He's talking fast, barely coming up for breath. 'I was going to send you a friend request on Facebook, or follow you on Instagram, but thought I might come across a bit stalky.' He moves away from the window.

I wouldn't have minded. I take a deep breath and open the door, am greeted by his smile and a bashful gesture of pushing his fingers through his hair. But there's something off. His eyes are puffy and bloodshot. 'Is everything OK?'

'It's fine, honestly.' He glances over his shoulder, his eyes narrowing as he looks towards the trees that line the street opposite.

'What's up?' I ask, the moment of excitement of finding him at my front door draining away.

His eyes are back on me. 'I had a weird feeling when I got out of my car, is all. Like I was being watched. Saw a flash of yellow.' He flaps a hand, smiles. 'Ignore me. I'm having a strange kind of day.'

'You'd better come in.' I open the door wider, and he steps onto the ceramic tiles. As he takes off his jacket, I poke my head out into the street. It's stopped raining, but it's dark out. There's nobody about that I can see. 'To be honest, I could do with a friendly face right now,' I say, closing the door and pulling the bolt across.

'Everything OK?'

'Yeah, yeah. Like you, it's been an odd sort of a day.'

I make some coffee. He sits in the armchair, and I perch on the edge of the sofa. 'You'll have to excuse my appearance,' I say. 'I don't normally look this awful.' It's a lie. It's actually quite commonplace on a Sunday for me to look on the wrong side of casual, and sometimes on a Monday, Tuesday . . .

'You look great to me.'

'Charmer.'

He laughs, but I notice once more his bloodshot eyes. 'I don't mean to pry, Tom, but is everything OK?'

After a moment, he says, 'I'm just finding it a bit hard being here in Ensley. Not sure why I came really.' His voice breaks.

I think about how he recently lost her, empathise with that gut-wrenching feeling of loss. I lean over, take hold of his hand. 'I'm so sorry about your sister.'

'Thanks,' he says. 'I suppose I thought coming here would help. But it hasn't. In fact, I think I need to head back to Norfolk.'

'When?' I sound far too disappointed.

'Tomorrow morning, I think. I just wanted to say good-bye, and, well . . . maybe I'll get to see you again sometime. I thought we hit it off pretty well yesterday.'

'We did. Yes. I thought so too.'

'So how are things with you?' He glances down at me clutching his hand, and I release it, realising I've been holding it for far too long.

'Fine,' I say, my worries seeming small next to his grief.

He smiles, tilts his head. 'Are you sure? You don't sound fine. Has something happened?'

'Well, if I'm honest, I've had an odd couple of days.' Maybe it's his gentle, caring eyes, but I suddenly feel I can tell him anything. 'I received an anonymous letter, saying someone is watching me.'

His eyes widen. 'Oh God, Riona, that's not good. You need to be careful. Can you take off for a few weeks, get out of Ensley?'

'That's a bit extreme, don't you think?'

He shakes his head, as though he wants to say more, casting a hand across his forehead. 'Do you have any idea who could have sent it?'

'No. Not really. I thought it could be someone on my client list, or a relative of someone who came to me who didn't get on very well. Erika got a letter too. Almost identical.'

His eyes widen. 'Have you called the police?'

I shake my head. Stare down at my hands. 'I'm not sure what they can do. It's probably just some weirdo. But with everything else that's been happening.'

'Everything else?'

'It's nothing, nothing at all.' I look up, stare into his eyes. I so want to tell him about the Instagram account, the odd figure in a yellow hi-vis in the field and by Quarry Lake. 'You don't need this, you've got enough to cope with.'

'No, it's OK, honestly.'

But I know I can't burden Tom any more than I already have. I sit for a moment, cradling my mug, before finally reaching over and touching his hand once more. He entwines his fingers with mine, and the fizz I feel is far too real.

'So, do you live alone in Norfolk?' It's a clumsy question, and a clumsy change of subject.

He nods, and half smiles. 'It's just me and the dogs, since my last relationship ended.'

'I'm sorry.'

'Don't be. We weren't right for each other, and both accepted that. We agreed we'd stay friends, but that, in my experience, rarely happens. I haven't seen her in almost a year. As I say, it's just the dogs and me. What about you?'

'Well, I was in a long-term relationship until a few years ago . . . he cheated on me.'

'Christ. Why would anyone do that?'

'You really are the charmer, aren't you?' I say with a smile. 'So, are the dogs with you in Ensley?'

He shakes his head. 'They're with my mum. I was going to bring them — wish I had now, they're a great comfort — but Mum was keen to have them. Since Becky died she's struggled, you know, and the dogs take her mind off things. I keep trying to get her to get a puppy or a rescue dog. She may do, in time.' He releases my hand. 'God, I'm sharing far too much. In fact, I better go.'

'Oh. OK.' I'm surprised, no, *disappointed*. He's only just got here, has barely touched his coffee. I want him to stay.

He rises, and seeming to register my disappointment, says, 'Would it be OK to get your number?'

'Yes.' I grab my phone. 'Great idea.'

Once we've exchanged numbers, he heads down the stairs, and I follow.

'Maybe we could see each other again sometime,' he says. 'It's only a couple of hours' drive.'

'I'd love that,' I say, though I can't see it happening, not if he's heading home to Norfolk tomorrow. We haven't had time to get to know each other. 'Take care, won't you?' I add. 'You know where I am if you need a friendly ear.'

'Thanks,' he says, as he pulls on his jacket and turns up the collar. He leans in and kisses my cheek. 'I appreciate that. And the same goes for you. Call me anytime if you're worried about anything at all, I'll come running. And please be careful, Riona.' He pauses for a moment. 'I still think you should think about taking off for a bit, get away from here.'

Once Tom has gone, I make beans on toast, and put on the TV, turning the volume up in an attempt to drown out my befuddled thoughts, as I watch an episode of *Friends*. But it's no good. I grab my mobile, drawn back to Instagram, needing to look at the photos once more.

I fumble open the strange profile, and as the account comes into view, my phone almost slips through my fingers. There are now four photographs. As well as the original two, there is one of me by Quarry Lake, and one of Stacey Roberts standing outside a semi-detached house, the number five clearly visible on a bright-red front door behind her. My heartbeat picks up speed, and nausea rises. What the hell is going on?

CHAPTER TWENTY

Charlotte

I stare out of the bedroom window into the darkness, my eyes landing at the foot of the garden. I blink, move closer to the grubby glass. The gate that leads to the lake stands open. I feel sure it was latched earlier. Suddenly a figure in yellow darts across the garden; someone is out there. But before I can see who it is, the garden plunges into a pool of black, the moon disappearing behind a cloud.

I descend the stairs, my heart drumming, careful not to fall. They're rickety, cluttered with piles of this and that, perhaps explaining Mother's demise. I need to clear them tomorrow. I wouldn't want to end up the same way, in a crumpled heap at the bottom.

A noise startles me, and I move slowly into the kitchen, peering in to see the backdoor handle moving up and down.

'Who's there?' I call out, my stomach churning. I snatch a knife from the rack. Hold it out in front of me in shaking hands. 'Who's out there?'

A *thump, thump, thump* on the door makes me jump. I step backwards, into the kitchen doorway, taking one hand from the knife and fumbling in my pocket for my phone.

'I'll call the police,' I cry, close to tears. 'Just go away. Leave me alone.'

The door handle rattles once more, and then there's silence.

My mind jumps to the man who came to the door earlier, warning me I wasn't safe. Did he know something I don't. I put down the knife on a pile of newspapers, pushing my glasses further up my nose, as I hover a shaking finger over the number nine on the phone screen. But I can't get the police involved. It was bad enough that they came round asking questions about Mother's death.

I wait, watching the door, motionless for more than five minutes. But there are no more thumps, no more rattles of the door handle. Whoever was on the other side of the door has gone, back through the gate at the bottom of the garden — back to Quarry Lake.

CHAPTER TWENTY-ONE

Me

The yellow hi-vis jacket hangs on the outside of the wardrobe. The mask hooked onto the corner of the bedstead. I picked the creepy mask up from a fancy-dress shop — it's perfect.

'Are you going to a party?' asked the woman in her sixties with big teeth and a nose ring, as she put the mask into a brown paper bag. 'Bit late for Halloween, isn't it?'

I wanted to scream at her to mind her own fucking business. But managed to stay polite, smiled at her across the counter. 'Everyone's after elves and Santas at the moment,' she added, taking my twenty-pound note, holding it up to the light as though she could tell if it was a fake, 'and I'm completely out of reindeers.'

I know you saw me from your window, Riona, when I was standing in the field behind your apartment. I didn't have my mask then, was worried you would see my face, but it seems you didn't.

You pulled down the blind. Out of sight, out of mind, isn't that what they say? I hope you saw the tag from the Instagram account too. Saw those lovely photos I took of you. I've got quite a talent for the natural shots, don't you think?

Of course, this is all just something to entertain myself while I wait for the right moment.

There's no rush.

No rush at all.

There's plenty of time, because honestly, Riona, I'm the last person you'll ever suspect.

CHAPTER TWENTY-TWO

Riona

Monday, 6 December 2021

After my run, I shower, pull on leggings and a jumper, and head down to the clinic. We're closed on Mondays, so I leave the blinds down at the front window and step into my office, where I open up the client list on my laptop and plough through all my regulars' details, attempting to find someone who may have something against Erika and me, enough to pen the two anonymous letters. But I honestly can't find anyone who would be so cruel. Perhaps I'm too trusting. Aunt Bernie once called me gullible, trying, in rather blunt fashion, to warn me what kind of person Stacey was, long before she made a pass at George.

I rise and grab my coat. Although it's the last thing I want to do right now, I have an appointment in Hitchin to have my eyes tested. After that, I need to pluck up the courage to approach Stacey.

It's later, as I come out of the opticians, that I see Tom on the other side of the road, striding along the pavement near the bank, his phone pinned to his ear. I raise my hand in a wave, but he doesn't seem to see me.

I wait for a gap in the traffic before hurrying across the road, seeing him turn up the Arcade. I don't know why I feel the need to follow. He said he's heading back to Norfolk. Whatever spark I felt when we were together, I need to put it out.

I zigzag through mothers with prams, an old man with a walking stick, before reaching the bottom of the Arcade. Tom is at the far end, and I hurry towards him, passing shops and huddles of people, finally seeing him pushing open the main doors of a block of flats, a fob in his hand. He steps inside. I'm frozen to the spot. He told me he was staying with his uncle and aunt on the Oakfield Estate, which is on the outskirts of town, that he came to Ensley alone. What is he doing with a fob to an apartment block?

Later, I drive to Bridge Court, hoping to find Stacey at home, trying to push out thoughts of Tom and focus on the odd things that are happening. I need to talk to Stacey, find out her thoughts on the Instagram account. Our estrangement needs to be put on hold — for now, at least. We don't have to become friends again, but she may have an idea who could be doing this.

I know it won't be easy. I haven't seen Stacey for so long, and our ten-year friendship ended so miserably. I can never delete the image of catching her and George together, and I wonder briefly how I forgave him at the time. I should have known, despite him insisting it was all Stacey, that he would do it again.

The weather has improved since yesterday, no sign of rain. It's cold, but the sun is bright through the car windscreen. I squint as I turn the corner into Bridge Court and pull up outside number five. I recognise the red front door, knowing immediately it's the house in the photo of Stacey on Instagram. I drag up the handbrake and kill the engine.

From the car, I glance about me. The area has a quiet, pleasant ambience, no sign of its traumatic history in the pretty gardens and brightly painted front doors. Some of the houses are already decorated for Christmas, one house with a giant blow-up Santa on a sleigh sitting on the roof, which makes me smile. I take a deep breath, get out of the car and head up the path towards the front door of the 1930s semi, passing a couple of white reindeers woven with lights. I ring the doorbell. A dog barks.

'Quiet, Minnie,' I hear from behind the coloured-glass panel, Stacey's voice so familiar, and a lump rises in my throat at the thought of seeing her again. I liked her once. Despite everything, we had fun in our teens.

The door swings open, revealing her tall, slim frame.

'Oh God, Riona.' She covers her mouth, her hazel eyes bright. 'Bloody hell, I can't believe it's you in the flesh.' Her shoulder-length, auburn hair is redder than it once was, dyed perhaps, and a cute pug is wedged under her arm. 'Long time, no see.'

I almost say I'm sorry for that — for never getting in touch — but remember, just in time, that she is the one who should be sorry. 'I got your email, I've seen—?'

'The photos on Instagram.' She steps aside, beckons me with her free hand. 'You'd better come in.' She puts the pug down, and the furry creature scampers away on little legs. 'It's all very worrying, isn't it?' she continues, leading the way into a large kitchen with patio doors opening at the far end. A red guitar is propped in the corner, and a memory flies in of Stacey teaching herself to play the instrument, because her mum couldn't afford lessons. 'Coffee?' she says, before the memory can fully form.

I shake my head. 'I won't stay long. I just thought we should, well, talk.'

'OK. Yes.' It's then that I notice the scar on her cheek, which hadn't registered in the photo of her on Instagram. I can't seem to tear my eyes away from it.

She touches her face, clearly seeing me stare. 'It was a wake-up call,' she says. 'Made me realise I needed to change who I was. Become a better person.'

'What happened?'

'I was attacked by a very upset wife five years ago, and I don't blame her one little bit. I was "a monstrosity, a blight on society" — her words, not mine, but she wasn't far wrong.'

'She cut you?' I cringe, feeling the pain Stacey must have felt.

'Not deliberately — she threw a plate at me when she caught me in her front room with her husband in my underwear. It hit the wall, shattered, and a sharp piece of china caught my face. I had six stitches.'

'Oh my God.' I covered my mouth.

'It was only what I deserved, Riona. I'm sure you would have done the same, given half the chance.'

I look away, unable to answer. I'm not normally a dramatic, 'throwing plates' kind of person, but at the time of Stacey's betrayal my anger was uncontrollable.

'I've been an idiot so many times,' she says. 'And I'm so sorry for the person I once was, really I am. I can only try to make good now.'

I'm not sure what she wants me to say, but I can't find any words that feel right. And anyway, I'm not here to discuss the past. I move my eyes away from her stare. 'I hope you don't mind me coming round.'

'Not at all, I'm so glad you're here.' She gestures for me to sit down, and I perch on a wooden stool at a breakfast bar. 'I spoke to Erika a few months back,' she says, 'and again more recently—'

'She told me. I was sorry to hear about your mum.'

She shakes her head. 'Weird one, that. You must recall how she wasn't the best mum growing up, but we'd grown closer in the last few years. She even got a job, would you believe? Street cleaner — she loved it. Gave her a sense of purpose, she said.' She smiles, a shimmer in her eyes. 'She died of a heart attack at fifty. She'd abused her body too much over the years, and it caught up with her.'

'I'm sorry,' I say again. I never liked her mother, was creeped out by her as a kid, when she turned up at my house, drugged up or drunk, demanding Stacey should come home. Her dad had died before I arrived in Ensley. A dealer who upset the wrong person — that's what the rumour was, anyway.

Stacey lowers herself onto a stool opposite me. 'I heard you and George—'

'Broke up, yes.' My jaw tightens. She's the last person I want to talk to about George.

'We had some good times, didn't we, Riona?' she says. 'Back in our teens. So many laughs. Remember that time—'

'Can I stop you there, Stacey.' I hold up my hand like I'm halting traffic, my tone snappy. 'I'm not here to go on a trip down memory lane.' I feel no qualms at being so blunt. No compunction for cutting her off.

She lowers her head, fiddles with her fingers. 'No, no, of course you're not.'

'So, you've seen the Instagram account,' I say, stating the obvious.

She nods. Picks up a packet of cigarettes and a lighter from the ledge beside her. Puts them down again. She didn't smoke when I knew her. 'I was tagged.'

'Have you any idea at all who would do this?'

She shakes her head. 'I've gone over and over it. Why someone would target the two of us. I mean, we haven't had any contact for almost twelve years.'

'I know. It doesn't make any sense.'

Three thuds on the front door makes me jump, and the pug flies from her bed in the corner and barks frantically, skidding across the black-and-white chequered floor tiles towards the door.

Stacey gets up, holding her chest. 'Minnie, for goodness' sake, it's only a delivery,' she says, leaving the room.

I look about me. Waiting. Her kitchen is modern, clean, the cupboards and surfaces white — too white, migraine inducing. The only splashes of colour are Minnie's furry, red bed and the guitar.

I rise, moving across the kitchen towards the fridge-freezer, where magnets pin paperwork to the door: an appointment with an estate agent, another with a dentist, a list of Christmas events in the area. There's a photo too, of Stacey and what looks to be her mother, and there's one of me, Stacey and Erika when we were in our teens. Did we really still mean that much to her?

'Riona! Riona!'

I start at the sound of Stacey's anxious voice and dash into the hall.

'You OK?' I ask.

She stares at me from where she's standing by the front door, holding a parcel.

'What's wrong?' I say, sure her panic has something to do with the parcel, and head towards her. 'Are you OK?' I repeat, but it's as though she's fallen into a trance. I look outside to see the courier pull away in a white van, but other than that, the road is quiet.

'Sorry.' She closes the door slowly, her voice shaky. 'I'm a bag of nerves — a total mess.' She takes a breath. 'The thing is — and please don't think I'm crazy — I keep seeing someone in a yellow hi-vis. You know, like the Ensley Killer wore.'

I cover my mouth with my hand. 'Oh God.'

'It's ever since I was tagged on Instagram, and it's as though whoever it is is watching me.'

The image in the field behind my apartment enters my mind, the vision by Quarry Lake. 'I . . .'

Stacey stares at me for a long moment before narrowing her eyes. 'You've seen them too, haven't you?'

I nod, hairs rising on the back of my neck. 'I think so.'

She closes the door and we return to the kitchen, where Stacey puts down the parcel and takes the packet of cigarettes from the shelf with shaking hands. 'Lots of people wear yellow hi-vis jackets.'

'Yes, yes they do.'

'But this feels different. In fact, and I know this sounds a bit barking, but it looked today as though they were wearing a mask. They're always so still, staring, watching me.' She takes a deep breath. 'I'm in a dreadful state, Riona,' she goes on. 'My frayed nerves can't handle this right now. I need a ciggie. Maybe you should go. We can talk another time.'

I had hoped we would get to the root of the odd Instagram posts. But Stacey heads away from me, opens the patio doors and steps out into her garden, Minnie on her heels. I watch her for a moment as she lights a cigarette, takes a long drag and blows smoke upwards out of the side of her mouth.

Before leaving, I jot down my phone number and put it on the worktop. I need to talk to Stacey some more, and the sooner the better.

It's later when I'm back at my apartment that I check the Instagram account. Another photo has appeared. It's of Stacey, standing on her doorstep, cradling the parcel.

CHAPTER TWENTY-THREE

Me

Nobody knows she's dead. That's the sheer fun of it. You're all going about your lives with no idea that I've already taken my first victim.

I sit on the edge of the bed, alone, but never lonely, and chuckle like a demented clown, excitement bubbling. I can't wait to move in for more kills.

But I need to be patient. Curb my needs, and savour the journey. But it is such a thrill I could almost burst. It's so good to see the fear I'm creating. The anxious looks as my future victims gaze about them, unsettled.

CHAPTER TWENTY-FOUR

Riona

Tuesday, 7 December 2021

I've been awake since 4 a.m., my thoughts chaotic, tangled, as I try to make sense of everything. Now it's gone six, and, with tired eyes, I trace a hairline crack across the ceiling, my head nestled against the soft pillow. I concentrate on my breathing, stay in the moment, aware of Wanda's gentle, rhythmic purr, but nothing more.

The sudden ping of a text invades my tranquil state. Startled, I lean over to the bedside unit, pick up my phone and hold it up in front of my eyes as I open the message:

> I must have eaten something rank, Riona. I've never felt SO ill. Throwing up big time. Can you cancel my clients for today please? Erika x

I sit up and swing my legs round, making Wanda jump. 'Sorry, sweetie,' I say, as I type an instant reply to Erika:

> Yes, of course! Get well soon, lovely. Do you need anything? x

She gets back within moments:

Just need to rest, will call you soon. x

Showered, dressed, cereal eaten and Wanda fed, I take the stairs down to the clinic and cross reception. Once in Erika's office, I search through her appointments. She keeps a physical diary, and I call her four clients for today, promising them that Erika will rearrange as soon as possible. I close her diary and sit for a moment, my mind drifting back to Saturday evening, the letters we both received.

I'm watching you.

I keep wondering if I should tell Aunt Bernie what's been happening. After thirty-five years in the police force, she may have some idea what I should do. I don't want to worry her, but she's always been strong, and I feel sure she would want me to confide in her — to turn to her.

The morning goes by fast: a mindful eating session with a group of women in their sixties who seemed to enjoy the cake a little too much, followed by two reiki healing clients. Now it's midday, and I haven't got any more clients until three o'clock.

As I sit at my desk eating my lunch, my mind drifts to Tom. Curious, I get up Facebook and track down his dog-walking page, scrolling through the gorgeous photos of dogs out on treks with him around Cromer: by rivers, in fields, on the beach, all different breeds and sizes, updates of the brown-eyed pups being promised liver cake and treats. Looking at him crouched beside them in selfies and out with them in all weathers, it's clear he adores those dogs. He even does what he calls a moonlight walk, where all the dogs have reflective bands around their necks and he's wearing a reflective jacket.

I close my laptop. There must be an explanation why he went into an apartment in Hitchin town centre. Why he told me he was staying with his aunt and uncle, when that doesn't seem to be the case. Or perhaps I'm overanalysing. Maybe he was simply visiting a friend. Tom's one of the good guys, I feel sure of it.

I glance at my watch and rise from my desk. I need to visit Aunt Bernie before my next client.

There's a small driveway next to the clinic, and I notice immediately that someone has parked across it, blocking my car in. It means I'll have to walk my usual route by Quarry Lake — something I hadn't planned to do. I take a deep breath, refusing to be frightened into changing my normal behaviour. It's a bright, frosty afternoon, so I decide to jog the route, and pop back into my flat and change into my running gear. As I jog towards the entrance, I take out my headphones, deciding I need to keep my wits about me, however determined I am not to be beaten.

Halfway along the lonely pathway, the haunting sound of someone humming echoes around me, bouncing off the tall trees, making my neck tingle. I stop and twist round, pinning the sound down to a clump of trees nearby. It's impossible to say where it's coming from, but I'm sure someone is here. I spot a flash of yellow in the trees, but it's gone within moments.

I take a deep breath. Convince myself I imagined the sighting. But still the humming continues, though it appears to be getting more distant. *I know that tune.* It's my father's Irish ballad, the one Erika and I sang in the Fox on Saturday night. It stops suddenly, and I freeze, staring out towards the boathouse, the sun's rays shining down, the water glittering.

Memories of the night we saw the candle burning in the window crash in uninvited. Who had lit it? Had someone been there? Had they hidden when they saw Erika, Stacey and I pile into the wooden shack? My mind jumps to the young woman who was murdered: Kerry Ann White. They never did find her killer. The case has tortured Aunt Bernie for years — still does, despite her being retired for eighteen months.

There's a sudden rustle in the trees, as though the leaves are talking, and my eyes dart across the woods once more. I can't stay here. I clench my fists, darting onwards, running past the rusting 'No Swimming' sign, my heart pounding by the time I reach the road on the other side of Quarry Lake.

I need Aunt Bernie right now. I need her to tell me to be strong, like she did when Alene and I were young, when we first arrived in England. It was her way: kind and loving, while asserting that life must go on. She told me once that our parents would live on in our memories, that they would want us to grow up happy. I loved her for that — strong and feisty, with a big heart.

I shove the key into her front door and let myself in. Bernie insisted we kept our keys when we moved out, wanting us to feel like it was still our home, should we ever need it.

'Bernie,' I call, as I close the front door with a click. I pick up the letters on the doormat and lay them on the oak cabinet in the hallway. 'Bernie, it's only me.'

She appears in the lounge doorway wearing a beige tunic over what I know to be stretch-top jeans. She's short, and veers on the plump side of thin due to her eating habits. She ruffles her short greying hair in an attempt to tidy it, and looks at me over trendy blue-framed glasses. 'Riona. It's great to see you, darling.' She races towards me, arms wide.

I'm glad of her embrace, and feel lost when she frees me.

'I've made homemade lemonade, fancy some?'

'Lovely.' The thought of it makes me wince, but I don't want to hurt her feelings. She has no culinary skills, never has had. Even joining a cookery course, a class in a long line of classes she's taken since she took early retirement, hasn't made any difference. She's tried so many hobbies, mainly because she misses work, though would never admit it.

'I've made rock cakes too. Or there's some carrot cake Alene sent over a few days ago.' She goes to turn away, but before she does, she looks into my eyes. 'Are you OK, love?'

I shrug, amazed how she can pick up on things. 'Not really, can we talk?'

'Of course.' She grips my hand and leads me into the kitchen, where sad-looking plants hang from the ceiling in wicker containers, and her pretty-average artwork — another of her many projects — fills the walls.

Once she has poured lemonade into pink glasses, I follow her into her cluttered conservatory, where piles of books — fact and fiction — litter every surface. She clears two chairs, and we sit down. 'So what's wrong?' she says. 'Tell Auntie Bernie all about it.'

I smile and pick up a rock cake, which feels even heavier than its namesake, and take a sip of the lemonade, trying not to pull a face as the bitter taste hits my tongue.

I start at the beginning, barely coming up for breath as I tell my aunt about the letter delivered to the clinic, the one Erika received, the strange Instagram account, and the fact that I think someone is watching me, though I leave out the yellow hi-vis. I know how much not catching the Ensley Killer got to my aunt, and I don't want to trigger that memory unless I really have to.

I see the worry in Bernie's eyes grow and feel bad for burdening her. 'This letter, have you any idea who it could be from?'

I shake my head. 'I did think it might be a client, but I really don't see how it can be.' I rub my neck, feeling the tension there, before picking up my phone and opening up the strange Instagram account. I hand the phone to my aunt and she taps the screen, enlarges the picture with her thumb and forefinger. 'Stacey Roberts,' she says. 'I see her about sometimes. Never liked the girl.' She hands back my phone. 'But why would someone put photos of the two of you on Instagram? You haven't seen Stacey for years, have you?' She sips her lemonade and winces, clearly not enjoying it any more than I am. 'You need to report the Instagram account, Riona. They'll take it down, I'm certain of it.'

'But it won't go away in here.' I tap my temple, feeling a surge of tears rising. 'And what if they set up another account?'

'Report everything that's happened to the police.'

I shake my head. 'We both know there's not much they can do.' I get up. 'I'd better go, I'm due back at the clinic by three.'

She rises too, straightens her tunic. 'Are you sure you'll be OK, love? You can stay here for a bit if you'd like to.'

'I'm fine.' Getting it all off my chest with Aunt Bernie has helped a bit, but I don't know what I thought she could do. She can hardly wave a magic wand and make things right. 'Honestly.'

I carry my glass into the kitchen and place it on the counter, feeling guilty that I've barely touched it.

Bernie follows. 'Have you seen anything of Alene lately?' she says.

'Yes . . . we had a bit of a disagreement.' I lower my head. 'I wish things were different between us.'

She screws up her nose. 'But I thought you two were getting on better?'

'Me too.' I bite down on my lower lip. 'She's met someone. Did you know?'

'Alene?'

'Mmm, she's only been exchanging messages so far, I think, but Kieran found out, and, well . . .'

'I'll give your sister a call later, see how she is.'

'Please don't tell her I told you, she's already angry with me.'

'Mum's the word,' she says, locking her lips in mime.

Bernie follows me to the front door, leans in and kisses my cheek.

'I'll call you,' I say.

'Be careful, love,' she says as I step outside into the cold day. 'You know where I am if you need me.'

CHAPTER TWENTY-FIVE

Riona

After waving me off, Aunt Bernie closes her front door, and I take a deep breath and head for home. The sun is bright but cool, shielding behind skittering clouds. It's a pleasant walk through the quiet village; the only person I see is an old man who nods and smiles a hello, and my thoughts begin to unclutter.

It's as I round a bend and the entrance to Quarry Lake comes into view that I feel a surge of panic at the memory of hearing someone humming my father's ballad. The thought of passing the lake once more fills me with sudden dread.

At this end of Quarry Lake there's a layby shrouded by trees. People park up here if they've driven from nearby Hitchin or further afield and want to take their dogs for walks or just enjoy the wildlife. I'm about to cross the road towards it when the vibration of a text startles me. I pull my phone from my pocket and stop on the kerb to open the message:

Hi Riona. I can't see me getting in to work tomorrow either. Feel like crap. I'm so sorry to let you down. Erika xx

Within moments a withheld call comes in.

'Hello?' I say, pinning my phone to my ear. 'Hello?'

I listen, feeling sure I can pick up on someone breathing. 'Is anybody there?' The line goes dead.

A wrong number, I tell myself, close to tears, taking long, deep breaths as I stand motionless, my head whirring.

I hear the car behind me.

Sense it speeding, but have no time to react.

I hear the thump as it suddenly bumps up onto to the kerb and mounts the pavement, giving me no time to move. The pain and shock as I fall to the ground is instantaneous. My head cracks against the kerb, and everything goes black.

* * *

Her yellow hi-vis jacket comes into view first.

'What's your name, love?' The paramedic has a kindly face. She's holding my hand in hers.

'Riona,' I say, but it doesn't sound like my own voice and is barely a whisper. The scene is bright — too bright — and voices around me sound as though they're coming from an ancient radio.

'We're going to get you to the hospital. We just need to do a few tests first. Can you remember what happened, love?'

I close my eyes. Open them again. Everything is fuzzy, but I can see the elderly man from earlier standing some distance away talking to a police officer.

'A car mounted the pavement.' I meet the paramedic's warm brown eyes. 'I was on my phone. I didn't see it.'

'Can we call someone for you?'

'Aunt Bernie,' I say, before everything goes black once more.

* * *

'They're keeping me in overnight for observation, that's all,' I say to Bernie, who, despite her strong exterior, is clearly worried about me. She is perched next to my hospital bed on the edge of a mock-leather chair with wooden armrests, eyes wide behind her glasses. 'I'm absolutely fine, honestly,' I add. And I am — physically. 'It's just a bit of concussion, some bruising.'

Psychologically, though, I don't feel so great. I'm sure whoever was driving the car that mounted the pavement did it deliberately. I just wish I could recall the car. And who had called my phone just before that? Had they been deliberately distracting me?

'The elderly man told the police that the car was red,' I go on. 'But he didn't notice the number plate or make. The police said his eyesight is poor.'

'You're lucky you're not in a worse state.' Bernie takes hold of my hand and squeezes.

I don't feel lucky, but I know what she means. 'I'll need to close the clinic tomorrow. Erika messaged earlier. She's too ill to come in too.'

'What a pair you are. I wish I hadn't let you leave my house.'

'That's silly,' I say with a smile.

'I'm going to buy a huge bag of cotton wool and wrap you up in it from now on.'

I laugh. 'Listen, could you put a sign on the clinic door, saying we've had to close due to illness? I know it's not very professional, and I'm particularly worried about Erika's clients needing grief counselling, but I don't know what else I can do.'

'No problem at all. And please don't worry, Riona, I'll sort out everything, you just get better. Do you want me to let Erika know what's happened to you?'

'No, best keep her in the dark for now. Knowing Erika, she'll come to the hospital, and I don't want her to worry when she's not well herself.'

'Plus you don't want her germs on top of everything.'

I run my hand over my forehead, stress making me feel warm. 'Please can you feed Wanda, and give her a big hug from me?'

'Yes, now get some sleep.' She releases my hand and rises. 'Call me tomorrow. I'll pick you up, OK?'

As I watch Bernie walk down the ward, my phone vibrates across the unit next to me:

Hey, Riona. I wondered if you fancied a day out on Saturday? I've decided to stay on for a bit. Tom x

I'm not going to lie, seeing Tom's message gives me a lift. I know I saw him letting himself into an apartment in Hitchin, when he told me he was staying with his aunt and uncle, but I've decided there must be a reasonable explanation for that. I feel sure I will be much better, physically at least, by Saturday, even if the haunting realisation that someone tried to knock me down might not be so easy to shake off. I hit reply:

I'm in hospital at the moment. Long story. But I'm sure I'll be well by then. Sounds great! Riona x

I put the phone back on the unit and close my eyes, my mind drifting through all the weird things that have happened over the last few days, before finally falling asleep.

When I wake, the main lights are out on the ward. I pick up my phone from the unit. It's gone ten o'clock. There are three messages, one from Alene saying Aunt Bernie has told her I'm in hospital, that she is sorry we rowed and hopes I'm OK; one from Kieran telling me to get well soon, and signing it 'your favourite nephew'; and the final one is from Tom saying he hopes I'm OK. I feel loved, and I really need that right now.

A nurse passes and pulls the curtains around the bed next to me. Despite sleeping for several hours, my eyes feel heavy. But I'm on high alert. The half-lit, silent ward makes me feel unsafe, uneasy.

I turn my phone over and over in my hands before opening the Instagram account that's haunting me. As I look down at my phone screen, nausea rises. 'Oh God,' I whisper into the silence, my panicked eyes darting around me, desperately searching the ward for whoever took the latest photo. But there's nobody about. Whoever took it is long gone.

CHAPTER TWENTY-SIX

Riona

A photo of me in the hospital bed stares back at me from my phone screen. It's just my face. My eyes closed. Whoever took it either zoomed the lens of their camera in close, or they were almost on top of me as I slept.

I'm shaking, a wave of nausea continuing to rise through my body, acid catching in the back of my throat. I reach for a cardboard bowl a nurse left for me earlier and ease myself up. The movement shifts the awful feeling, but my whole body hurts, and I cry out in pain.

The nurse peers from behind the curtain that's draped around the bed next to mine, her brown eyes wide.

The pain eases a little. 'Sorry. I'm OK. Honestly.'

She dashes over, takes the bowl from me. Makes me comfortable, puffing my pillows, the coarse blanket rubbing against my skin. 'I'll get you some painkillers,' she says.

'Do you know if I had any visitors while I was sleeping?' I ask.

'I'm afraid I've only just come on duty. Sorry.'

'Oh. OK. No worries.' The pillow against my head gives me some comfort. 'Thank you.'

She turns and, plastic apron crackling, takes quick, silent footsteps out of the ward.

I pick up my phone once more, scroll through the photo of me singing, the pictures of Stacey Roberts, me asleep in the hospital bed. Who would do this? Why? I want to call Aunt Bernie and pour out my fears to her, but it's late, she'll be in bed. I look around the quiet ward at the sleeping patients. Whoever took the photo must be long gone, but I won't sleep. Panic mounts inside me, making my skin prickle. Someone is stalking me, and I'm starting to realise they could be dangerous.

* * *

Wednesday, 8 December 2021

It's 10 a.m., and I'm sitting on the chair next to my bed, waiting, when Aunt Bernie appears at the end of the ward, swaddled in a padded jacket.

'Ready?' she says, approaching. I rise, exhausted from lack of sleep, gripping my discharge letter, keen to get home. I ache like crazy, which will put paid to any running for a while, but I've been given the all-clear. Other than concussion, which they have given me a list of things to look out for, it's just bumps and bruises, no broken bones.

Bernie gives me a much-needed hug, and we make our way out of the ward as I button my jacket. We approach the main entrance of the hospital, and my eyes dart from patients to visitors, wondering if one of them is watching me. We head through the doors and into the multi-storey car park, and I suddenly realise Bernie is talking.

'Sorry?'

'I was just saying, I need to pay for parking.' She's turning a yellow disc over in her hand, furrowing her forehead. 'Are you sure you're OK?'

'Yes, yes.' I realise I'm trembling. 'I'll just be glad to get home, that's all.'

Later, as Bernie pulls out of the car park and onto the main road, I open my mouth to speak. But her usual rosy complexion is drained of colour, shadows cradle her eyes, her hair is tousled — it's clear she hasn't slept. I close my mouth, deciding to stay quiet for now.

As though sensing my attempt to confide in her, she glances my way. 'I'm worried about you, sweetheart.'

My resolve to stay silent evaporates with her kind words. 'I have to admit I'm a bit of a mess,' I whisper, tears burning the backs of my eyes. 'I keep thinking someone may have mowed me down on purpose.'

'Oh, love. I'm sure it was some drunken fool.' But I hear the doubt in her voice. She's worried too.

I desperately want to tell her about the new photograph of me in the hospital bed, but stay quiet. It's ridiculous that I want to protect Bernie, when she has such strength, has coped with so much — not only as a police officer but with the death of her beloved brother, and taking on Alene and me — but I do.

* * *

Wanda races down the stairs to greet me as soon as I step through the front door. I lift her into my arms and cuddle her close, her soft fur comforting me. 'Have you missed me, little one?' I say, as she kisses my chin and purrs.

'Would you like me to stay for a while?' Bernie hasn't ventured inside the front door, just stands on the step in the cool morning air. 'I won't be offended if you'd rather be on your own for a while.'

'Are you sure?' Oddly, I need just that — to be alone with my thoughts in the safety of my apartment. 'I'll call you later. I promise.'

'You'd better.' She leans in to kiss my cheek before turning and taking off towards her car. I close the door and pull the bolts across, something I rarely do, before heading up the stairs, reluctant to put Wanda down, despite her sudden wiggling.

Once I've taken some painkillers, I settle on the sofa with a mug of coffee and a plate of marmalade on toast. Not that I'm hungry, and I sense already that I'll struggle to swallow it down. Before I attempt to eat, I dial Erika's number. It rings for a while before going to voicemail.

'Hey, Erika, I hope you're feeling a bit better,' I say into the phone, trying to sound upbeat. 'I'm not too great, got knocked off my feet by a car, would you believe? Just general aches and pains and concussion — could have been a lot worse. I'm home from hospital now, but won't be in work for a couple of days.' I pause for a moment. 'Anyway, can you give me a call to let me know how you are? Not rushing you back to work, but if you have any idea when you'll be well enough to return, I'll contact your clients. Take care, lovely.'

Next, I call a couple of my own clients, but I'm shattered, can barely string my words together. I lean my head back against the softness of the sofa and close my eyes, letting my toast and coffee go cold. I'm beginning to drift off, when the phone rings, startling me. Without looking who it is, I answer, assuming it's Erika getting back to me. 'Hi, how are you feeling?'

'Sorry?'

I realise my mistake. It's not Erika. 'Oh, sorry . . . I was expecting someone—'

'It's me, Stacey.'

'Oh, hi.'

'I hope you don't mind me calling. Is it a good time?'

It's far from it, but I need to hear what she has to say. 'It's fine.'

'Thanks for leaving your number, and I owe you an apology. I'm sorry I was a bit off when you came round to see me. All of this . . . well, it's a bit worrying, don't you think?' She pauses for a moment but I stay quiet. 'I saw the photo of you asleep on Instagram. Have you seen it?'

'I have, yes.' I gulp down a wave of panic. *This is real.*

'I thought I'd better call.' There's a slight tremor in her voice. 'There's another photo of me standing on my doorstep the day you came to see me.'

'Yes. I saw it.'

'I wasn't sure who else to turn to, Riona. I haven't got anyone to talk to since Mum died.'

She sounds close to tears, and I suddenly feel for her. 'Listen, do you want to get some coffee or something? Maybe if we go through all of this together, we can find out who's doing this. Get to the bottom of it.'

'OK. Yes. I'd love that.' I hear the relief in her voice and realise, despite this being the woman who let me down, I'm relieved too, glad that I'll have someone to talk to who will understand what I'm going through.

'Though I'm not feeling so good today,' I say, deciding not to tell her about the hit and run — that the photo of me was taken in a hospital bed — not yet, anyway. 'Maybe we could meet tomorrow, at Lola's café?' I say, hoping I will feel well enough.

'I remember you working there.' There's that reminiscing tone again. 'You loved it, used to give me free leftover Bakewell tarts at the end of the day.'

I don't want to talk about the past. 'Say, about ten?'

'Sounds good. Thanks, Riona.'

She ends the call, and I discard my phone onto the table and sprawl full-length on the sofa, covering myself with the throw, pulling it up around my shoulders and closing my eyes once more.

It could be the strong painkillers, but I wake with a start from a dream about a faceless man in a yellow hi-vis. Gasping, I sit upright, my heart beating too fast. The room is shrouded in darkness. I must have slept the day away.

I glance towards the window. The curtains are open, the sky black, and I realise I'm shivering, that the room has dropped in temperature.

I peel the throw from my body. Despite the nightmare, I feel better for catching up on my sleep, and my aches and pains have eased. I rise, turn up the heating and hobble into the kitchen. Once I've fed Wanda, I search the freezer for something to shove in the microwave, settling on a ready-meal curry that looks about as appetising as cardboard.

As the carton turns on the glass plate and the microwave hums, I pull down the kitchen blind and make my way back into the lounge intending to close the curtains. I'm about to drag them across, when I see someone standing opposite my apartment. I gulp back a wave of fear. They're wearing a yellow hi-vis, their face shrouded by shadows.

Determined, I hobble across the room, pick up a vase for protection as I go, and take the stairs, holding onto the handrail for support. I need to catch this person who is messing with my head. I don't care how dangerous they are, I can't live like this any longer. But by the time I get to the foot of the stairs, fumble the bolts across and open the door, there's no sign of anyone.

It's around 7 p.m. when I go down to the clinic. Erika has yet to reply to my voicemail — which is unlike her, she normally gets back to me within minutes — so I concentrate on calling my remaining clients.

Once that's done, I attempt another call to Erika, but the call again goes to voicemail. I'm growing anxious about her. It's not like her to be so unreachable. Though to be fair, she does have moments when she prefers to be alone. But what if she's so ill she can't get to her phone? Or worse, been rushed to hospital? She lives alone. Her mother returned to Sweden when her father died. Who would know if she was really sick? I need to go round and see her, and I'm about to call Bernie to ask if she'll drive me to Erika's house when a text flies onto my phone:

> Hey, Riona. Sorry for the delay getting back. I've slept most of the day. Still feeling awful, had the doctor out, he's suggested bed rest. I can't believe you've been in an accident, but SO glad you're OK. If you're up to cancelling my clients for the rest of the week, that would be great. Thanks, sweetie. x

I reply straightaway:

No problem, lovely. Take care of yourself. I'll pop round and see you soon. x

Her reply is instant:

No, please don't do that. I would hate for you catch my bug on top of everything else. x

CHAPTER TWENTY-SEVEN

Me

Going into the hospital was a risk. But it's funny how nobody seems to notice you if you're wearing a yellow hi-vis — so bright, glowing and yet somehow invisible. There's something safe about them. If you see someone approaching wearing a reflective jacket, you don't panic or run. I realised that back in 2009.

I was armed with a bunch of grapes when I entered the ward, just in case someone asked what I was doing there. But nobody did.

I wasn't sure if I would be able to get away with it. Was going to make a quick exit if you were awake, as I wouldn't have wanted you to see me. But when I peered into the ward, I could see you were sleeping like a baby. I wonder what you were dreaming about, Riona. Were you dreaming about me?

Snapping a photo was easy enough. Nobody noticed me raise the phone for a moment and take it. I got out of there quickly then. Didn't want you to wake up.

I wish I could have seen your face, dear Riona, when you opened up Instagram and saw the photo. I know you'll have checked in. It's far too hard to resist.

CHAPTER TWENTY-EIGHT

Charlotte

I slide the two new bolts I've fitted across the garden gate and drop the screwdriver into the toolbox at my feet.

Whoever came into the garden and tried the back-door handle will hopefully be deterred by them and with luck won't return.

I shiver, the cold seeping through my jumper, chilling my skin, and pick up Mother's toolbox.

As I head back towards the cottage, the feeling of being watched makes me uneasy. But there's nobody about that I can see, the six-foot fence surrounding the garden keeping out prying eyes.

As I continue towards the back door, my leg throbs, and a shooting pain stabs my thigh. Gordon flashes into my head. The surge of relief I'd felt when I found him dead at the foot of the cliff was the same kind of solace I'd felt when Mia disappeared under the water. What kind of person is relieved when someone dies?

Back inside the house, I shove the toolbox back into the walk-in cupboard on top of the mountains of accumulated junk. I was surprised earlier that I even found the tools, the box was buried so deep amongst the clutter. As I close the door, the box tips, scattering the contents.

I crouch down, picking up a plastic tub of nails, the screwdriver I used earlier. A hammer I didn't notice before. It must have been at the bottom of the box. It's heavy, the handle wide, a reddish-brown stain on the thick metal head. Without thinking too deeply, I throw it into the box with the other tools, slam shut the lid and push the door closed.

I rise to my feet. This is my house now. Mother didn't leave a will, but I'm her only child. It will automatically come to me. But I can't live here. I'll sell the place, and with the money maybe Ryan and I can move abroad. Sweden or Norway, perhaps — or Italy. I've always wanted to go to Italy. But wherever we go it will need to be somewhere isolated. Somewhere we'll never be found.

I take my jacket from the hook by the door. I need to go into Ensley. Go to the council offices, look at development plans. But I can't help thinking Mother lied — that she'd found out the truth about Mia. Lured me here knowing I wouldn't be able to ignore her words. Had she seen Mia fall from the white cliffs into Quarry Lake from the cottage window, that night back in 2009? But if she had, why did she wait until now to mess with my head?

CHAPTER TWENTY-NINE

Charlotte

Thursday, 9 December 2021

I spoke to Ryan first thing this morning. He seemed vague and unresponsive, much like he'd been when we first moved to Cornwall in 2009. I know all of this is unsettling him, bringing back painful memories, but we have to get through this. We have to.

I told him he must stay put. That he can't leave Cornwall. That if he comes to Ensley everything will unravel, and we can't have that. But I wasn't sure he was listening. I worry he'll do something stupid.

Now I sit at the dining table by the window, my laptop open in front of me, conscious of how lonely the country lane is. I haven't seen a car pass in over an hour. I skim my fingers over the keys of my laptop, not pressing them hard enough for letters to appear on the screen. I've never looked at reports about the Ensley Killer — not at the time, or through the years. I overheard in a shop just after Kerry Ann White died that the killer wore a yellow hi-vis, and that was it for me. That was when I closed off, refused to go there.

I suppose I've always been afraid I'll see something I don't want to see, that will make me suspect Ryan further. But now something's pushing me to know more. Perhaps it's being back in Ensley. Suddenly my fingers are pushing down on the keys, and I'm searching the internet for articles about the case.

There are several pieces from 2009: quotes from an Inspector Blake, and a Sergeant Foley who I remember vaguely from school, requests for witnesses, and photos of the young women who were attacked that give me an uneasy feeling in the pit of my stomach. They haven't got much on the killer other than he put on his online dating profile that he was a heavy metal fan, that his favourite film was *Iron Man*, and that he worked in construction. *Surely my Ryan isn't capable of this.* I snap closed my laptop, tears stinging my eyes, the excruciating pain that my son could be a killer slamming into me once more, reducing me to sobs.

CHAPTER THIRTY

Riona

Ensley High Street has a bite-sized Spar, a pub and Lola's café, where I worked in my teens before heading off to uni.

It's a bright day, but the pavement is slippery from a sprinkling of snow that settled during the night.

It's as I glance into the supermarket window, checking out how busy it is and wondering if I've got time to pick up a pint of milk before meeting Stacey at ten o'clock, that I see a man in the reflection, racing across the road towards me. I turn as he approaches. He's tall, slim, about my age — handsome under his shabby appearance, his hands deep in his jean pockets.

'You're Alene's sister, aren't you?' he says, stopping about a metre or so away from me. 'She told me all about you.' He pauses, stares into my eyes. 'How is she? I often think about her.'

I don't know this man, whose dark hair is shaggy past his shoulders. His overall air is one of defeat, neglect. His shoulders rounded as though the whole world is resting on them.

'She's OK,' I say. 'Can I tell her who's asking after her?'

He stares for a moment before shaking his head. 'She won't want to hear from me,' he says, his dull eyes scanning my face. 'You look a bit battered and bruised.'

I touch my forehead.

'What happened?'

'Hit and run.'

'I'm so sorry to hear that. Are you in pain, Riona?'

His questions are invasive. The fact he knows my name, and I have no idea who he, making me uncomfortable. 'Who are you?'

He shakes his head. 'Nobody,' he says. 'Nobody at all.'

I step away, and he reaches out, goes to touch my arm, and I take another step backwards.

'Sorry.' He lowers his hand. 'I seem to have forgotten how to communicate these days.'

'I really should go.' I look at my watch. 'I'm meeting someone at ten.'

I leave the man, feeling his eyes on me as I hobble down the road towards Lola's café, trying to focus my thoughts on my meetup with Stacey. Planning the words I want to say. I glance over my shoulder as I reach the café. The strange man has gone.

Lola's has changed since 2009, and is now the prettiest building on the High Street, with jade paintwork and hanging baskets brimming with winter flowers.

Through the window, I see Stacey sitting at a table for two, her red hair falling about her face as she cradles a mug, her dog curled on her lap. If I'm honest, I still don't feel too well, and the man accosting me a moment ago hasn't helped. Plus the frustration I feel at having to mix with the woman who tried to seduce George still isn't sitting right. A huge part of me wants to go home, but I need to talk to Stacey about the Instagram account, about everything. Could it all be connected?

As I open the café door, I'm greeted by the sweet smell of freshly baked pastries mingling with the aroma of strong coffee. I raise my hand to Stacey as I order a drink at the counter from a young girl who reminds me of myself at eighteen. Stacey smiles and waves back, and I notice a Bakewell tart on a plate in front of her.

'Hey,' I say, mug of coffee in my mitts, as I join her at the table.

'Hey.' She's free of make-up, the scar on her cheek more vivid today, and she's wearing grey sweats and a black zip-up fleece — a far cry from my glamorous friend of twelve years ago. 'How are you?' she goes on, eyeing my bruises, though she doesn't ask questions.

'I've been better.' I sit down, smiling at her dog, whose little pink tongue is sticking out. 'She's cute.'

'Did you hear that, baby dog?' Stacey's mouth is close to the pug's silky ear. 'Riona thinks you're a little cutie.' She kisses the dog's head noisily three times before looking about her. 'We love these dog-friendly cafés, don't we, Minnie?' She pauses and stares into my eyes, making me oddly self-conscious. 'You know I'm sorry,' she says. 'About George—'

'So,' I say, cutting her off. I don't want to hear her apologies or talk about the past — plus, I feel awful mentally and physically. 'Do you think we should get this Instagram account taken down?'

'I've thought about that.' She takes a gulp of her coffee, doesn't touch her Bakewell tart. 'Wouldn't whoever it is just set up another one? If we were to wait it out, maybe we'll catch them taking a photo.'

I want to say we're not a couple of amateur detectives, but instead simply shrug and take a sip of my drink. She mirrors me, takes another long gulp of hers. *This feels uncomfortable.*

The café is busy. There's a woman with a little girl who's whinging about wanting more orange juice; a middle-aged, balding man tucking into a slab of cake, stabbing the plate with his fork rhythmically; a younger man in the corner, his head down looking at a laptop; a group of older women laughing. It's noisy. My head thumps. I really don't want to be here.

I return my gaze to Stacey. Her wide hazel eyes stare back at me. 'There's something else,' she says, moving forward in her seat before opening her bag and bringing out an envelope.

I recognise the scrawling handwriting on the front immediately. 'Oh God.'

'What?'

'I'm wa—' My words catch in my throat.

'Watching you.' She pushes the envelope back into her bag. 'How did you know? No wait, you got one too, didn't you?'

'Yes. And Erika.'

'Erika?'

I nod. 'When did you receive it?'

'Yesterday. It was shoved through my door.' She pushes her hair from her face, her voice agitated. 'And, as I said before, I keep seeing someone hanging about wearing a yellow hi-vis, too far away for me to see them properly.' She takes a breath. 'God, it feels so good to talk to you, Riona. After all this time.'

'I'm only here because of what's happening, Stacey. This isn't about us. I'm not here to mend our relationship.'

She looks hurt. 'Fine. I get that.' She pauses for a moment. 'But I can't get it out of my head how the Ensley Killer wore a yellow hi-vis.'

I shiver and pull my jacket round me. 'This can't have anything to do with the murder of Kerry Ann White. Why would the killer turn up again after all this time and target us?' I'm not sure who I'm trying to convince, her or me. 'This doesn't even fit the MO.'

'MO?'

'OK, so I watch too many crime dramas. But I know enough that killers tend to stick to a pattern.'

'How do you know this isn't their pattern? That Kerry Ann White wasn't stalked before she was killed?'

'Well, I don't, but I'm sure this has nothing to do with her death.'

'Well, even if it doesn't, it's still freaking me out.' She sighs, moves forward and rests her elbows on the table, a faint smell of tobacco on her breath. 'Whoever is doing this is deliberately messing with our heads, Riona. I just wish I knew why.'

I take a deep breath. 'The photo of me in bed was taken when I was in hospital the other night.' I pause for a moment, as Stacey's eyes widen. 'A car mounted the pavement and—'

'Oh God. That explains your bruises.' She squeezes the dog so hard its eyes bulge. 'That's so scary. Christ, Riona, I think we have to agree we're in danger. What did the police say?'

'They think it was possibly someone drunk at the wheel. They don't think I was victimised, just unlucky — wrong place, wrong time.' I feel my anxiety rising. Want to yell that I could have been anyone walking along the pavement. I turn my ring around my finger.

'Did you tell them what else has been happening?'

'No, I—'

'You need to tell them. What if it was deliberate, Riona? Oh God, I'm going to be looking over my shoulder all the time now.' She glances at her watch and drains her mug. 'Listen, I've got to go. I'm teaching at eleven o'clock.'

'Teaching?' I realise I know nothing about who Stacey is now.

'A guitar lesson for a gifted teen.'

I'm impressed at what she's achieved for herself. Despite her awful upbringing, she's taught herself to play and now teaches.

'That's amazing,' I say, annoyed at myself for sounding interested, for softening.

She smiles. 'Yes, it turns out music is my solace. Though most of my students won't get past grade one before realising they're not going to be the next Hendrix.' She pauses for a moment. 'It was good to talk to you again, Riona. I understand you don't want to be friends, but it feels better somehow that I'm not in this alone.' She rises, puts the pug down on the floor and lifts her jacket from the back of her chair. 'Can we keep in touch? Please? Deal with this together, yeah? Maybe text each other if we have any new worries.'

'I'd like that,' I find myself saying, despite everything.

'And be careful, Riona,' she adds, before cutting through the tables, waving as she leaves, the door closing behind her, her Bakewell tart untouched. And I realise I don't feel quite so alone.

CHAPTER THIRTY-ONE

Riona

I stay seated in the café for a while, aware for the first time of Bing Crosby's dulcet tones as he sings 'It's Beginning to Look a Lot Like Christmas'. I cast my eyes about me, taking in the tastefully placed decorations. I loved Christmas as a child, before my parents died, but it's never really been the same since then. Bernie often worked over the festive period, and Alene and I would tag onto our neighbour's Christmas and Boxing Day events. Later, George and I would put up decorations, but he wasn't a fan. In fact, on the days leading up to the festive season he always wore a black Santa hat with 'bah humbug' on it. Maybe if we'd had children things would have been different.

I tune out from the song, going over and over my conversation with Stacey before finally getting to my feet. My legs wobble, and I stumble as I attempt to walk, taking hold of the back of the chair as the café spins. I close my eyes, continuing to grip the chair, until the feeling stops.

I cross the room, spotting a yellow hi-vis jacket on a hook by the entrance. Heart thudding, I step closer and run my hand over the fabric. On impulse, I pull it from the rack, begin searching the pockets, not sure what I hope to find.

'Hey!' I turn to see a middle-aged man dashing towards me, eyes wide. He snatches the jacket from me. 'What the hell do you think you're doing?'

He's heavily built, his tone slightly aggressive. Within moments he puts on the jacket and leaves the café.

I rest my hand on the wall to stabilise myself as another wave of dizziness takes over.

'Are you OK?' The woman behind the counter appears in front of me. 'You don't look so good.'

'I'm fine.' I take a deep breath. 'Thanks, but I'll be OK.'

'Do you need to sit down?' She pulls a chair out from a nearby table, but I shake my head and stumble through the door and out into the cold air, almost slipping on the settled snow.

My body shakes and my head starts pounding, the sound of passing traffic too loud. Dizzy and nauseous, I lean against the cafe window, hoping the feeling will pass, knowing I was a fool for coming out. I'm not even sure I'm capable of driving home.

On the other side of the road, I'm aware of movement in a quiet area between the butchers and a private house, the dingy space that leads to the car park. I narrow my eyes, my vision blurring, but I see a figure dressed in a yellow reflective jacket.

I drag myself away from the window. I'm not sure if it's the man I've just seen in the café and want to get a closer look, study the person's features. I step into the road. A driver blares his horn, and I dart back, a wave of nausea flooding my body. 'Oh God.' I cover my mouth, unable to move for fear of splattering my recently ingested coffee over the snowy pavement.

When I look across the road again, the figure is approaching in fast, long strides. I let out a scream as they reach me.

'Take it easy.' It's the bloke from the café. 'You almost got knocked down. I wanted to check you're OK.'

'I'm fine,' I say, but I'm far from it. I was almost knocked down for a second time. 'I'm fine, honestly.'

'You sure?' he says, before leaving me to it.

My car is in the short-stay car park near the Spar, but it feels like miles away, and however hard I try, my feet won't move. I pull my phone from my pocket. Call Aunt Bernie.

* * *

My world is still swimming when Bernie pulls up beside me in her car. She jumps from the driver's seat like a paramedic at the scene of an accident.

'Why the devil have you come out, love?' She shoves an open plastic bag into my hand before taking my elbow and walking me slowly to the passenger seat of her car. 'Didn't the hospital suggest a couple of days' bed rest?'

At this moment I can't recall what the nurse told me. My head throbs and I feel fragile. If I were made of glass, I would shatter.

'We'll go round to the car park and pay for a couple more hours on your car,' Bernie goes on, easing me into her Kia. 'I'll come back for it later, once I've got you home safely.'

'Thanks.' I rub my temples with the tips of my fingers as she climbs in next to me. 'Sorry.'

'It's not a problem, Riona,' she says, starting the engine. 'I worry about you, that's all. You know that, don't you?'

'You shouldn't worry. I'm a big girl,' I mumble, covering my face with my hands. 'I can look after myself.'

'Not from where I'm sitting.' She pulls away from the kerb with a screech of tyres. She has always been a bit of a girl racer. In fact, she went through a phase, just after she retired, of going up to the local go-karting track, but got banned for reckless driving.

'Slow down, please,' I say, and she takes her foot off the throttle.

Once we're back at my apartment, Bernie lowers me down onto the sofa and covers me with the throw before going into the kitchen to make some tea.

'What made you go out?' she says returning with painkillers and perching herself on the arm of the sofa. 'Riona?'

I stare up at her. 'Another photo appeared on Instagram,' I say, before taking a breath. 'It was of me in the hospital bed, asleep.'

'Good God.' She reaches over, takes hold of my hand.

'I know. Pretty unnerving, right?' I take another deep breath. 'I went to see Stacey.'

'Stacey Roberts?'

'Yes.' I nod. It hurts. 'Odd things are happening to both of us, Bernie, and I wonder if whoever mounted the pavement is the same person putting up the pictures. But then I can't think who would be so cruel. What I could have done to deserve this.' My eyes well up. I want to mention the sightings of someone in a yellow hi-vis too, but I wonder deep down how relevant it is. Someone standing by the lake, and another time in the field behind my flat — well, it's not exactly evidence of a stalker, even if Stacey's seen the figure too. Lots of people wear reflective jackets, and anyway, I know if I start tying in the murder of 2009, it will stress Bernie out. She never really got over the fact they failed to catch the Ensley Killer.

'Can I see the latest picture?' she asks.

I point towards my bag on the floor, knowing if I bend down I will feel worse. 'My phone's in there.'

She leans over, pulls it out and hands it to me. As I tap the screen, I see immediately that more pictures have been uploaded and lose control of my already volatile emotions. I feel my chin crinkle as I attempt to gulp back tears. 'I don't get it,' I cry. 'Why would anyone do this?'

There's a photo of me standing outside the café, leaning against the window, pale and fragile, and one of Stacey and her little dog. She's inside the café, her head down, her hair falling about her face, just as it was when I entered earlier. I try to think back to the customers in there when I arrived this morning, but apart from the man in the hi-vis, I can't bring any of them to mind — and the picture could so easily have been taken through the window by anyone passing by. The strange man who'd approached me asking after Alene springs into my head. Who was he? Could he have taken the photo?

Bernie takes the phone from me, looks at the screen. 'Oh, love,' she says. 'We need to go to the police with this right now, and you must report the account to Instagram.'

'I can't go to the police station,' I cry, closing my eyes, a tear escaping through my lashes. 'I feel too awful.'

'Then I'll go.' She hands me my phone, rises, and brushes the creases from her trousers. 'I've still got friends on the force. We'll get to the bottom of this. Can you send me a link to the account?'

I tap my phone, copying and pasting the link into a WhatsApp message and sending it to her.

'Great,' she says, bringing out her phone. 'I've got it.' She grabs her jacket from where she threw it over the back of the chair earlier and shuffles into it. 'Now, are you going to be OK?'

I rub my eyes, and they squelch under the pressure of my fingers. 'I'm just tired. I'll be fine.'

'Righty-ho. I'll walk to your car and bring it back here. Then I'll go to the police station. In the meantime, sit tight about reporting the Instagram account, I'll need to show it to them.'

'Do you really think they can do anything?'

'They will if I have anything to do with it.' She smiles, kisses my forehead and, with a flurry of plump fingers, leaves me alone.

CHAPTER THIRTY-TWO

Charlotte

I bash down fears that Ryan is capable of murder, just as I've done for over twelve years now. Convincing myself that if my son killed Kerry Ann White there would have been further murders in the area of Cornwall where we've been living. Surely someone who kills random young girls as a teenager wouldn't stop because they've moved house.

I head down the path towards the front door of Willow Nook Cottage. I've asked a few questions in shops, and been to the planning department. Plus I've ploughed through all the requests for planning permission subbed to the local council over the last year, and that's on top of emailing all the building companies and housing developers in the area. I've come up with nothing. What else can I do? It's clear Mother was lying. It's time to return to Cornwall. Hide away once more.

I go to put the key in the front door and it creaks open before I can. My stomach tips as I push against it, a chill sliding down my spine.

I step inside. 'Hello!'

I tell myself I didn't close the door properly when I left earlier. My mind is so full. It wouldn't surprise me if I hadn't latched it.

Something catches in the corner of my eye, not quite registering, as I move through the hallway and into the kitchen. I put the bag of groceries I picked up from the supermarket on the counter, pushing an unsettling feeling away as I unload the shopping into the fridge and cupboards. And then it hits me, what I saw in the hallway a moment ago.

I stop, turn, a jar of jam slipping through my fingers, shattering on the quarry tiles. Heart racing, I dash into the hall. Mia's porcelain doll sits on the sideboard by the door. I shudder. Look around, turning on the spot. How the hell had it got downstairs from the bedroom?

Propped up against the doll is an envelope, my name scrawled on the front. I fumble it open, pull out the sheet of paper, my eyes leaping across the three words:

I'm watching you.

I go into the dining room, my eyes flicking about me. Next I head into the lounge, searching for an intruder, before thundering up the stairs.

'Mia?' I find myself calling, my voice raspy. But I know I'm being ridiculous. *Mia is dead.*

I peer round the door of the bedroom she used when she stayed here for that brief moment in time, my eyes scanning the freestanding wardrobe, the bedside cabinet. I creep across the landing, poke my head into Mother's room and finally into the bathroom, where I snatch back the shower curtain — but there's nothing. Nobody is here. Whoever came into the house has gone.

I hurry down the stairs. The doll has vanished, and I notice a pool of water near the unit and splashes of water leading into the kitchen.

Slowly, fear rising in my chest, I follow the droplets of water to the back door. It stands open, letting the cold air in. I slam it shut, pull across the bolt and lean my back against the door, trying to get my breath.

Eventually I move towards the window. Through the glass I see the back gate standing wide open. Whoever has been here has returned to the lake.

CHAPTER THIRTY-THREE

Riona

I'm propped up against a gnarled oak tree, singing my father's Irish ballad. The fact that I should be afraid, alone here in the dark wood near Quarry Lake, seems to have escaped me. Footsteps approach. It's a man in a reflective yellow jacket, the full moon highlighting his large frame, his facial features a white blur.

A ringing sound forces its way into my nightmare. My eyes spring open. I pick up my phone from the table beside me and answer it. 'Bernie,' I say, my voice croaky.

'Did I wake you? Sorry, love.'

I ease myself up, stretching. Wanda, who has been sleeping on my chest, rises to her feet and digs her claws into my jumper. 'What's the time?'

'Just gone five. Listen, I've spoken to the police.'

'And?'

'Well, I'm so sorry, I really shouldn't have got your hopes up, as there isn't much they can do. They said you're to monitor everything that's happening. Keep a diary.'

My heart sinks.

'And you need to report the account, get it taken down.'

'Whoever put it up will just set up another one.'

'You don't know that, Riona.'

'The hit and run? Did you ask—?'

'They're still looking into it, but they're not sure it's connected to the photos.'

'But surely it's got to be.' I want to cry, my throat is so dry.

'I agree. But they haven't much to go on. I'm so sorry, love,' she says again. 'I thought there might be more they can do, but—'

'Did you mention the letters?'

'I did. As I said, they said to keep a diary of everything that happens. And you're to call them when you feel up to it to discuss it further.'

'So basically they're doing nothing.' I'm pissed off and upset. Bernie said she had contacts in the police force, and I felt sure she would make everything right, like she always did in the past.

'Well, not nothing. They said they will discuss it further with you, and if anything else happens that worries you, you're to give them a call. And they're still doing checks on the red car.' Another pause. 'Are you OK, love?'

'Yes, fine.' But I'm not. I feel as though I'm falling apart.

'You know I'm here for you.'

'I know. Thanks, Bernie. I'm grateful for that.'

'So you'll keep me updated with everything?'

'Of course.'

'And you'll contact Instagram and get rid of that awful account? They may even be able to tell you who set it up. The IP address, perhaps? And Riona, please be careful.'

'I will.' I end the call and throw the phone onto the table, where it bounces and falls to the floor. I'm angry. Not with Aunt Bernie — it's obvious she has done her best — but with myself for letting everything that's happened crawl under my skin and fester into fear. I need to get a grip, practise mindfulness, maybe even indulge in a couple of hours of binge-watching my favourite TV shows.

* * *

I'm watching *Friends* — 'The One with Ross's Wedding' —
when the doorbell rings, making me jump. I don't even feel
safe in my own apartment anymore. I press pause on the
remote control and head downstairs.

'Tom!' I say as I open up. He's standing on my doorstep
in a black wool coat, a dark green scarf wrapped around his
neck, brandishing a bottle of wine. 'So you never went back
to Norfolk, then?'

'No, change of plan.' He hands me the wine with a
smile. 'And I know we said we'd meet Saturday, but when
you mentioned you've been in hospital, well . . . I wanted to
check you were OK.'

'Thanks, that's kind of you.'

'So, how are you?'

'I've been better.' I step back, allowing him to enter.

As he passes he stares at me, narrowing his eyes. 'Ouch,
what happened?'

I touch my forehead and wince. The bruising is fully out
now. 'I had an argument with a car.'

'Christ, are you OK?' He sounds sincere.

'You should see the car.' I cringe at my poor attempt at
humour. 'As I say, I've been better.' I lead the way up the stairs.
It's good to see him. There's something about him I really like.
But I still feel I should ask him about the apartment I saw him
go into in Hitchin, why he said he was staying with his aunt and
uncle on the Oakfield Estate. It might seem like nothing, but
the way I'm feeling, he needs to be honest and upfront with me.

'*Friends*,' he says, seeing Joey's face frozen on the screen.
'"The One with Ross's Wedding".'

'You like *Friends*?'

'Grew up on it. I've seen this episode a million times. It
never gets old.'

'I know. I still laugh at the same jokes over and over.' I
head into the kitchen and pour two glasses of wine. When I
return, he has taken off his coat and scarf and laid them over
the back of the chair. He turns, takes one of the glasses from
me. 'So, the car versus your face — what exactly happened?'

'Hit and run,' I say as we sit down on the sofa. 'A car mounted the pavement, knocked me off my feet. It was the fall that did most of the damage.' I sigh. 'Anyway, enough about me, *how you doin'?*'

He smiles at my terrible impersonation of Joey from the show.

'Not too bad,' he says. 'Up and down, you know.'

'So you decided not to head home.'

He nods, takes a sip of his drink. 'I'm going to be honest with you, Riona,' he says, 'and sod the consequences.'

'That sounds ominous.'

He stares into my eyes for some moments, before taking a deep breath. 'The point is, life's been so hard for a while. You know, after Becky died, and the only good thing lately was meeting you.'

'Wow,' I say, feeling my eyes brighten, a flutter in my chest. 'Well, I'm glad to be of assistance.'

He laughs. 'I'm not trying to come on all heavy. I just want to get to know you better, see how things turn out, you know.' He takes a long gulp of his drink, averts his eyes. 'Sorry, I don't want to freak you out or anything.'

'No, no, you haven't. I'm glad you've stayed.'

'That's good to hear. At least we're on the same page.'

I have to say it. It's in my head and demands to be freed. 'So where did you say you were staying?'

He puts the glass down on the table, pats his pockets. It's as though I haven't spoken. 'Sorry, I've left my phone in the car.' He rises. 'Better get it, never know if Mum might want to get hold of me.' He heads across the room, glancing back once. 'Won't be a minute,' he says, disappearing through the door.

I lean my head against the back of my sofa and close my eyes. Had he avoided my question on purpose? Within seconds, my phone buzzes across the table. It's a message from Erika:

Sorry I keep missing your calls, Riona. I will ring you later. Promise. Erika x

I'm still staring at the phone screen when the front door slams and Tom thunders back up the stairs. 'Got it,' he says, waving his phone as he sits back down next to me.

Erika's message has washed away thoughts of finding out exactly where Tom is staying. I'm getting worried about my friend. 'Listen, I know this is a bit cheeky,' I say, 'but you couldn't take me to Erika's house, could you?'

'Erika?'

'You met her the other night at the Fox.'

'Ah, yes, I remember.'

'She's unwell, and I'm getting a bit concerned about her. I keep thinking she might be more poorly than she's letting on.' I turn my ring around my finger. 'The thing is, I daren't drive as I keep having dizzy spells.'

'Of course, where does she live?'

'Hitchin. Is that OK?'

'No worries at all.' We get to our feet. 'Happy to help.'

He puts his coat back on, wraps the scarf around his neck. I reach for my jacket, and we make our way down the stairs and out into the cool evening.

He points his key fob at a bright yellow Mini and the car bleeps. I look at him and tilt my head. I somehow hadn't imagined him driving a yellow Mini.

He smiles, as though reading my mind. 'What can I say? I love Minis. My dad had a 1965 Austin Mini Cooper, red with a black roof. I used to work on it with him before . . . he went downhill after Becky became ill. Severe depression. Died a few years back.'

I place my hand on his arm. 'I'm so sorry, Tom,' I say.

'Somebody said once that God — or whoever is up there watching over us as we scramble through life — only gives us the heartache he knows we can cope with.' He shakes his head. 'Perhaps it's true for some, but I know my father would say different.'

'And what about you?'

He sighs. 'I'm dealing with things in the only way I can.'

* * *

Once we reach Hitchin, I direct Tom to the Victorian terraced cottage Erika rents near the train station, and he parks up outside. We make our way up the short path, and the porch light springs on. I ring the doorbell.

'Maybe she's gone out,' Tom says, as I press it again.

'No. She has to be here. She's ill.' Concern rises as I step onto the cobbled frontage, and, avoiding the empty terracotta pots, I place my hand over my eyes and peer into the window. 'I can't see any sign of life.'

Tom knocks hard on the door with a tight fist, and I return to the path, try the bell for a third time. After a few moments of stepping from one foot to the other, I bend and call her name through the letterbox, finally taking a set of keys from my bag.

'What are you doing?' Tom looks at the keys before glancing about him.

'I have her spare set in case of emergencies.'

'And you think this is an emergency?' He looks concerned, as though we're breaking and entering.

In truth, I'm not sure if it's an emergency either, but I shove the key into the lock anyway.

'Erika,' I call out, opening the door and heading in. 'It's me. Riona . . . I'm with Tom Evans. Remember him from the other night?'

There's a noise in the kitchen and I hurry down the hallway, aware of the warmth of the place, the heating on high, and into the kitchen.

It's only the cats, and they glance up at me from where they are feeding. Their litter tray is clean, and there is fresh water in their bowls.

'Erika,' I call, heading back through the house. There's a pile of opened letters on the table in her narrow hallway. I poke my head into the lounge. It's neat and tidy. A bland room with no hint of Erika's witty personality in the décor, only a photograph of her mum in snowbound Kiruna, where Erika lived before coming to England. She told me once this house is a temporary fix until she can afford to buy, but she's been living here for over two years now.

There's no sign of Erika being ill. No tablets. No crumpled tissues. No throw and pillow on the sofa.

'Erika?' I call again.

'Where does this lead?' Tom points at a door in the hallway.

'The cellar — Erika won't be down there. She's a bit freaked out by it. In fact, it almost put her off renting the place. She told me once that she thinks something lives down there.' I half smile at my friend's silly fears. 'But I've checked it out for her. Apart from the creaks of the old building and the squeaks of a family of mice — who have so far escaped the cats — it's as silent as a graveyard.'

'We should probably check the bedrooms.' I head up the stairs, Tom right behind me. 'Erika! Erika, are you up here?'

Her bedroom is tidy, much like the lounge, her bed neatly made. 'Where the hell is she?'

'Perhaps she's gone to stay with family,' Tom offers, as we head back down the stairs.

I shake my head. 'She wouldn't have just taken off to Sweden without telling me. Plus, she isn't the kind of person who would lie about being ill. She loves her job. It's our own business, so she wouldn't let her clients down if she could possibly avoid it.' I hear the worry in my voice. *Where are you, Erika?*

We make our way back into the kitchen, and I study the photos of my friend and me pinned to a corkboard. We look so happy, hugging, our eyes sparkling. 'I just don't get it.' I take my phone from my bag and call her number once more. But just as before, it goes straight to voicemail.

'She can't be far.' Tom's tone is light. 'It's clear the cats have been fed recently, and the heating is on. She's probably gone to the shop for something. Try not to worry.'

'You're right. I'm probably overreacting. Maybe we should go.' I give each of the cats a cautious head tickle

— they're not the friendliest of pets — before jotting down a note for Erika. We move into the hallway, and as we head back outside, I try to convince myself she'll have a right laugh at me panicking so much.

As we travel back, my head throbs and a wave of dizziness takes over, though I'm not sure if it's to do with my accident or if it's been triggered by anxiety.

Tom pulls up outside my apartment. 'Maybe I should make a move.' He shrugs, and I guess he senses I'm not feeling good. I'm not hiding it well. Fidgeting all the way back and fiddling with my phone are dead giveaways. I desperately want him to come up to finish the wine, but know in my vulnerable state I'll end up melting into his arms. One thing may lead to another, and I can't afford to get this wrong, not after George.

'I must admit I'm not feeling too great,' I say, opening the car door and getting out. 'But another time, yes? And I so appreciate you taking me to Erika's.'

'No worries,' he says. 'I hope she's OK. Are we still on for Saturday? Maybe a walk, something to eat?'

'I'd like that,' I say, and close the door. As he pulls away, I raise my hand, watching the rear lights of his car disappearing into the distance. I realise I haven't asked him why he was letting himself into the apartment in Hitchin, but convince myself once more that it could have been for any number of reasons. Perhaps, as he's staying longer than expected, his aunt and uncle couldn't keep putting him up.

Once he's out of sight, I feel lost and a little afraid, the comfort of his presence missed already. I turn and head towards my front door.

As I'm fiddling with my keys, a sudden rustle in the bushes opposite makes me turn quickly. A chill runs down my spine. I study the shadowy darkness for some moments before a cat shoots out and darts across the road.

'Get a grip, Riona,' I tell myself, as I push the key in the door with shaking fingers.

CHAPTER THIRTY-FOUR

Riona

Friday, 10 December 2021

'Kieran!' I'm pleased to see my nephew the following morning, though I wish he didn't look so pale and downhearted. I usher him into my apartment and give him the biggest hug, hoping it will go some way to lifting his spirits. 'How are you, sweetie?'

'More's the point, how are you, Auntie Ri?' he says as I release him. 'Mum told me what happened, that someone knocked you down.'

'I'm not too bad,' I say, brushing over it, not wanting him to worry. 'I'll live to fight another day.'

He smiles. 'You look as if you've done six rounds with Tyson Fury.'

I touch my forehead then move my hand to my cheek, my whole face feels tender, swollen. 'Well, I'm feeling better than I was.' It's true. Since getting up a couple of hours ago, I haven't suffered any waves of nausea or dizzy spells, and my head doesn't hurt quite so much. I feel stronger mentally too, after some mindfulness sessions when I got up.

I heard from Erika last thing yesterday, which was a relief. Her tone was upbeat and jokey in her text, asking if I broke into her house and stole cuddles from her soppy cats. I know she's joking, she always is. Her cats aren't soppy at all, and far from the cuddling kind. She said in the message that I must have missed her by a few minutes, as she'd popped out to the shops for some cat food.

Stop worrying about me, Riona, she added, *though I love that you care.*

I've decided to leave her be for a few days. She must need some time out right now — some space — like we all do from time to time. So I will give her that and stop being such an overprotective friend.

Kieran hands me a bag of grapes and pushes back his heavy fringe. 'There you go, don't eat them all at once,' he says. 'They're from Mum. She knows I'm here.'

'And she's OK with that?'

'Yep. She's gone to the Spar. I've got to text her when I leave, and she'll pick me up.'

'She's not coming in?' I sound far too hurt.

He shrugs. 'Sorry, Ri.'

'Oh, sweetie, it's not your fault. She's busy, is all.' I lead the way up the stairs. 'These grapes look yummy.'

'I prefer biscuits.'

'Well, I'm sure I can find some of those.'

'Great, I'm starving.'

'So how are things with you and your mum?' I say, once I've poured two glasses of cola and found a packet of custard creams.

We sit down in the lounge, and he takes a bite of biscuit, crumbs sprinkling down his hoodie. 'She's finally told me a bit more about this bloke she's messaging.' He takes a swig of his drink, moves to the edge of the sofa. 'She says it's early days, and the reason she didn't tell me about him is she doesn't want me to get to know him, for him to disappear like Vince did.'

'That makes sense.'

'I s'pose.' He shrugs, takes another bite of biscuit. 'She says as soon as she knows whether it will work out, she'll let me meet him. But at the moment they've only been talking to each other through messages. She said he's making her happy so far, but she doesn't want to rush into anything.'

'And you're OK about it?'

Another shrug. 'Not really, I haven't met him yet and nor has Mum. I said to her the other day she should make sure she's not being catfished, but she just laughed.'

'She must have seen a photo of him.'

He takes a gulp of his drink. 'Yeah, I think so. I'm not sure how she met him, but if it was online I worry it could be anyone, Aunt Ri. It happens all the time, people online not being who they say they are. There was this programme I watched where a bloke online pretended to be twenty-five and really fit, and it turned out he was, like, in his eighties with a crinkly face and achy bones.'

I laugh, but his face is serious.

'It's not funny, Ri.'

'No, I know.'

'This bloke Mum's talking to could be anyone.' His eyes are fixed on me, wide and worried.

'I guess. But sometimes you have to have a little trust.'

'I will once I've met him and I know he's OK.'

'He could turn out to be good for your mum.'

He nods. 'I guess so. She may even start thinking she looks OK and stop getting surgery.'

'Oh, Kieran, sometimes you sound so much older than eleven. You're good for your mum, do you know that?'

'Yeah.' He nods proudly. 'She calls me her life support.' He smiles, a biscuit crumb on his chin, and I wonder, as I often have in the past, whether my sister puts too much onto his young shoulders.

'Anyway, Mum says she's going to meet him soon.' He sniffs, drains his glass and puts it down on the table. He gets to his feet, biscuit crumbs falling to the floor. 'Thanks for the drink.'

'You're welcome.' I rise too, and we hug.

His heavy footfalls thump against the stairs as he makes his way down. The door opens and slams closed behind him.

I lower myself onto the sofa, where I sit for ten minutes wondering — no, hoping — that this new man in Alene's life, whoever he is, turns out to be a good one.

CHAPTER THIRTY-FIVE

Riona

I look out of the front window of my apartment, my body pressed against the warm radiator. It's dark, gone 6 p.m., and a frost is settling.

I spot Stacey walking across the road, her hair scooped into a high ponytail, her hands deep in the pocket of a thigh-length red woollen jacket, a beige scarf wrapped around her neck, a bag over her shoulder. She looks up at the window, picks up speed when she sees me watching.

Within moments the doorbell chimes, and I pull myself from the radiator and head down the stairs.

'Riona!' she cries as I open up, a wobble in her voice. 'Have you seen it?'

I guess immediately there must be another photo on Instagram, and move to one side so she can enter, the thud of my heart kicking my ribs.

'Don't worry, there are no more pictures of you,' she says, once we're sitting in my lounge. She doesn't remove her jacket, too busy fumbling in her bag and bringing out her phone. 'But there's another of me, and I'm not going to lie, it's completely freaked me out. I had to come. I didn't want to intrude, but—'

'It's fine,' I say, hearing the agitation in my voice. I'm still struggling being in her company, but our shared problem forces me onwards.

She continues to faff with her phone. 'I thought I might find you at the clinic. I'm so glad I spotted you at the window.' Her hand is shaky as her fingers touch the screen. She passes her phone to me, eyes wide. 'Who is doing this, Riona?'

The new photo is of Stacey playing her guitar. Her eyes are closed as though lost in her music, her dog curled asleep on the sofa beside her.

'I'm in my lounge. In the privacy of my own home.' Her voice is tense with anxiety, her eyes watery. 'Someone must have taken this through my window without me knowing. They must have come into my back garden, looked in at me.' A tear escapes, rolls down her cheek.

'This is getting out of hand,' I say, handing back her phone. 'I'll make us a drink, shall I?' I rise, struggling to come to terms with yet another invasive photograph.

She follows me into the kitchen, where I fill the kettle and take a couple of mugs from the cupboard.

'Who would do this?' she repeats, as we wait for the kettle to boil.

'I've no idea, but I think it's time we talked to the police together.'

She nods, leans against the worktop. 'I know I've said it before, but do you think there could be a connection to the Ensley Killer?'

'Because of the person in the yellow hi-vis?' I'd pushed that idea from my thoughts, deciding that seeing someone in a yellow hi-vis doesn't constitute a killer returning to the village after twelve years. 'I feel sure this has nothing to do with the murder.'

'But we've both seen him, Riona.'

'No. I've simply seen two people in a yellow hi-vis, Stacey. Seriously, lots of people wear them. I'm not going down that road. We need to stick to what is actually happening: the anonymous letters we received, the Instagram account.' *The hit and run?*

'OK. Yes. Fine.'

I make some instant coffee, conscious of Stacey watching me with watery eyes. I hand her a mug.

'I'm probably wrong,' she says. 'But don't you think it's more than a coincidence that this is all happening as Charlotte Carter arrives back in Ensley?'

'Maybe,' I say, but I'm not sure. I've no connection to Charlotte Carter, and I'm pretty sure Stacey hasn't either.

Stacey's eyes move to the window. 'Jesus!' She clutches her chest. 'What the hell?'

I spin round, look to where her eyes have landed, but I can't see anything. It's dark outside, the field behind my flat a sheet of black. 'What?'

'Let's go!' She slams her mug down with a thud, liquid splashing the work surface.

'What? No! It's dark out there.'

'But I saw him, Riona.'

'Him? What are you talking about? I didn't see anything.'

'Someone is out there. I saw torchlight, a flash of yellow.' Stacey's eyes are back on the window. 'I swear I saw someone.' She shudders. 'We should go out there, Riona. See who it is.'

I lean over the sink and drag down the blind with a clatter. 'No! We'd have to be crazy to go out there if some bloke is lurking about.'

'But what if it's the Ensley Killer?'

'Especially if it's the Ensley Killer! And I didn't see anyone, Stacey. Are you sure you didn't imagine it?'

She bursts into tears. 'This is all too much,' she cries, heading into the lounge and dropping onto the sofa with a thud. 'I can't cope anymore, Riona.' She buries her head into her hands and sobs.

I approach, sit down next to her, and place my arm loosely around her shoulders. 'It's OK,' I say.

She looks up at me, dashes away her tears and sniffs. 'We should call the police.'

'And say what? That you saw a flash of yellow in a field?'

Her wide eyes trap me in their gaze. 'Let's go out there, Riona. Please. We need to get to the bottom of this before I go completely crazy. If you won't come with me, I'll go alone.'

My body trembles, but I can't let her go alone. 'OK . . .'

'Thanks, Riona,' she says, rising, but I know already that the idea is ridiculous.

I throw on my jacket, and we hurry down the stairs and out through the front door into the cold evening. We make our way towards the field, to where an uneven path runs between the rear of the houses and the field. The steep embankment shields our view of the field. I shudder. Pull my jacket tightly round me. 'Is this really such a good idea?'

Stacey ignores me and scrambles up the embankment. She stands at the top with her hands on her hips, looking out across the field. 'I can't see anyone.' She reaches out her hand towards me and yanks me up the bank.

'Come on,' she says.

I grab her jacket sleeve before she can head off. 'I'm not coming, Stacey. This is a stupid idea. I don't know why I'm here.'

'It's freaking me out too, Riona, but we have a chance to find out who's doing it.' She shakes her head, climbs over a stile into the field, her ponytail swinging. 'We need to get closer than this. Find out who it is.' She stops, glances back.

'I can't.' I step backwards, my whole body crying out in fear. 'And you shouldn't go out there either.'

Mature trees that fringe the field rustle and fidget, there's a hum of distant traffic, a crow caws — but I can't see anyone.

'I'm out of here,' I say, turning and stumbling down the embankment, dropping onto my bottom as I reach the road, covering myself in mud. I look back, expecting Stacey to follow, but she's disappeared into the darkness.

'If this person is uploading those photos, Riona,' she yells, her voice getting smaller, 'putting us through all of this, we need to confront them.'

'You're crazy,' I call, standing at the foot of the embankment.

I wait, my phone torch throwing out a weak beam of light. Most of the houses that back onto the field are in darkness. It's so quiet. Cold. My fingers are starting to go numb.

Time *tick*, *tick*, *ticks*, and I tell myself it was Stacey's choice to take off, that I did my best to stop her going, that she is no friend of mine. She was the one who let me down all those years ago. But guilt for allowing her to take off alone gets to me. I scramble up the bank once more and climb over the stile. Holding my phone torch towards where she headed, I dash across the field. It's not long before I pick up the sound of quick breathing, the stomp of anxious footsteps crossing the field, getting closer. I slow, dart the beam across the area, catching Stacey's wide, hazel eyes in the light. 'Oh God, Riona,' she cries, racing towards me. 'I saw someone. I saw someone.'

She dashes past me, and without hesitation I turn and run too. We stumble as we go, finally reaching the stile. We climb over it and slip down the embankment, my pulse thudding.

On the pathway we stop, and her shocked eyes freeze on me. 'Whoever it was, they took off into the trees,' she says, breathless. 'But I got photos, Riona. I got photos of the figure in the hi-vis.'

CHAPTER THIRTY-SIX

Riona

'Somebody is out to scare us, that much is obvious.' Stacey fumbles with her phone as we reach my front door. 'Oh God, my battery's dead.' She looks at me with shiny eyes, her breathing ragged, her tone a little manic. 'I must have used it up taking pictures.' She shoves her phone in her pocket. 'God, my heart is bouncing in my chest like a ping pong ball.'

I push my key in the door, feeling unsettled. 'Maybe you could come up, I may have a phone charger.'

'Have you got wine?'

I recall the bottle Tom left. 'I have indeed.'

'Great, I could do with a large one after that.' She pulls her loose ponytail tight as I push the door open. 'I shouldn't be too long, though. Minnie will be crossing her legs.'

Once upstairs, I search for a charger to match her iPhone, with no luck, before pouring two glasses of wine.

I sit down in the armchair and Stacey settles onto the sofa, both of us calmer now.

'Oh, I meant to say earlier,' she says, reaching for her bag, 'I've got you something.' She pulls out a small parcel wrapped in tissue paper and hands it to me.

'What is it?' I say, feeling awkward, certain my cheeks flush.

'It's just a little something I got on eBay, nothing much. I just saw it and thought of you, us.'

I don't want to open it. I don't want a gift from Stacey Roberts. I pull free the tissue. It's a bracelet: an Edward wooden bracelet from *Twilight*. I've seen them on eBay and they're not cheap. I hold it up, studying it, struggling for the right words.

'Remember how we loved *Twilight*?' she says, a dreamy look in her eye.

'Yes. Thanks. It's lovely.'

Wanda jumps onto Stacey's lap, moving our focus from the bracelet, and I put it down quickly onto the side table.

'She's a gorgeous cat,' Stacey says, tickling her silky grey ears with her free hand, as Wanda purrs, loud and rumbling.

'She's such a floosy,' I say with a smile. 'She's anybody's for a fuss.'

Stacey stares into my eyes. 'Are you afraid, Riona?' she says.

'Afraid?' I take a gulp of wine. Maybe I am. 'Well, it's not exactly normal, is it?'

She shakes her head, continues to stroke the cat. 'I keep trying to think why someone would be targeting both of us. I mean, we haven't been friends for so long. What's the connection?'

I look down, run my finger around the top of the glass. 'It's not just us though,' I say. 'It's Erika too.'

'Of course, yes, you said.'

I meet Stacey's eye, recalling how Erika turned her down for bereavement counselling because of me. 'Her letter was shoved under the loo door when we were out at the Fox.'

Stacey's hand flies to her mouth. 'What could we possibly all have in common that would make someone be so cruel?'

'I keep thinking the same thing.'

She takes a long sip of her wine. 'I'm sorry for how things worked out between us,' she says. 'I'm sorry for what happened with George. I was young. Stupid. Though it's no excuse.'

I think back to the things Stacey told me in our younger years, how her father had a reputation on her estate as a ruthless drug dealer. Nobody dared cross him. She'd hated her life, the way her mum was afraid of her father, how she'd been a junkie who fell into his world when she was only seventeen. It's a wonder Stacey didn't end up in care. It was no life for a child.

'Let's leave the past in the past, shall we?' I say, keeping my tone even, feeling my barriers lower.

'If I could go back and change it I would, you know that, right?'

She sounds sincere, but I'm still not sure I will ever be able to fully forgive her. She crossed a line the day she kissed George, proved she was no friend of mine.

She drains her glass. 'Right, little cat, I really should make a move.' She shifts, gently easing Wanda from her lap, and brushes fur from her trousers. 'How about we meet up tomorrow afternoon? Talk things through, look at the photos I took together.' She rises. 'Decide what we should do now.'

I get up too. 'I can't make tomorrow, I'm afraid.'

'Oh?' She tilts her head.

'I'm meeting someone.' I decide not to tell her about Tom. My private life has nothing to do with her.

She takes a tissue from her pocket and wipes it across her nose, and I try to read her expression, but find it impossible. 'How about Sunday, then?' she says. 'I've got a private guitar lesson first thing in the morning, but maybe come to mine around midday?'

'OK.'

'And I'll send you the photos I took in the field once I've charged my phone. If we have a clear picture of who's doing this, we can go to the police.'

I'm not convinced. Even if she has a photo of someone in the field wearing a yellow hi-vis, what does it prove?

'And in the meantime,' she goes on, 'please be careful, Riona.'

'You too, Stacey,' I say, as I follow her down the stairs and open the front door.

She steps out, and I watch as she makes her way down the road, swallowed by the darkness. I sense the bond that was destroyed when we were in our teens repairing a little. Knowing we are going through this together makes it less painful somehow. Perhaps people can change.

Back upstairs, I go into the kitchen and, against my better judgement, pull the cords on the blind, raising it halfway up the window. The field is a block of solid black. I can't see anything, but I can't help wondering if someone is out there watching me. I shudder and drag down the blind once more, almost knocking my row of tiny cacti off the windowsill in my haste. I doubt I will sleep tonight.

* * *

Saturday, 11 December 2021

'Wanda!' I cry, waking to find her nibbling my nose. She straightens up, looking proud of herself as she stares down from where she's balanced on my chest. I drag myself to a sitting position and ease her gently away. She mews, annoyed, starts licking her fur.

'I suppose you think you're clever waking me up,' I say, stroking her silky head.

It's 8.30 a.m. when I clamber out of bed. Once in the kitchen, I glance at the window, take a breath and reach for the cord on the blind. I need to face the view from my kitchen window. But it's no good. Despite doubting that a figure in a yellow hi-vis will be staring in at me, I can't take that risk. I lower my arm. I need coffee.

I feed Wanda, make my drink and head into the lounge, the warmth of the steaming mug comforting.

As I lower myself onto the sofa, a message pings onto my phone:

Hey, are we still on for today? Shall I pick you up around two? Tom x

I observe the kiss and smile:

Yes, looking forward to it. See you then. Riona x

Coffee drunk, I return to the kitchen, take a deep breath, and before I can change my mind, pull up the blind. The sky is pale blue, and the sun's rays cast a brilliant light over the field. There's no sign of a figure in yellow.

* * *

It's good to be back working in the clinic this morning, even if it's only for a few hours. My clients, as they arrive, give me a sense of purpose that's been lacking since the hit and run. Focusing on them rather than my own problems goes some way to helping me find my inner strength once more, for now at least.

I close the clinic at one, locking the door and pulling down the blind. It's been odd here without Erika. I miss our banter, her cheery presence, the way she makes a mean cup of coffee. Despite regular texts saying she's improving and will soon be back, I wish she would hurry up and get well. Her insistence that I shouldn't go round to see her, that she's not up for a chat at the moment, are making me wonder if she's suffering with anxiety or depression. Sometimes the life and soul — the one who makes us laugh — is the very person who is going through turmoil and putting up a front. I battle down an urge to go round to see her, arguing the merits of descending on her if she needs space.

I head back upstairs to my apartment and change into an orange jumper and jeans, and put on some make-up, a splash of perfume. I'm looking forward to seeing Tom despite all the unanswered questions swirling round my head.

* * *

'Hey,' I say, opening the door to him just after two o'clock. I pull on my padded jacket, woolly hat and gloves, and step out into the chilly afternoon, glad to be getting out of the apartment with someone I hope I can trust.

'Shall we take a drive out?' he says, pulling his woollen coat around him. 'It's a lovely, bright day. What do you think?'

'Sounds good.' It really does. 'Where were you thinking?'

'There's a Christmas market in a village on the other side of Stevenage. I looked it up online, and there's a nice pub nearby.'

I'm not sure I'm up for a Christmas market, but nod and smile anyway, go along with it.

'We can do something else, if you like,' he says, seeming to pick up on my slight reservation. 'I just thought—'

'It sounds good. It will be nice to get out in the fresh air. Get to know each other.'

He nods. Points his key fob at the yellow Mini and presses the unlock button.

Once in the car, he fires up the engine and pulls away, heading out of Ensley. I fumble around in my head for something upbeat to talk about. I desperately need to push everything that's happened to the back of my mind. 'So, what are your dogs' names?'

'Oh.' He looks across at me for a moment before returning his gaze to the road ahead, squinting into the hazy sun. 'Agatha and Christie.'

I laugh. 'Brilliant.'

'Though Agatha has been shortened to Aggie, so the impact isn't quite the same.'

'They must miss you.'

'Apparently they haven't mentioned me once.'

I laugh again. There's an easiness about Tom, and I find myself relaxing as we head along the A1, passing signs for Knebworth House.

'It's haunted,' he says.

'Sorry?'

'Knebworth House. By a Victorian novelist, apparently.'

'Creepy. I saw Robbie Williams there in 2003.'

'I think half of the UK were there that weekend at some point.'

I nod. 'I was about twelve at the time. My aunt was a huge fan and dragged me and Alene along.'

'Are you and your sister close?'

I shrug, glance out of the side window. 'We were once.'

A silence descends as Tom pulls off the motorway, and we hit winding country roads.

Finally, he indicates to pull into a field full of cars. 'Thank goodness for that,' he says, driving into a space. 'I thought that car was going to ram us at one point.'

I look towards the road. 'What car?'

'Just some random, tailgating us for the last half a mile or so. Didn't you notice?'

I shake my head and glance over at the wooden huts laden with sparkly lights and spilling with Christmas ornaments.

'Ready?' he says.

I snap free my seatbelt. 'Ready,' I say.

CHAPTER THIRTY-SEVEN

Riona

Tom slips his gloved hand in mine as we head towards a wooden shack selling mulled wine. I smile up at him, noticing the deep blue of his eyes. We've had a great afternoon exploring the Christmas market, watching excited children racing around eating pretzels, Christmas cookies and gingerbread men, their parents enjoying jugs of beer or mulled wine. I've even bought a Christmas ornament for Erika – a handmade Swedish Christmas gnome called a tomte – it looks rather cute with its tall red hat and long white beard, I'm sure she'll love it.

It's dark, around half five, when I climb onto a stool at a high round table, with a paper cup full of mulled wine. I feel good. The worries of the last week are, for this brief moment in time, drifting further to the back of my mind.

Tom loosens his scarf and sits down next to me. I lean across the table, cinnamon and orange tickling my nostrils, and kiss his cheek. 'Thanks so much, Tom,' I say. 'It's been a great day.' I feel myself blush. But this is exactly what I needed. And I like him. I like his company, a first for me since George.

'It's been good,' he says. 'I'm glad you've had fun.' He raises his cup. 'Shall we have something to eat at the pub after these?'

'Sounds good to me.' I smile as he takes a sip of his drink. It's as though magic dust has sprinkled over my worries, blocking them out, if only temporarily.

He pats his pockets and rises. 'I've left my phone in the car. I really should check it.'

'Oh, OK.' I go to get down from the stool.

'No, stay here, I won't be a minute.' He takes off before I can argue, getting lost in the crowd.

I take a sip of my drink, enjoying the warm, comforting flavour. The atmosphere is charming, even the carol booming from one of the booths sounds pleasant to my ears. Perhaps the Christmas spirit has got me for the first time in years. I sigh. I need to rein in my feelings. Tom is dealing with his sister's death. He'll be heading back to Norfolk soon.

It's as I'm enjoying the ambience that I see, through the crowds, someone standing by the entrance, and my mood plummets. At first I try to ignore the staring figure. Convince myself that lots of people wear yellow hi-vis jackets. But it's the way they are standing so still, looking my way, that makes my neck prickle.

A throng of people shift in unison, blocking my view, and the figure disappears from sight. I slam my drink down, splashing some on the table, and jump to my feet, pulling out my phone. *I'll snap a photo if I can.*

Ducking and stretching, I attempt to see through the crowd and finally catch sight of the figure once more, still not moving, hands dangling by their side — so still.

Maybe it's a paramedic, or someone clearing up litter, or maybe security. Am I being ridiculous? Starting to lose the plot?

But it's as though they only see me, as though they're picking me out of the crowd, pinning me down — yet I can't actually see their eyes, I can't make out their features.

Despite my fear, I've had all I can take. It's dark, but surely whoever it is can't hurt me with so many people about. I dart from the table, leaving our drinks, and race across the crowded market towards the entrance, gripping my phone. I dart through the throng of people, and I'm halfway there when a group of youngsters cuts across my path, laughing and talking, one wearing a reindeer hat, clearly no idea how desperate I am to get by. I stumble, and the kids look at me. 'I'm fine,' I say, not that they seem bothered.

I gather my wits. I can still see the figure through the throng. I will confront whoever it is. Find out what they want from me.

'Riona?'

I turn to see one of my clients, holding her little boy's hand, and carrying a holly wreath. 'Are you looking forward to Christmas?' she says, as though settling in for a chat, her smile wide.

I don't want to be rude, but need to get by. 'Yes. Yes, I am,' I say, standing on tiptoe, attempting to see over her shoulder. But the figure has gone, no longer standing at the entrance. 'Listen, let's catch up later,' I say. 'Sorry. I just need to see someone.'

'Oh. OK. No worries.'

I dash past her, and straight into Tom coming in through the entrance.

'Did you see him?' I cry, my voice shaky, my heart thudding. I spin round, my eyes flicking across the backs of the temporary buildings and out towards the car park.

'Who, Riona?' Tom looks startled.

'He was just here.' Tears fill my eyes. 'I saw him. I know he was here.' I turn to the guy behind the counter in a nearby wooden chalet, selling handmade candles. 'Did you see him?' I ask. 'He was wearing a hi-vis.'

The bloke shrugs and looks at Tom. 'Didn't notice anyone,' he says, but he looks a bit vague, as though he wouldn't have noticed Prince William if he'd walked up to him delivering a pizza.

Tom wraps his arm around my shoulders and moves me away from the entrance. 'What's going on, Riona?' he says. 'Is everything OK?'

I take several deep breaths and brush away my tears with the back of my hand. 'I'm fine,' I say, pulling away from him, but I'm a mess and I'm not sure how much more I can take.

* * *

We drive back to Ensley in silence.

After frantically racing out of the Christmas market, leaving Tom looking bewildered as I searched the area, diving around the backs of the wooden huts, searching in the shadows like I was demented, I finally gave up. There was no sign of anyone in a yellow reflective jacket.

Tom put his arms around me again when I'd finished hunting for the elusive figure, and I broke down and cried. He seemed worried, kept asking me who I thought I saw, and I suddenly felt ridiculous. Cross with myself that I'd let Stacey's theories get under my skin.

'Do you still want to go to a pub?' Tom asks now, as he pulls onto the motorway, into the slow lane.

I don't, and I sense he doesn't either. I shake my head. 'Just take me home,' I say. 'Please.'

He pulls up outside my apartment, doesn't turn off the engine.

'I'm sorry,' I say. 'I didn't mean to act like such an idiot.'

'It's OK.' He turns to look at me. 'I just wish you'd tell me why.'

'It was nothing. I had a lovely day,' I say. 'I'm so sorry I spoiled it.'

'You don't have to keep saying sorry, Riona.' He pauses for a moment. 'I just hated seeing you that way. I was worried more than anything.'

A tear rolls down my cheek.

'There's some tissues in the glove compartment,' he says, gently.

I sniff, open it and reach in for a pack of tissues. A chunky gold bracelet catches my eye, and I glance over at Tom, who is looking the other way. It doesn't look like something he would wear. I snap the glove compartment closed and pull a tissue from the pack.

'Listen, why not come up for a bit?' I press a tissue against my nose. 'We could maybe order a takeaway.'

'Sounds good. I'd like that.' He smiles and kills the engine. 'And you can choose what takeout we have, as long as it's Chinese.'

CHAPTER THIRTY-EIGHT

Riona

'So, why did you need your phone?' We're standing in the kitchen, serving Chinese food onto plates, and the words have spilled out before I can check them.

Tom looks up, his eyes meeting mine, a forkful of beansprouts suspended in mid-air. 'Sorry?'

'When we were at the Christmas market, before my ridiculous outburst, you said you needed your phone, but didn't say why.' I'm not sure why I'm being like this.

'I was expecting a call from my mum. I may have said before that she worries if I don't pick up. She's been in a bad way since my sister died, likes to be able to get hold of me.'

'Yes. Yes, of course.' I feel bad for bringing it up. Maybe I am being paranoid.

I reach for two trays, hand him one, and we head into the lounge. We sit with our food on our laps and begin to tuck in, our cutlery hitting the plates loud in the silence.

'So, this person you saw,' he says after a swallow, 'have you seen him before?'

'A couple of times, but I don't even know for sure it's a man, or that it's the same person. Whoever it is, they're always too far away to see properly. It's nothing, honestly. I'm not feeling myself at the moment, that's all.'

'Because of the letter you told me about?'

I'm desperate to tell him everything that's been going on, so he fully understands my outburst. I rise, put my tray on the table and go into the kitchen to grab my phone. 'Things have been happening to me,' I say, returning.

'Things?'

I open up the Instagram account on my phone and show him the screen.

'What's this?'

I sit down, conscious of his closeness. 'I was tagged in some photos on Instagram that I had no idea were taken. All the photos on the account are of me and an old friend of mine. On top of the anonymous letter and getting knocked down, it's made me a bit jittery.'

'This really doesn't sound good, Riona.' He sounds sincere, dashes a hand across mouth. 'Have you told the police?'

'Yes, my aunt has. They suggested I report the Insta account and keep a diary of everything that happens. They said to call them, talk things through.'

'And have you?'

'Not yet.'

He rubs the back of his neck. 'You need to get the account taken down, Riona.'

'Yes, I realise that. And I will.'

He nods, blinks. 'So how does this tie in with what happened at the Christmas market?'

'It all started when I saw someone in a yellow hi-vis by Quarry Lake, and then again in the field behind my apartment. I thought it was nothing, but then Stacey — the other woman in the photos — said she's been seeing someone in a yellow hi-vis too. She was round last night and saw whoever this person is from my kitchen window.'

'They were hanging about?'

'Yes, in the field behind the apartment.' I shake my head. 'I'm unsettled, is all. So when I saw someone today dressed in a yellow hi-vis, I lost it. I don't know if you know, but there was a murder here in 2009, and two other women were attacked. The killer wore a yellow hi-vis.'

'Really?'

'Uh-huh, and he was never caught.'

'This is really strange, Riona.' He looks again at the pictures on my phone. 'I don't like it at all.'

'I'm not too keen myself,' I say, trying to smile. 'Whoever is taking the photos must be watching us all the time. This one—' I point at the photo of me asleep — 'was taken when I was in hospital.'

He runs his hand across his jaw, discards his tray. His face flushes as he hands my phone back to me. 'You need to be careful, Riona.' He rakes his fingers though his hair. 'You need to get away for a couple of weeks. You could come to Norfolk with me, maybe.'

I smile, surprised he would want me to join him. 'I'd love that, but I can't close the clinic. Between Erika and me having to cancel appointments, we've probably already lost clients.'

'Well, if you change your mind . . .'

He stares at me for some moments, moves in closer. His kiss is sudden, passionate, and I'm instantly swept into it, letting myself go. I need his closeness right now. I need the comfort of him, the smell of him.

After making love, I fall asleep in his arms, feeling safer than I have since the letter was pushed through the clinic door. Though I know, without doubt, this feeling of security won't last.

CHAPTER THIRTY-NINE

Riona

Sunday, 12 December 2021

I wake, eyes gritty, and reach my arm across the bed in the hope Tom will still be there, but he's gone. The sheet is cold, and a surge of panic rises inside me. I'm not myself at all, and I hate this feeling of helplessness.

Wanda is curled on the chair by the window in her favourite spot, where the sun's rays reach in, like golden fingers, through a gap in the curtain and caress her silky body. She opens her eyes as though sensing me watching her, unfurls and stretches, before making her way over to me. I stroke her warm fur — it's comforting.

I reach over and pick up my phone from the bedside cabinet. There's nothing from Tom or Erika, and my heart sinks.

I know I should get up. Go for a walk to clear my head. Spend some time meditating, perhaps. But I seem to have lost my self-preservation routine. I just want to hide away from the world, from everything that's happening.

I'm about to snuggle back down and drag my quilt over my head, when I remember I've arranged to meet Stacey at midday.

'Crap,' I mutter, as I force myself out of bed and push my feet into my slippers.

* * *

I drive to Stacey's, making up my mind that once I've seen her, I will go into Hitchin to see Erika whether she likes it or not. I'm frustrated by her constant text messages. It's been over a week since we last spoke. She's my friend — my closest friend — and she may not need me right now, but I sure as hell need her.

I pull up outside Stacey's semi just before twelve. It's quiet here, as though nobody lives behind the closed doors.

I get out of my car, make my way up her path and buzz the doorbell.

Inside, Minnie barks.

I wait.

And wait.

I ring the bell once more before pulling out my phone and calling Stacey's number. It goes straight to voicemail.

'Hey, it's Riona. I'm at your front door. I thought we said midday.' I step back and look up at the bedroom windows, my phone pinned to my ear. Minnie is silent now, and I shake away a feeling that something doesn't feel right. 'Maybe I got the time wrong,' I continue into the phone, though I feel sure she said twelve. 'Get back to me when you can, and maybe we can rearrange.'

I'm about to get back into my car when I see her dashing along the road towards me, wearing joggers and a hooded sweatshirt, a carrier bag swinging by her side.

'Riona! Sorry!' She waves frantically, her pace quick, erratic.

I raise my hand to let her know she can slow down, that I've seen her.

'Sorry,' she repeats as she reaches me out of breath. 'I realised I was out of milk.' She lifts the carrier bag higher. 'There was a queue in the Spar, and—'

'It's fine. No worries at all,' I say with a smile.

'Right . . . well, let's get the kettle on, shall we?' She turns, hurries towards her front door, and I follow.

Once inside, Minnie calmer after excitedly greeting her owner, and a steaming cup of tea in front of us as we sit at the kitchen table, Stacey opens her laptop.

'I didn't send the photos over, because . . . well, I uploaded them and there isn't that much to see, to be honest,' she says. 'I really hoped we would be able to see the figure more clearly, but . . . well . . . be ready for a shock. It's quite creepy, in fact.'

My heartbeat quickens. 'What is it?'

'Well, I thought the photos would show the person's face, as I got pretty close.' She clicks on a link to her downloads and opens the first picture. 'But . . .' She moves the screen across the breakfast bar so I can see it clearly. 'I've tried to lighten it, but . . .'

I stare at the screen. Slam my hand to my mouth. 'Oh God.' The creepy sight makes me shiver. Whoever is in the picture is wearing a white, featureless mask. 'Christ, that's so freaky,' I whisper, a crawling fear tickling my neck, making me shudder.

'Mmm. I thought so too.' She opens another photo, enlarges it. It's an image of someone in a yellow hi-vis retreating into the trees. 'These ones are completely useless. I guess it's not enough to take to the police. What do you think?' She turns from the screen, her eyes locking with mine, her face unreadable.

I rub my neck, fear refusing to release me. 'I don't know. I guess we could see what they say.'

Her eyes dart to my mug. 'Ooh, would you like a biscuit?' She goes to rise.

'No, I'm fine, honestly.'

'I've got chocolate digestives.'

'No, really, I don't think I could swallow right now.'

She lowers herself back down and closes her laptop. 'I'm a bag of nerves,' she says, looping her hair behind her ears. Her face is pale, the scar on her cheek vivid.

A sudden thump comes from upstairs, and my stomach leaps. 'What was that?' I'm so on edge it's ridiculous.

She looks towards Minnie's empty basket and up at the ceiling. 'Only the dog jumping off the bed.' She reaches over, touches my arm. 'God, you're so tense.' She takes hold of my hand, squeezes. 'We'll be OK. We just need to stick together in this. We could go to the police together, if you like.'

'Maybe.' I drain my tea, pull my hand away and rise. I don't want to be here any longer than I need to be. 'I'd better go,' I say, making my way to the door. 'Let me know if anything else happens.'

She follows me to the front door as Minnie trots down the stairs and appears by her side. She bends to fuss her. 'It's so good that we have each other, Riona,' she says, moving in close. 'I don't think I could get through this without you.'

CHAPTER FORTY

Riona

Alene is standing on my doorstep when I arrive home, her beige coat tied a little too tightly at the waist, her collar up against the cold weather. I pull up beside her and drag on the handbrake.

'Hey,' I say, climbing from the car. 'To what do I owe this pleasure? Would you like to come up?' I head past her, shove my key in the door.

'Yes, for a moment, if that's OK.'

'Of course, it's always good to see you.'

'I wanted to talk to you.'

'About?'

She doesn't reply, and I push open the door. She follows me in, takes off her mac and hangs it on a hook near the door, slips off her shoes.

'It's about the man I've been messaging,' she says as we make our way up the stairs and into the lounge. 'There's something I need to tell you.'

'Oh, OK,' I say, shocked she's confiding in me.

'The thing is, he's invited me to his house for a meal.'

I sit down in the armchair, hug a cushion, and she perches on the edge of the sofa, cracks her knuckles.

'Well, that shows things are progressing. That's a good thing, right?'

She shrugs. 'I don't know what to think. It's a big step. I mean, we haven't seen each other for so long, and—'

'He's someone you know?' I'm aware she still hasn't told me his name, and wonder now if that's been deliberate.

'Knew,' she says, as Wanda winds her body around her legs. Alene fusses her head, has always been an animal lover — we both are. 'I just need to talk to someone, Riona,' she goes on, her eyes locked on mine. 'And despite our differences over the years, you really are the closest I've got to a friend.'

'I am?' I curse the doubt in my voice.

'Don't look so surprised – we were close once, remember? When Mum and Dad died we were inseparable.'

It's true. 'I regret that we grew apart,' I say.

'I blame Stacey for that. She moved in on you.' She fiddles with her pearl pendant. 'Drove a wedge between us.'

'I—'

'But we can get past that, I know we can. Lately, I've felt closer to you than I have in a long time.'

I'm not sure that's true. It was only the other day she threw me out of her house. 'I want us to be friends,' I say. 'I really do.'

'Good. Me too.'

'So, this man?'

'I don't know how I feel about him, exactly,' she begins. 'I'm struggling to make sense of my feelings. I couldn't believe it when he dropped a note through my door asking me to message him and enclosing his phone number.'

'It's not Vince again, is it?'

'God no.' She shakes her head, looks down at her hands.

'But you said you knew him.'

'I do, yes.'

'Who is he, Alene?' I lean towards her, place my hand on hers, surprised when she doesn't pull away. 'Do I know him?'

She shakes her head, takes a deep breath. 'It's Ryan Carter.'

'Ryan Carter?' I rub a hand across my mouth. Get to my feet.

'I worked with him at the construction company back in 2009. We became close.'

'And he's in Ensley? Is he staying with Charlotte? Is Mia here too?' I'm aware I'm bombarding her.

'All I know is Ryan has a house in Little Ashley, works as a freelance graphic designer.'

'Does he?' the uncertainty in my voice is obvious.

'And he hasn't mentioned his sister. They never got on.'

'So you were seeing him twelve years ago?'

'Yes, for a while, and then he left for Cornwall. I really liked him, thought he liked me.'

I feel my eyes widen, the influx of new knowledge whirring round my head. I've never met Ryan, had no idea my sister was seeing him all those years ago. 'I didn't know.'

'No, well you didn't know much about me back then. You were so wrapped up in your own friends. Your own life. Yourself.'

I feel as though the last few moments have been stripped away, and I've been slapped sharply across my face.

She takes a deep breath. 'I used to tell him how much I missed being part of your world — he was so understanding.' She pauses for a moment. 'To be honest, it wasn't just you who we didn't tell. We never told anyone, we kept our relationship quiet. His sister had acted a bit psycho around his previous girlfriend, so he didn't want her to know about me . . . and then he took off, never even said goodbye.'

I sit back down, push my head into my hands, catching my fingers in my curls. And then it hits me. I stare up at her, noticing her eyes shimmering with tears. 'Oh God, he's—'

'Kieran's father?' She nods, a tear rolling down her cheek. 'Yes. That's why I can't let Kieran know who I've been talking to. I need to be sure.' She dashes the tear away with the heel of her hand.

'But why tell me now, after all this time?'

'It's like I said, I'm struggling to work out how I feel.' She takes a breath before adding, 'It's all a bit fast, when I haven't actually spoken to him yet.'

'You haven't?'

She shakes her head. 'We planned to talk a few times, but each time we tried the connection went down. All contact has been via text or WhatsApp.'

My mind drifts to Kieran's words, *Mum needs to be sure she's not being catfished*. 'But you know for sure it's him?' I say. 'I mean, you're certain it's Ryan?'

'Of course it's him, Riona. Why wouldn't it be?' Her tone is sharp. 'He knows things only he would know about where we met, things we did together. It's definitely Ryan.'

Perhaps I'm projecting my anxiety and paranoia, but I don't trust the situation. It seems bizarre that she hasn't once spoken to him.

'Listen, Charlotte Carter is in Ensley at the moment, let me talk to her, ask her about Ryan.'

'Christ, Riona.' She gets to her feet. 'Why can't you just be happy for me?'

'I am happy for you. If it is him, and—'

'What part of *it's definitely Ryan* don't you understand?' She's angry now. 'Nobody else knew about our relationship twelve years ago, so it must be. And it's not like I'm jumping back into a relationship with him without being sure. That's why I didn't want Kieran to know too much. Why I'm talking to you now.' She shakes her head. 'God, I wish I hadn't come.'

'No. Wait.' I reach across, take her hand in mine, and eventually she sits back down. 'I can tell this means a lot to you, and I'm sorry for the cross-examination. I haven't been feeling too great lately, and I'm taking my own worries — my paranoia — out on you.'

She's silent for a few moments before saying, 'It's OK, I understand.'

'I'm just being an overprotective big sister. I'm glad you told me about him. And I really hope this works out for you, and for Kieran. You both deserve happiness.'

She rises once more, my hand still in hers. 'Thanks,' she says with a grateful smile. 'And once I'm sure about my feelings, I want you to meet him.'

I nod. 'I'd like that.'

I follow her as she moves through the door and down the stairs, and as we reach the front door she leans in and gently kisses my cheek, and I can't help but hope that Alene and I might be on the right road to mending our fragile relationship.

But once I've closed the door, the bizarreness of Ryan contacting my sister after all this time, the uncertainty of why he won't talk to her directly, hits me once more. I need to keep an eye on my sister, and make sure, if Ryan has come back into her life, that he has the best of intentions.

CHAPTER FORTY-ONE

Riona

Sunday, 12 December 2021

'Riona! Thank God.' It's Stacey on the other end of the phone, her voice high with panic, her dog barking frantically in the background. 'Shit! Someone's trying to get in. Someone's trying to get into my house, Riona.'

'On my way,' I say, grabbing my car keys and dashing down the stairs. 'I'll call the police.'

'Hurry, Riona, please.'

By the time I get to Bridge Court, a police car is parked outside Stacey's house. I pull up against the kerb and get out of my car.

The front door stands ajar, and I push it open, step inside, the warmth of the house hitting me. 'Hello?'

Minnie races along the hallway to greet me, wagging her tail. 'Hello, sweetie,' I say, bending to ruffle the dog's head. 'Where's your mum?'

'I'm in here, Riona,' Stacey calls from the kitchen.

She's sitting at the breakfast bar, two uniformed police officers standing close by.

'Oh God, what happened?' My eyes flick from the broken glass panel in the back door to a wound on Stacey's forehead.

'I'm fine,' she says, touching the cut, blood smearing her fingers.

'Whoever it was has long gone,' says one of the officers, a woman in her twenties with cropped black hair. 'We've searched the area.'

'You should go to A & E, Stacey,' I say.

'That's what we've been saying,' says the male officer, older, forty-something.

Stacey shakes her head and moans. 'I'm fine. Honestly. I don't want to sit over at the hospital for hours, I'd only worry about Minnie.'

'I can look after Minnie,' I say, wondering if Wanda would be OK with the little dog, as I'm not sure I would want to stay here at Stacey's house.

'No really, Riona. I'll be fine.' She turns to the police officers. 'You can go, honestly.'

'We will need you to make a statement, when you're ready.'

Once the police officers have gone, I nod towards the back door. 'You'll need to get that fixed. I know a builder I can call.'

'Thanks,' she says, close to tears, but forcing a grateful smile. 'I'm glad I've got you, Riona, that we're friends again.'

I'm still not sure I consider her a friend, but I've mellowed towards her. She was only eighteen when she made a pass at George. Perhaps we all do stupid things when we're young that we come to regret. Perhaps our teenage self is a very different person to who we are later in life. I definitely regret who I was at eighteen, a person who wasn't there for my sister when she needed me — someone who only thought about myself. I appreciate the chance Alene has given me to change that, and maybe I need to cut Stacey the same kind of slack. She's been attacked. She needs me right now, and she doesn't seem to be the same person I once knew.

'Did you tell the police about the other things that have been happening?' I ask.

She shakes her head. 'I didn't think, maybe it's the shock. I'll tell them everything when I give them a statement.'

'I think we need to go down to the station together. Tell them everything that's happened. Make them see how it's all connected. We need to be proactive, not just roll over and accept all of this.'

'You're right. Tomorrow.' She closes her eyes. 'My head is killing me.'

'Have you taken painkillers?'

She nods, holds her head, the gesture clearly causing pain. 'We will get through this, Riona — find out who's doing these awful things.'

'I hope so. Listen, can I make you a sweet tea or something?' I point to the kettle. 'Or have you got anything stronger?'

'There's some brandy in the cupboard,' she says. 'Medicinal, obviously.'

I find it and pour her a glass. 'So, did you see who it was?'

She shakes her head, takes a sip of her drink. 'Someone was hammering on my back door, rattling on the handle. There was a blur of yellow. That's when I called you. Moments later the window was smashed.' She closes her teary eyes, gulps the brandy before continuing. 'It was the glass shattering that did this.' She touches her forehead gently, winces. 'It was like déjà vu.' She moves her hand to the scar on her cheek. 'I obviously need to beware of low-flying china and glass.' She tries for a smile.

'You should get the cut checked out.'

'No, it's fine.' Her voice is firm. 'I've cleaned it, no real damage done. Whoever it was took off when Minnie barked. My baby girl clearly sounds more frightening than she is.'

I smile down at the little dog, now fast asleep in her bed.

'I guess there's a possibility it's not even connected to . . . well, everything else. It could have just been some thief chancing their luck.'

'I doubt that.'

As she sips her brandy, I call the builder I know, explain it's urgent, and he promises to come round within the hour.

'Thanks, Riona,' Stacey says when I go to leave half an hour later, pulling me into a tight hug. 'I don't know what I would do without you.'

* * *

Later, I send Erika a message to say I'm on my way. I get an instant reply:

I'm feeling so much better! I'm out at the moment.
Won't be back 'till later, sorry. I'll be back at work
on Tuesday, so we can catch up then.
Erika X

I can't help but feel a bit hurt that she's out and hasn't been round to see me. I bash down my sadness. It's great news that she's well again, and I should be happy with that.

Apart from a text from Erika, the rest of the day is thankfully uneventful. But my mind won't settle, whirring through events like a film on fast forward.

In fact, when I hit the pillow around midnight, I can't sleep, and I'm still wide awake, tossing and turning, at one o'clock. I throw back my quilt, rise and head over to the window, hearing the *boom, boom* of a car sound system.

I pull back the curtain. A car is parked in the layby, shrouded by trees. I peer closer to the glass. It's impossible to see the make or colour of the vehicle, but I'm sure someone is sitting in the driving seat. Despite trying to convince myself it has nothing to do with me, I feel uneasy. I shudder and drag the curtain back across the window.

CHAPTER FORTY-TWO

Me

She's in the boot of my car, thud, thud, thudding *the metal chamber with tired fists. I will keep her there until all my plans are locked in place. Until I take her to Little Ashley.*

I yawn, but I'm alert, my mind brighter than it's felt in a long time, despite the late hour — that's how I can run rings around you. That's how I will punish you, Riona.

I like watching your window. Was thrilled to see my music roused your curiosity, and you poked your head out from behind the curtains. I hope you saw me here in the shadows. I hope I scared you. Left you wondering.

Fear is such a wonderful weapon, don't you think? Better than any knife or gun. It gives such power. Fear. *The word itself ignites spasms of joy inside me. I can't wait for everything to reach fruition. Watching you shiver and shake and shudder, scared of your own footsteps, gives me such pleasure. I literally cannot wait to ramp things up.*

I start the engine. I'm afraid I can't stay here chatting with you all night. I have so much to do.

Thud, thud, thud.

'Shut up,' I yell. 'I can't hear myself think.'

I pull away. I will see you very soon, Riona. You can count on it.

CHAPTER FORTY-THREE

Riona

Monday, 13 December 2021

Dusk settles as I take a slow jog along the road, the light exercise going some way to clearing my head. I haven't heard from Stacey all day. She didn't pick up when I called her first thing, and hasn't yet answered my text about going to the police, so I doubt we'll go today. If I don't hear from her, I'll go alone tomorrow. So much has happened now — the police will have to do something.

I reach the entrance to Quarry Lake, bending and resting my palms against my thighs for some moments. I'm frustrated that I'm too afraid to head through the iron gates. That whoever's tormenting me is disrupting my life. But I know, for now at least, my exercise routine needs to take place on the streets of Ensley, and not via Quarry Lake.

My mobile rings out, startling me.

I answer the call. Press the phone to my ear.

'Mum's gone to stay with him,' Kieran says before I can speak. 'She didn't tell me. She said she would tell me.'

'Calm down, sweetie.'

'But she's not here, Ri.' His voice is high, anxious. 'I'm staying over at Josh's house, but his mum's brought me home to get my game controller, and Mum isn't here. I texted her, and she says she's having an overnight break, but I know she's with him.'

'Kieran, your mum seems to like this man, but she doesn't want you involved until she's sure about things, especially after Vince. You know that, right? We've been through this a thousand times.' I realise my tone is edgy. Too much is cluttering up my head, to the point that I'm now getting agitated with my lovely nephew.

'She hadn't expected me home. That's why she didn't tell me. Why wouldn't she tell me?' He's so young to have such a bite of anger in his voice. I try to bring my focus back to him, but there's someone approaching through the canopy of trees that lead to Quarry Lake.

'You need to give your mum this, Kieran,' I say, trying to word things carefully, wishing I didn't know that she could be meeting with Ryan Carter — *Kieran's father*. 'Give her time to sort things out.'

There's silence for a moment, and then, voice calmer, he says, 'Yes, I get that. You're right. Sorry, Aunt Ri, I don't know what got into me.'

The figure approaching is wearing yellow. They're getting closer and my heart kicks into overdrive.

'Ri?' Kieran says.

I realise with relief it's a woman in a yellow mac walking a Labrador. I'm stupidly on edge. I need to get a grip.

'You still there, Ri?'

'Yes. Yes, of course.' The woman passes, throwing me a smile, and my heartbeat returns to normal. 'Listen, try not to worry.'

'Yeah, sorry . . . I'm fine. Josh's mum's waiting for me, so I'd better go.'

We say our goodbyes and I hang up, watching the woman and her dog disappear around the corner.

I blame Alene for the way Kieran is. She really has made him into a mini adult — relying on a child, who should be relying on her. But I bat down my negative thoughts; they won't help me mend my relationship with my sister.

I continue onwards, my mind in overdrive. What if Alene has been catfished? What if she's been lured away somewhere by a stranger? I desperately need to know more about Ryan, and there's only one person to ask. I turn back, knowing I need to talk to Charlotte Carter as soon as possible.

CHAPTER FORTY-FOUR

Charlotte

Monday, 13 December 2021

I've packed my case and plan to leave in the morning. It will be good to get back to Cornwall. I don't feel safe here.

I don't think I'll ever get to the bottom of why Mother sent me that email. There's no development, no dredging of Quarry Lake. My daughter will remain beneath the water. Nobody will ever find her remains. Not in my lifetime, anyway.

I had a call earlier from the funeral directors, wanting me to set a date for Mother's cremation. I've paid them with Mother's cash. Ordered a nice casket. But I won't be there to send her off. I'll be long gone.

I called Ryan earlier, told him I'll be doing the five-hour drive home tomorrow. Promised him we'll be coming into some money soon. He seemed vague, jittery. I wonder if he's been forgetting to take his medication. 'We're wrapped up in this together for eternity,' I told him.

It's dark outside, gone six o'clock, when the doorbell rings, shrill through the house. It's been a long day, and I'm in no mood for visitors.

I put the chain on the front door and open up to see a young woman huddled in a winter coat, wearing low-heeled, fur-topped boots. I've seen her before.

'My name is Riona Foley,' she says. 'I wondered—'

'It's not a good time.'

'You don't know what I was going to say. It's important. I just want to talk to you for a moment, that's all. It's about Ryan.'

'Ryan? What about Ryan?' I take off the chain and open the door. Whatever this woman wants to say about Ryan, I don't want it said on the doorstep. 'You'd better come in.'

I follow the woman's gaze as she casts her eyes over my battered suitcase in the corner. I lead the way into the dining room. 'What's this about?' I ask.

She turns. 'Do you know where Ryan is?'

I press my hand against my chest. 'My Ryan?'

'Is he living in Little Ashley?'

'What? No. He lives in Cornwall. He's there now.'

She widens her eyes. 'Are you sure? Absolutely sure?'

I gulp down a surge of panic. I want this woman with crazy, spiralling hair to leave. I should never have let her in. 'Of course I'm sure.'

'So he hasn't got a place in Little Ashley? He doesn't work as a graphic designer?'

'No.' I shake my head, frustrated now. 'For God's sake, I have no idea what you're talking about. We left Ensley to live in Cornwall twelve years ago. He's there now.' I move towards her, grab her arm. 'Now, get out of my house.'

'No, wait.' She pulls away from me. 'The thing is, he's been in contact with my sister, Alene.'

'Ryan?'

'It seems he . . . well he used to see her, when you were here in Ensley before—'

'Impossible.' Anger flares. Riona is ruining everything. 'I want you to leave. I want you to leave right now.' I bury my nails into the woman's coat and pull her across the room with force and out into the hallway.

'Christ, you're hurting me, Charlotte,' she cries, pulling herself free. 'I only asked you a simple question.'

'My life, my son's life, is private.' I fling open the door and push the woman through it, where she falls to the ground with a thud. 'And none of it — none of it, you hear me — is any of your bloody business.'

'It is when Ryan's my nephew's father,' Riona screams at me, her face full of anguish.

I stare for less than a moment before slamming the door.

Inside, I turn and lean against the wall before slowly slipping down to the floor, where I cradle my head in my hands and sob.

This mess — this awful mess — is all my fault.

CHAPTER FORTY-FIVE

Riona

Tears roll down my cheeks, and my head spins as I walk along the road towards my apartment, my hands stinging, bleeding from where I fell. I can't believe Charlotte threw me out of her front door.

Is it true that Ryan's living in Cornwall? Does that mean it wasn't him who contacted Alene? And if not, who did? Or was Charlotte lying? But the worst thing of all is I blurted out that Kieran is Ryan's son. Alene will be furious with me. I can't believe I was so stupid.

I reach my apartment, and I'm still fumbling in my bag for my front door key when I receive a text from Alene:

Hi Riona. I'm in Little Ashley, and I've met up with Ryan. We're planning dinner, and he's suggested I stay over, but I really don't know — is it too soon? And there's something not right. He seems different to how I remember. I can't explain it exactly. He's locked my car in the barn, and we're miles from anywhere, and I really don't want to overreact, but, well, you couldn't come, could you? Maybe stay for dinner? I just feel a bit vulnerable, and if you were here with me all would be OK. Love, Alene x

I stare down at my phone, reading my sister's words over and over. Alene has never asked anything of me since I let her down when she was pregnant. I owe her. I owe her big time:

Of course, send me the address — I'll be there. x

She replies instantly:

Yew Tree House, Little Ashley, Near Tring.

I get into my car and start the engine, and I'm about to key the address into my satnav when my phone rings. It's Tom.

'Hey,' I say, glad he's called, though my mind is on Alene. I'm not sure I've got time, even for him.

'Sorry I haven't been in touch,' he says. 'That I left yesterday morning without saying goodbye.'

'It's OK, no worries.' I put my car in gear, place the phone on hands free and drive away.

'How are you?'

'I'm good. Stacey and I are going to go to the police about everything that's happened, hopefully tomorrow.'

'Good. You need to get them involved. I don't suppose you're free tonight?'

'No, sorry.' I indicate to turn out of the road. 'I've had a message from my sister.'

'Oh. OK.'

'It's complicated. I can't really talk about it.'

'Is everything OK? You sound a bit—'

'I'm fine. I'm sure it's something and nothing, but I need to go to Little Ashley, check in on her.'

'Little Ashley? Near Tring?'

'That's it. She's at an old boyfriend's house, but things don't seem to be going that well. She's asked me to go rescue her.' I laugh, though there's no humour in it, and I have a horrible sense of foreboding I can't quite shake. 'I'll probably get there and all will be well, and I'll be a giant gooseberry, but—'

'Little Ashley,' he says again, his tone almost a whisper.

'Yes, do you know it?'

There's a silence for a few moments before he says, 'I do, yes. It's in the middle of nowhere, only one house that I know of.'

'Yew Tree House?'

'That's it . . . Riona, can you hang on? Wait for me, and I'll come with you.'

'I should really head off—'

'It's just, after everything you've told me—'

'This is something different, Tom.' But I'm not sure it is, and suddenly my mind is joining all the painful dots. 'I'm sure I'll be fine,' I say. 'Listen, I really have to go. I owe my sister this, and if I get there, and anything looks dodgy, I'll call the police immediately.' I pull up at a red light. 'I really need to go, Tom. Can we talk tomorrow?'

'Be careful, Riona,' he says, then the line goes dead.

* * *

Bernie

I make my way down the stairs. I've been talking on an online forum, in the room I converted into an office when I retired. I signed up for a creative writing course a few weeks back, and it was my fourth session. We discussed juxtaposition and alliteration. Next week we move on to structuring a novel. 'Move over Stephen King, my tutor thinks I've got very, very hidden talent.' I laugh to myself, as I pad down the hall and into the kitchen, glancing at my homemade lemonade, before turning to fill the kettle.

Once I've made a mug of coffee, I pick up my phone from where I left it charging. There's a voicemail:

'Hi, Aunt Bernie, it's Riona. The thing is, I'm not supposed to mention this, and I know Alene will kill me, but I needed to let you know where I'm heading, just so you're aware. Nothing to worry about at all, but . . . well, anyway, I don't know if you even know this, but apparently Alene was seeing Ryan Carter back in 2009, and he's recently got back in touch, invited her to his house near Tring. Except . . . well . . . well, anyway, she's asked me to meet her there. I'm sure it's all good, but, well . . . if you never see me again, you'll know why . . . sorry, that's not even funny. Anyway, sorry for babbling on and on, but I've texted you the address where I'm heading, just so you know where we are. Bye for now. Love you.'

The address on the text message seems familiar, and I'm aware Riona isn't telling me everything. I rub my hand across the back of my neck. How hadn't I known about Alene seeing Ryan back then? But then she's always been a secretive girl.

On impulse, I bring up the Instagram account that Riona showed me. There are two new photos. But they're not of Riona or Stacey. I stare down at them. There's one of Erika walking alone in the dark, next to the graveyard in the village, and another of her asleep on her sofa with her cats. I get an uneasy feeling in my stomach. There's no doubting that whoever took the last picture has been in Erika's house.

CHAPTER FORTY-SIX

Riona

I've been driving for almost an hour, the darkness wrapping around the car like a blanket.

I look in my rear-view mirror for what must be the fifth time, sensing someone following. Whoever is driving the car is keeping their distance, but with every turn I make, they do the same.

I inject a burst of speed until the car is no longer visible in my rear-view, and pull sharply onto a driveway with a screech of brakes. I kill my lights and slip down in my seat. The house is set back from the road, in darkness; the owners don't appear to be home, thank God.

The car I suspect was tailing me races by, and I wait for some time, my breathing ragged, before starting the engine once more. Still trembling, I pull back out onto the road. There's no sign of the other vehicle now, and the sky seems blacker than ever, not a star to be seen.

Narrow roads take me deeper into the countryside, the snake-like bends and shadowy verges adding to my unease. I've never been the most confident of drivers, and the feeling of being followed hasn't helped my anxiety.

I haven't seen anyone for a few miles, when the satnav tells me I've reached my destination, and I spot Yew Tree House. It's a grotesque building, almost like a prison. The walls are grey, the roof flat — a giant toad of a thing.

I pull onto the cobbled front drive, my eyes moving across two towering barns that fringe the property. I return my gaze to the house, taking in an orange glow radiating from a downstairs window.

I pull up the handbrake and continue to look about me. There's no sign of my sister's Fiat, but then her message mentioned Ryan putting it in one of the barns. I kill the engine and roll my tight shoulders, trying to ease my tension. There's no sign of life at all. Reluctant to climb out, I take my phone from my bag, deciding to call Alene — check she's here. It rings a few times before kicking into voicemail. I don't leave a message.

Bashing down paranoia, I grab my bag from the passenger seat, take a deep breath and get out of the car. Alene has asked me to come here. She must be inside. As I head towards the grey front door, the porch light springs on, the beam bouncing off the opaque glass panels. The wind has picked up since I set off from Ensley, and the house backs onto a wood where tall trees sway, branches creaking, leaves fidgeting. I shiver. It's cold, but it's more than that, this place gives me the creeps.

'Alene?' I call, thinking I see movement in the trees. I freeze. My imagination is on overdrive. I need to calm down. I take another deep breath — then another. Feet crunching the pebbles, I dash towards the front door.

I go to knock, but the door eases open.

'Hello! Alene?' I call, poking my head inside. 'Ryan? Hello!' The hallway is spacious, uncluttered apart from a black hatstand near the front door. I recognise Alene's beige coat hanging from it. She must be here. *Thank God.*

Three doors stand open, one leading to a large modern kitchen, another a lounge, the third a dining room. The hallway is gloomy, the only light the one radiating from the lounge. I spot a light switch and flick it on.

'Alene?' I step into the lounge, where two black leather sofas and a chair hug an open fireplace — embers glow in the grate, almost burnt out. Pale grey curtains hang at the window. A black bookcase is crammed with books, and a large silver-framed photograph of a dark-haired woman with an older man, a chunky gold bracelet hanging from his wrist, stands on the top, next to a clock that *tick, tick, ticks* into the silence.

I move into the kitchen, spotting a note propped against a microwave:

Riona.
So sorry, realised we may not have enough wine. Won't be long. Make yourself at home — there's white wine in fridge, red wine in the rack. Alene and Ryan x

I don't recognise the handwriting. It definitely isn't Alene's neat, small lettering.

I glance at three bottles of red wine on a rack. And in the fridge is an unopened bottle of white. It all feels very odd. I try to think back to Alene's text — what she said in her message. I get it back up on the phone:

Hi Riona. I'm in Little Ashley, and I've met up with Ryan. We're planning dinner, and he's suggested I stay over, but I really don't know — is it too soon? And there's something not right. He seems different to how I remember. I can't explain it exactly. He's locked my car in the barn, and we're miles from anywhere, and I really don't want to overreact, but, well, you couldn't come, could you? Maybe stay for dinner? I just feel a bit vulnerable, and if you were here with me all would be OK. Love, Alene x

I turn, and lean against the worktop. There's no sign of a meal being cooked or prepared. In fact, the fridge is empty apart from the wine. Perhaps they're planning a takeaway? But then we're miles from anywhere. I shiver. This place is cold, soulless, as though its heart has been ripped out and discarded.

I return to the hallway, where I run my hand over Alene's coat. Wouldn't she have taken it? It's cold outside. I fumble in the pockets, not sure what I'm hoping to find. Empty. No phone. No car keys. Nothing.

I look up a wide staircase towards a landing and back at the front door. Curiosity triggered, I climb the stairs.

The first room is a bathroom. The door stands open, revealing black-and-white décor. Fluffy white towels are folded neatly on a rack, and a row of men's toiletries and packet of tablets are on a shelf near the sink. There are several more rooms, the doors all firmly closed. I glance over the slatted balustrade to check Alene and Ryan haven't returned without my knowledge, before opening one of the doors.

The room is decorated in shades of grey. The double bed is covered with a charcoal-grey duvet, plump pillows propped neatly against a wooden headboard. There's a tall bookshelf rammed with books, just like the one downstairs, and a pale grey wardrobe, the door standing open, men's clothing hanging inside. On a matching chest of drawers is a bottle of aftershave. I move across the room, lift up the bottle and sniff it. It's strong and spicy. After one more look around, I leave the room. I'm about to move on, when I hear a car pull up outside. I glance out of the landing window to see Tom's yellow Mini on the drive next to my car. *Thank God.* I head down the stairs at speed and fling open the front door, so relieved to see him.

Batting down an urge to run into his arms as he climbs from his car, I call from the doorstep, 'Tom, what are you doing here?'

He shrugs. 'What can I say? I had a bad feeling is all.' He slams the car door. 'I was worried about you.'

'Well, I'm fine, honestly.' I'm not sure I am. This all feels weird, and I'm beginning to worry where my sister is. 'Alene and Ryan have gone out for some more wine,' I go on as he approaches. 'Though I'm sure there's enough here.'

He reaches me, kisses my cheek, and I lead the way inside, closing the door behind us.

As he slips off his coat, revealing a checked shirt and black jeans, and hangs it on the hatstand next to Alene's, I glance down, noticing a dark, reddish-brown mark on the carpet at the foot of the stairs in the otherwise immaculate house. I want to mention it to Tom. Tell him the whole house is giving me the creeps, but keep quiet.

'There's wine, but not much else,' I say, as he follows me into the lounge. 'I thought there might be signs of the meal they were meant to be having, but there's nothing in the fridge.' I'm talking far too fast.

He seems on edge too, his eyes flicking around him as we sit down, him on the sofa, me in the armchair.

'Are you OK?' I say, noticing his knee bouncing.

'Yeah, I'm good.'

'I'm sure my sister won't be long.'

'So, has she been seeing this bloke long?'

'Ryan? No. This is the first time she's met up with him since . . .'

'Since?'

'She knew him when she was young, and they're back in touch. I had no idea he'd ever been in her life.' I fiddle with my ring. Should I tell him my fears? Should I tell him that Charlotte said Ryan was in Cornwall? That, if she's telling the truth, her son doesn't live in Little Ashley at all — and whoever contacted my sister may not be Ryan?

Tom looks towards the fire dying in the grate, and I realise, once more, how cold it is — that I haven't even taken my jacket off. I shiver, even my nose is cold, and wrap my arms around myself, as much for comfort than anything else.

'I noticed some logs out there near the barn,' he says. 'Shall I bring a few in?'

I know we need to keep the place warm. 'Yes, OK, if you don't mind.'

He rises and playfully flexes his muscles. 'I may have to chop a few, but it won't take long.'

I go to get up too. 'Can I help?'

'No!' He places his hand on my shoulder, pushes me gently down. 'I won't be long. Try to relax, I'm sure everything will be OK.'

But as he leaves the room, glancing back at me with a smile that doesn't reach his eyes, I know relaxing is the last thing I'm going to be able to do.

* * *

Bernie

I stand on Erika's doorstep, looking up and down the silent road, the Instagram pictures I saw earlier fresh in my mind. Riona told me Erika's been ill, that she hasn't spoken to her directly for a while, and my cop instincts tell me something is wrong.

I'm about to ring the doorbell for the third time when a female voice interrupts me. 'I haven't seen Erika for a while.'

I turn to see a woman of around seventy, dressed in a beige duffle coat and ankle boots, a West Highland Terrier by her side, wagging its tail. 'She's unwell, but her friend's been going in and out,' the woman continues.

'Her friend?'

'I knocked a couple of times but got no reply, wondered about letting myself in. Wasn't sure whether to take Erika some magazines or a bunch of grapes or something. Though, to be honest, I didn't want to catch anything nasty. You can't be too careful these days.'

I give up on ringing the bell and move towards the woman, my neck tingling. 'This friend, what was she like?'

The woman runs a hand over her chin, looks towards the night sky.

'Well, I say friend, but I couldn't honestly tell you who it was, or even if it was a woman, I only ever saw them from a distance. But they wore one of those yellow hi-vis jackets like the police wear, and a woolly hat.'

'A yellow hi-vis?' I can't help a jolt of fear, as a memory of the Ensley Killer pushes into my thoughts.

'Yes. Though if I'm honest, Humphrey here—' she nods towards the dog now tugging on his leash — 'is always in such a hurry to get to the park, I didn't have time to ask. But whoever it was, they had a key.'

'You said you were going to let yourself in?'

'Aha, yes. I have a key too, you see. I always feed Mr Spoon and Eggbert, if Erika's away.'

'Could you let me in now?' Bernie looks at the house. 'I'm worried Erika might be too ill to answer the door.'

The woman furrows her forehead. 'Well, I'm not sure.' She bites down on her lower lip, seeming to weigh me up. 'I don't know who you are—'

'Erika is my niece's closest friend. She may have mentioned her. Her name's Riona?'

The woman shakes her head and bites down on her bottom lip, then her eyes light up, as though she's had a lightbulb moment. 'Oh, yes, Riona, her partner at the clinic.'

'That's right.'

The woman looks at the house in darkness and back at me. 'Well, I guess if I'm with you it won't hurt to check Erika's OK.'

We head up the path, the ground icy, and the woman takes a set of keys from her bag and unlocks the door. The dog gives a little growl. 'Actually, I'll wait outside. Humphrey and the kitties don't get on too well.'

'OK.' I push the door open and step inside, hit by how warm it is. I move my hand across the wall, find the light switch and flick it on. 'Erika? Erika, love, it's only Bernie.'

Like bullets from a gun, the cats race from the kitchen to greet me, mewing, making me jump.

'Christ!' I grab my chest, clearly out of practice. When I was on the force I would never have got so rattled by a couple of cats. 'Well, I heard you two weren't very friendly,'

I whisper, as they wrap their bald bodies around my legs. 'So you're either two different cats, or you're hungry.'

There's a strong, unpleasant odour of used litter tray in the air as I follow the cats into the kitchen, where they continue to mew. I pour dried food into their dishes, water into their bowls. 'Where's your mum gone?' I say, as they tuck into their dinner.

My gaze slides to the cork memo board full of photos of Erika and Riona. 'Where are you, Erika?' I whisper.

The kitchen is small and narrow. A couple of mugs are turned upside down on the drainer, a cat crate is wedged by the back door, but there's no real sign that Erika has been here lately.

I head back into the hallway and glance into the lounge, which is empty, before making my way upstairs, which is equally deserted, Erika's bed neatly made.

'Any luck?' the neighbour calls from the doorstep, as I head back down the stairs.

'Erika doesn't seem to be here,' I say, shaking my head. 'I felt sure she would be.'

'That's most peculiar.'

'Mmm, you're right, it is. In fact, she doesn't seem to have been here for a while, if the litter tray is anything to go by, and the cats seemed pretty hungry.' I lower the handle of the cellar door, go to push it open.

'We should probably go,' the neighbour calls, looking up and down the street. 'I would hate for Erika to come back and find us snooping.'

I return to the woman. 'Well, thanks so much for letting me look.'

As I step outside, I wait for her to turn her back before flicking on the latch and pulling the door closed behind me. I need to return once the neighbour has gone. Something feels wrong inside this little terraced house, and I need to trust my instincts. I need to find out what it is.

CHAPTER FORTY-SEVEN

Bernie

As Erika's neighbour disappears into the darkness with her dog, heading towards Ransoms Recreational Park, I take a deep breath and get out of my car once more. The road is still, silent, as I hurry back up the path towards the Victorian terrace.

I've always liked Erika — the Swedish girl who came into Riona's life when she was seventeen. She's witty, from a good background, intelligent — a positive influence on my niece, unlike Stacey Roberts.

I push open the front door and step inside. The cats don't race to greet me this time, their stomachs full. And a quick glance into the lounge tells me they are curled up on the sofa, asleep — content.

I head straight for the cellar and lower the door handle, a horrible sense of foreboding washing over me. I open the door and step onto the concrete landing. The air is musty, and there's that odd smell again. I take one step and freeze, searching the wall for a light switch, cobwebs catching on my fingers as I flick a switch. An orange bulb buzzes and flickers, illuminating the dusty basement below.

I take the steps slowly, my mind working overtime. Should I call Erika's name? But somehow I already know it is futile. I've had too much experience not to recognise the stench that gets stronger the deeper I go.

I hear a noise above me, and twist round to see one of the cats staring down at me from the doorway, copper-coloured eyes flashing. 'Christ! You scared the hell out of me,' I say, clutching my chest.

I reach the foot of the stairs.

The basement is small.

Square.

I see her immediately. Lying on the floor.

Erika.

I fall to my knees, tears burning my eyes, and take hold of the young woman's wrist with shaking fingers. But as I search for a pulse, I know I won't find one. Rigor has already set in. This young woman is dead, and she's been dead for a while.

* * *

I climb the cellar steps to the sound of sirens approaching. Since finding Erika fifteen minutes ago, I've stayed with her, holding her hand as though the young woman knew I was there.

The copious amounts of blood tell me she's been murdered. Bludgeoned to death. I feel sick, helpless. Who could have done this to a woman who only helped others? A woman who spent hours counselling grief-stricken people.

I recognise Chief Inspector Blake. He's here because I mentioned when I called that Erika's neighbour saw a so-called friend wearing a yellow hi-vis. He knows, like I do, that there could be a connection to the Ensley Killer of 2009.

Detective Sergeant Brown — an enthusiastic young officer with neat dark hair and wearing a three-piece suit straight out of a Next catalogue — dashes through the front door. 'Inspector,' he says to me, seeming to have travelled back in time. I vaguely recall the sergeant. Our paths crossed several years back. Him on his way up, me on my way out.

'Not anymore,' I say, and he flushes. 'Her name was Erika Danielsson,' I tell the officers. 'She was thirty years old.' I'm surprised by the break in my voice, how tears prod my eyes. This never happened when I was an officer. Not because I didn't care. I always cared. But I guess I was stronger back then, squashed down emotions when I was on a job. I had to.

This is different.

This was Riona's best friend. A woman I'd known for over thirteen years.

I show the officers the Instagram photo that had drawn me here. 'Erika was afraid of the basement,' I say. 'How the hell did she end up down there?'

As the team make their way down the cellar steps, I feel lost. Even though I've been retired a while now, it feels strange not to be of some use. I head into the lounge. The cats look up from where they are curled up on the sofa, and I sit down, tickle their ears. The rumour that these cats don't like people doesn't ring true, as the furless creatures rise and move closer to me, seeking comfort. It's as if they know already that Erika has gone.

Later, once the DS has taken down everything that happened leading up to the discovery of Erika's body, I rise. 'I'll take the cats,' I say, 'just until they can find a good home. It's the least I can do.'

I head into the kitchen to collect the crate.

Detective Chief Inspector Blake is looking out of the window at the garden, as though deep in thought. He turns. 'Could he be back after all this time?' he says. He almost looks younger now than he did when we were in the thick of the case, but I know the murder in Ensley still haunts him, as it does me. He loosens his tie, unfastens the top button of his shirt. 'I'm hoping forensics will come up with something. It can't be a coincidence, surely.'

'But the killer had a type, remember? Kerry Ann, Clare and Rebecca all had dark hair. Erika's hair was blonde, streaked with purple.'

He shakes his head. 'I'm not ruling out that this is the same killer, Bernie.'

'But why would they wait all this time to kill again?'

DS Brown enters, scans the photos on the memo board of Riona and Erika looking so happy.

'Do you know who the other woman is?' he asks me.

'My niece Riona.' I move closer, pushing down a surge of emotion.

'Erika was her best friend.'

* * *

I head from the house, the two cats in the carrier, thoughts bouncing around my skull like grenades. Someone knocked Riona down, put odd photos on Instagram, and now Erika is dead. It has to be connected.

I open the back door of my Kia and put the mewing cats on the seat, then try Riona's and Alene's numbers alternately, but they both keep going to voicemail. I bring up the address that Riona sent me. *Where do I know this address from? Think, Bernie, think.*

Whatever's going on, I don't like it one little bit, and I won't be happy until I know my nieces are OK.

'Buckle up, cats,' I say, climbing into the driving seat and putting the address into my satnav. 'This is going to be a long ride.'

* * *

Charlotte

I pull my car onto the grass verge opposite Yew Tree House, taking in a yellow Mini and Riona's car shrouded by shadows, the glow from a downstairs window leaving a pool of orange on the drive. I need to know what's going on. I need to ask her questions.

I tried calling Ryan after I threw Riona out of Willow Nook Cottage, but he didn't pick up, and I'm glad now that I couldn't get hold of him. No point in worrying my already troubled son. Could Riona have been telling the truth about Ryan being a father? If she is, he can't know. He can never know.

I regret tossing Riona onto the pavement. It wasn't a sensible thing to do. Apart from anything else, it will make her wonder why I was so defensive. I should have let her explain, told her, calmly, she's got things wrong.

I keep the engine running, not sure what to do next — how to handle this the best way possible. I had no choice but to follow Riona. I need to ask her why she thinks Ryan lives in this grotesque house. Why she thinks he's been in contact with her sister. Why she thinks he's the father of her nephew. The thought sends shivers of fear down my spine.

I lost sight of Riona's car a while back, but thankfully remembered her mentioning Little Ashley when she turned up on my doorstep, and this is the only house for miles.

I cut the engine, open the door and climb out onto the icy grass verge. From here I study the weird house in front of me. It looks so out of place here in the countryside. Why has Riona come here? Why would she think Ryan lived in Little Ashley? She must be inside, but I can't help wondering if there is there someone else within the walls.

It's as I'm making my way across the road, pulling my coat around me against the freezing weather, that I sense movement in the darkness. I hurry onwards, a sudden sense of unease making my body tingle. Somebody else is here. Somebody else is close.

As I hesitate, unsure whether to head back to my car or carry on to the house, someone emerges from a clump of trees and paces towards me at speed. Whoever it is, they're gripping something solid — *a metal bar? Oh God.*

'No!' is all I can muster, as I turn away from the fig-ure and attempt to run. But whoever this person is they are quicker, more agile. They catch me up, push me to the floor, and I fall on my back.

The white mask is chilling — vague indentations where features should be. The yellow hi-vis takes me back to the Ensley Killer, to the fear I've carried all my life that my son took Kerry Ann White's life.

I raise my hand in defence, opening my mouth to scream as the figure raises the metal bar and cracks it down hard against my skull.

CHAPTER FORTY-EIGHT

Riona

Tom has been outside getting logs for a fair while now, and not only am I cold, I feel restless, uneasy. *Where is my sister? Ryan?*

I head towards the window, and peer through the gap in the curtains. A hazy beam radiates from one of the barns, but I can't see Tom. My eyes move across to the other unlit barn as I recall what Alene said about Ryan putting her car inside.

The rest of the area is shrouded in darkness, but I sense movement. Hairs rise, prickling my neck, as glowing yellow eyes meet mine — a fox, caught in the light from the barn. It scampers into the shadows.

I turn from the window and make my way across the room and into the hallway, noticing, once more, Alene's coat hanging on the hatstand next to Tom's. I wonder once more why hasn't she taken it with her? She'll freeze without it.

I'm about to climb the stairs once more when the front door swings open. 'God, it's cold out there, you wouldn't believe,' Tom says, ambling in with an armful of logs, cheeks glowing pink. 'You OK?' he adds, heading into the lounge with a sniff.

I follow him, and he drops to his knees in front of the fire. He places the logs on the dying embers and adds screwed-up newspaper from the pile on the hearth. The flames ignite, and within moments the fire is alive once more, flickering wildly. He twists round, looks at me over his shoulder, and as though sensing my anxiety says, 'Maybe we should go home, Riona. You have to admit something doesn't feel right here.'

I sit down on the sofa, and push my head into my hands. I want to go home more than anything. 'But what about Alene?' I look up, my eyes meeting his. 'I need to be sure she's OK, Tom. Maybe I should call the police.'

'What would you say?' He suddenly sounds agitated. 'I'm not sure they could do anything if they came here.'

He's right. Nothing has happened to warrant a police call-out. 'I just don't understand why they would both go out for wine. I mean, Alene could have stayed while Ryan went, or vice versa. It doesn't make sense. And she did sound worried in her text.'

'You're right. It does feel weird.' He runs a hand over his mouth. 'I'm guessing you've tried calling her.'

A stupid question – and I can't help thinking he's acting a bit strange. 'Of course, several times, and she isn't picking up.'

He shakes his head and gets to his feet. 'I need the loo,' he says. 'It's this cold weather. When I get back, maybe we should search the house and the grounds.'

'Really?' The thought of searching the place turns my stomach. 'The bathroom is—'

'I know where it is,' he says.

'You do?'

He's silent for a moment before saying, 'I noticed it when I came in, the door was standing open at the top of the stairs.'

He leaves the room, and I lower my head into my hands once more. 'Where are you, Alene?' I whisper.

* * *

216

'Have any more of those odd photos appeared on that Instagram account?' Tom asks, coming back through the door a few minutes later.

I shake my head. 'To be honest, I haven't looked for a while. I decided if I can't see it it's not there.'

'But it is still there?' He narrows his eyes.

I nod. 'I think so.'

He moves across the room and sits down in the armchair. 'So you haven't reported it to Instagram yet?'

I shake my head, fighting back tears. 'Stacey and I were meant to be going to the police today, but I couldn't get hold of her.'

He leans forward, rests his hand on mine. 'This must be hell for you, Riona. I'm so desperately sorry it's come to this.'

I shrug. 'It's hardly your fault.' I pause for a moment before adding, 'I just can't think of anyone who would be so cruel. I thought I'd always led a fairly blameless life.' I say it like a joke, attempting to make light of it.

He leans back in the armchair. 'So, were you and your sister brought up in Ensley?'

I feel sure we've already talked about this, but decide he's trying to relax me. He's clearly forgotten his suggestion to search the house and grounds, and for now I'm not sure I want to remind him. 'We were originally from Ireland, came here when we were eight.'

'You're a twin?' he asks.

I shake my head. 'No, I'm ten months older than Alene.' I pause. 'Were you and your sister close in age?'

He shakes his head. 'I'm five years older. The protective older brother.' He looks down. 'Though I didn't protect her as well as I should have.'

'You can't blame yourself for that.' I realise he hasn't told me much about how his sister died. But before I can ask more about her, he rises and heads for the window, rubbing his arms, despite the mounting heat of the room. He moves closer to the glass, his body tensing as he looks over his shoulder at me. 'There's someone out there.' His eyes return to the window.

I get to my feet and hurry towards him, but by the time I'm standing next to him, there's nothing to see. 'Who was it?'

He's shaking. 'I don't know.'

'Alene?'

'No.' He looks at me, colour draining from his cheeks. 'Someone in a yellow jacket was standing there, staring towards the window.' He rubs his hand over his chin. 'Their face was so white. It looked like a mask, Riona. We need to leave — now.'

'You're right, let's go.' I race towards the lounge door and stop. 'But what about my sister?' *We can't just walk out. What if this person, whoever they are, has Alene somewhere?* 'I'll call the police,' I say, trying to track down my bag.

'I'm going out there. I need to see what they want.' He bolts across the room, pushing past me and out through the lounge door before I can argue.

I follow, watching as he makes his way into the kitchen and rummages through drawers, in cupboards, until he finds a torch. He flicks it on before snatching a knife from the rack. 'We need to get to the root of this. You'll never rest as long as they keep taunting you.'

I grab his arm as he goes to race by me. 'Don't go out there, Tom. You don't know what they're capable of. We need to lock ourselves in the house and call the police.' I spot my bag on the counter, take out my phone, but there's no signal.

He shrugs free, heads down the hallway towards the front door. 'Lock up after me, yeah?'

And then he's gone, the front door slamming closed behind him.

CHAPTER FORTY-NINE

Riona

I run towards the front door, part of me wanting to dash out after Tom, call him back. But self-preservation kicks in. I turn and lean against the door, trembling, my body on hyper alert. I need to check the back door. The thought of this person, who could be the Ensley Killer, coming in that way sends shivers down my spine. I hurry through to the kitchen, relieved to see two bolts are already pulled across the back door.

Back in the lounge, I turn off the light and look out through the window, my eyes skittering across the darkness, over the two towering barns, searching for Tom, my heart thudding. I can't see him, and I wish he hadn't been such a hero.

I move into the hallway, look up the stairs towards the landing, realising I can't see the bathroom from where I'm standing, and a sudden niggle of doubt rises about Tom. *How did he know where the bathroom was?* It's not the first time he's raised my suspicions. I never did find out why he lied about where he was staying. Had he been searching for me in the Fox just over a week ago? Had he asked the landlady who I was? I force down the worry, tell myself I'm being distrustful, that he came to Yew Tree House because he cares about me.

Suddenly I'm climbing the stairs, almost trance-like. Slow and steady, as though pulled by an invisible thread. Halfway up, I run my hand over a mark on the wall – it looks as though someone's scrubbed it hard, taking some of the beige embossed wallpaper with it. At the top I open one of the doors, reach in my hand and fumble across the wall until I find a light switch. I flick it on.

The room is large, and I notice immediately that the windows are barred. The wallpaper is cream with pale pink roses, the carpet shagpile. The bed is six foot at least, with a cream satin canopy fringed with lace. The curtains, quilt and scattered cushions are the same as the wallpaper: cream with pale pink roses.

I move into the room and pick up a gold-framed photo of a dark-haired child of ten or eleven.

A noise downstairs startles me, and the picture slips through my fingers, bouncing onto the dresser. I swing round, knocking a freaky-looking porcelain doll to the floor as I move across the room at speed, flicking off the light as I go, and heading onto the landing. 'Tom? Is that you?'

I creep down the stairs, my breathing quick and shallow. I'm halfway down when the front-door handle rattles up and down. 'Tom?'

I race down the rest of the stairs, my pulse loud in my ears. There's someone on the doorstep, a hue of yellow moving behind the glass. My stomach twists as the handle rattles up and down again. My heart bangs against my ribs. I panic, and dart down the hallway into the kitchen, where I rummage in my bag, dropping the contents as I search for my car keys, the sound of glass shattering in the hall ringing loud in my ears. Finally, I fumble my keys from my bag and yank across the bolts on the back door. I need to get to my car, get out of here. Whatever this person wants from me, I'm not going to stick around to find out.

I hear the front door swing open as I throw open the back door. A shard of freezing air hits me as I stumble out into the night. Disorientated, the only light coming from the house, I follow the grey, prison-like wall, attempting to get round the building to where I parked my car.

Within moments, I hear footsteps behind me, getting closer. I take a swift detour into a copse of trees and make my way deeper into the wooded area, scratching my arms on sharp brambles. Finally, I crouch down in the undergrowth, hiding, acid rising in my throat as I pray they don't see me.

I wait and wait, feeling sick to my stomach, the sound of my ragged breathing too loud in the silence. I wobble, and reach down to support myself, gripping hold of what I think is a tree root. But I instantly know that whatever is beneath my fingers is no tree. It's cold, stiff. I snatch my hand away, shaking uncontrollably. *Oh God.*

I gingerly run my fingers back over the ground, my breath bursting in and out. There's no doubting it. It's a hand, and whoever it's attached to is buried here under the soft earth. I retch, my stomach churning, sweat cold against my forehead.

Sudden footsteps startle me. They're getting closer. I cower, curling into myself as a torch beam flashes across the trees. A glint of a blade catches my eye. Should I get up? Run? But I can't move, the shock has seized my body, and I seem to be getting smaller and smaller, a tiny mouse afraid of a cat.

'Riona?'

It's Tom, shining a torch in my face.

I blink, blinded. 'Thank God.' I pull myself up, stumbling into his arms, pushing my face against his chest. I'm afraid, so afraid.

'What are you doing out here?' he says, his eyes wide as I release him. 'I saw you run into the trees. You should have stayed in the house.'

'Did you see . . .' I cry, unable to get my sentence out.

He looks about him. 'No, but—'

'Someone got into the house, Tom.' My voice is shaky, my body alive with fear. 'And someone's buried here.' I point to the ground, and he flicks the beam of his torch across the disturbed earth, his eyes widening as he sees the hand. 'We need to get out of here, Tom. Now.'

He takes hold of my hand and pulls me through the copse of trees, towards the driveway. 'We'll take my car,' he says, once we're on the drive. He unlocks the doors with his fob. 'This has to end here. It's gone too far.'

I see it before he does. The tyres on his Mini, and those on my car too — all slashed, as though someone deranged has hacked them with a knife. 'Jesus, what the hell are we going to do?'

'It's OK, Riona. When I was chopping wood I noticed a Fiat in the barn.'

'Alene's car,' I whisper as he pulls me along, but I'm not sure I trust him anymore.

He opens the barn door and flashes his torch towards the shiny, mint-green Fiat 500. But before I can say anything, I sense movement behind us.

The pain across the back of my skull is sudden and excruciating.

The ground rises up to greet me.

Everything goes black.

CHAPTER FIFTY

Bernie

I'm about five miles from Yew Tree House, my shoulders aching from tension, when it hits me. I know who owns the place, remember the address from when we were working on the Ensley Killer case, and a catapult of fear shoots through me. *Why the hell would he invite Alene to his house?*

'Hang in there, cats,' I yell, pushing my foot further down on the throttle as I whiz down dark country lanes, my headlights picking out the frost settling on the hedgerow. 'Almost there.'

Once on a straight stretch of road, I key 999 into the phone pinned to my dashboard. 'Police,' I cry, when the call is answered, my voice breaking with fear. 'It's urgent. You need to come to Yew Tree House in Little Ashley now. My nieces are in danger.'

* * *

Riona

The sickening pounding in my head is unbearable. My feet and hands, numb from the cold, are bound by coarse rope.

It takes a moment to adjust my eyes to the dim lighting, to become aware of three limp figures propped up against the barn wall in the shadows — bound, as I am, with hessian sacks over their heads. Blood thumps in my ears. *Who are they?*

I look towards the closed barn door and across to the figure wearing a yellow hi-vis spattered with fresh blood, a mask covering their face. Whoever it is watching me from behind the plastic has been waiting for me to come round. *Waiting to kill me?*

'What do you want?' The angst inside me is loud, boisterous, but my voice is a frightened whisper. 'Who are they?'

The person behind the mask moves slowly towards me. Touches my face with icy fingers, and I shiver, repulsed. Afraid.

'Are they dead?' I nod towards the motionless figures slumped in the shadows. 'Have you killed them?' Tears spill from my eyes, roll down my face.

A laugh. Tinkling. Cold. 'Not yet, but I will. The truth must come out first, Riona. You all need to know why I'm doing this, otherwise there's no point.'

The voice is familiar, and a memory attached to it flutters around me like a butterfly. And then it lands. Clear. I know exactly who it is behind the mask.

CHAPTER FIFTY-ONE

Riona

The three hostages remain motionless, barely visible in the shadows. *Please be OK, whoever you are.* But it doesn't look good; they are so still, like the waxworks Alene and I saw at Madame Tussauds as children.

I look back at the eerie figure in front of me.

'Mia Carter,' I say. It's not a question. I know it's her. I remember her voice, her Northern accent, from that brief conversation we had in Lola's café so long ago.

She pulls off the mask. 'You remember me?' She sounds flattered.

'Yes, I remember you.' I feel as though I might choke on my words. It never once occurred to me that the person in the yellow hi-vis was a woman. Did it mean Mia killed Kerry Ann White all those years ago? That she was the Ensley Killer?

'It's so good of you to come, Riona,' she says, mist appearing in front of her mouth, hovering for a moment in front of her pale, chapped lips before vanishing.

A slight defiance pushes through. 'It's not like I had a choice.'

She looks over at the three trussed-up people, twirling a strand of her hair around her finger so tightly her skin turns white. 'It was quite a coup to get you all here. I couldn't believe it when my mother arrived.'

'Charlotte?' I whisper, realising one of her hostages must be Charlotte Carter.

'I wasn't sure how I would get to her before she scurried back to Cornwall with my brother, her precious son. I should have killed her straightaway, really, when she arrived at Willow Nook Cottage. But then, what would be the fun in that? She wouldn't have suffered, and I need her to suffer. I need you all to suffer.'

'Why? What have we done to deserve this?'

She places a finger against my lips, and I cringe, shy away. 'All in good time, Riona, all in good time.' She removes her finger and looks at the three lifeless figures. 'My mother was so obliging, following you here. It was all so convenient.' She snaps a look back at me, and however much I want to turn from her stare, I find myself studying her. She looks almost as she did when she came into the café twelve years ago. The same unconditioned hair hanging down her back, the same freakishly pale face. 'He took me,' she says, as though I'm meant to know who she's talking about.

'Who, Mia?'

She digs her thumbnail down hard into the palm of her hand, draws blood. 'You should have helped me.'

'I don't know what you mean. I thought you were in Cornwall.'

Her head snaps up, her eyes meeting mine. 'That's what they wanted everyone to believe.'

'Who?'

'Mother and Ryan.' She moves closer to me, strokes my hair, and I realise her skin is tinged with grey — unhealthy. 'Your hair is quite out of control, Riona, did you know?'

I try to move back, but she moves with me. Continues to stroke my hair, catching her fingers in a tangle, making me wince.

'So where have you been if you weren't in Cornwall?' I ask, trying to keep her focused. If I'm going to die here, I want to know why.

She pulls a pair of scissors from the pocket of the hi-vis jacket.

'Please don't kill me,' I say, grovelling, sounding pathetic. 'Just tell me what happened, Mia. Let me help you.'

'No one can help me,' she says, and taking a strand of my hair between her thumb and forefinger, she snips it off. I flinch as it falls to the floor, a shiver running across my neck.

'Where's Tom?' I say, looking over at her prisoners.

'Oh, he's not over there, Riona, if that's what you're thinking.' She takes another strand, pauses mid-snip, the scissors wide. 'He's not on my list.'

'Your list?'

'Everyone on my list must pay. But Tom, well, he's one of the good guys. I like Tom. Tom doesn't need to be punished.'

My thoughts swing to the man I once thought I could trust. 'You know him?'

'That's no concern of yours.' She puts the scissors back in her pocket, and I let out a breath.

'What did we do to you, Mia?' My eyes fix once more on her hostages, trying to work out if one could be my sister, catching sight of a pearl pendant around the neck of the middle figure. 'Alene?'

Mia looks to where my gaze has fixed. 'Ah, you've guessed it — ten out of ten. Go to the top of the class.' She lets out a peal of crazed laughter. 'Yes, she's there. Can you guess which one?' She says it like I'm taking part in a game show. 'Poor, gullible, Alene. I remember following her and Ryan back in 2009. They thought they were being secretive, but I knew. I know everything. Alene really thought Ryan wanted to come back into her life and sweep her off her feet. Shame I'm going to have to kill her.'

'She has a son, Mia — a little boy . . .' I want to add *your nephew*, but would that make things worse? 'What did she ever do to you?'

She rolls her eyes, as though my questions are merely an irritation. 'Alene was just a pawn to lure you here, Riona.' Her smile is manic. 'She'll have to die, of course. You all have to die. I can't leave loose ends, that would be incredibly careless.'

CHAPTER FIFTY-TWO

Riona

'He found me that day,' Mia says after a silence.

'Who found you?' I wiggle my wrists. Feel the rope gnawing into my skin as it loosens. 'What are you talking about?'

Tears shine in her eyes. 'He pulled me out of the water. At first I thought I was safe. Thought it was Ryan, saving me.' A pause. 'But when he shoved his big hand over my mouth, I knew I wasn't safe at all.' She stares deep into my eyes. 'You could have done something, Riona. You should have done something that night.'

'How, Mia? How could I have done something?'

'You were there in the boathouse, twelve years ago. You, Stacey and Erika came in, looked around. Blew out the candle. You must have heard me struggling in his grip, trying to get away.'

I recall the night vividly and suddenly feel sick. Had I heard something? 'I don't remember hearing you that night, Mia. If I had, I would have done something. Honestly.'

'You left me there, Riona, and he took me away. Here to this awful house.' Her voice is growing in volume. 'He made me spend the next twelve years in a room with bars at the window. Here in hell.'

'Who, Mia?' I say. 'Who kept you here?'

'He did. But it's OK. He's dead now. Gone for ever.'

I think of the makeshift grave I found earlier. Has she killed her captor?

'When you girls came into the boathouse I kept thinking, *they'll save me*, but you didn't. You didn't.'

'We didn't know you were there, Mia. If we had we—'

'Too late.'

'Oh God, why are you doing this?' I sound frantic, desperate. 'You said yourself he's gone, you can move on with your life now. If you let us go, we can get you help.'

'He would have killed me eventually, if we hadn't got to him first.'

We?

'Who, Mia? Who did you kill?'

'There was so much blood that day — so difficult to clean up.' She shook her head. 'There's a stain on the carpet at the foot of the stairs. I couldn't get it out, however hard I tried.'

My eyes skitter across the barn, the rope around my wrists loosening further. Tools are propped against the walls. A car is parked in the corner, a grubby sheet thrown over it, one wheel arch in view — a red car. *The car used in the hit and run?*

'Yes, that was me,' she says, looking to where my eyes have landed. 'I didn't intend to kill you that day. Just scare you. I called your phone to distract you, and the rest was easy. Even coming into the hospital was a doddle.'

'Mia.' A small voice echoes from the corner.

Mia swings round, moves towards one of the figures and pulls off the hessian sack. Charlotte's head is slumped to one side, blood caked on her forehead, matted in her blonde curls.

'Hello, Mother,' Mia says, pulling the scissors from her pocket. 'You are quite the survivor, aren't you? I thought that metal bar against your skull had taken you out.'

'I thought you were dead,' Charlotte blurts, her voice husky, laced with panic. 'You have to believe that. I saw you go under the water, you didn't come up — I can't swim, Mia.'

'Ryan can.'

'It was dangerous in there. I didn't want to lose you both.'

Mia's eyes shine with tears. 'You never told a soul.' Mia clenches the scissors. 'When I turned up on Gran's doorstep a few weeks ago she said she thought I was in Cornwall with you and Ryan. She was shocked to see me. Though not as shocked as she was when I pushed her down the stairs.'

'You killed your gran?' Charlotte's voice is high with anxiety. 'Why? Why would you do that?'

'Oh, come on. She wasn't a good person. You must have been relieved to see the back of her.'

Tears roll down Charlotte's cheeks. 'I've created a monster.'

Mia crouches down, moves her face close to hers. 'So that must make you Frankenstein.'

'Did you send me the email about the development?'

'Of course.' Mia stands up straight. 'It wasn't that difficult to get into Gran's email account. Her password was flimsy. I needed you to return, Mother, so I could kill you. I'd hoped Ryan would come with you, that I could kill him too, but it seems he's in hiding. But I will find him. I will kill him.' She glances back at me. 'And it didn't take much to get my head round Instagram either, and set up an account to mess with your heads, Riona.'

'Please let me go, Mia. Please, darling,' Charlotte says. 'We can get you help.'

'Darling?' She laughs, hysterically, too loud, an echo of her insanity bouncing around the barn. 'I'm not your darling. You left me—'

'But I keep telling you, I thought you were dead. Ryan—'

'Precious, perfect Ryan,' she spits.

'Please, Mia. Your brother and I have been through hell.'

'You've been through hell?' Mia screams, her face distorting. 'What do you think I've been through?'

'But I didn't know.'

'You'll get caught, Mia,' I say, my wrists springing free, though my ankles are still tied. 'You'll never get away with this.'

She swings round. 'I don't care. My life is over anyway.'

'But it doesn't have to be, not if you stop now.'

Charlotte attempts to move. 'We can come back to Ensley. Ryan and I can take care of you, Mia.'

'I've killed people. No court will let you and your precious Ryan look after me.'

'You have to end this now,' Charlotte cries. 'Please.'

Mia laughs. 'You'll never understand what it's like to take a life.'

'Oh, but I do,' Charlotte whimpers. 'I came so close to killing your stepfather several times.'

Mia kneels down in front of her mother, her hand tight around the scissors. 'But then Ryan did that for you.'

'What?'

'I saw him push Gordon from that cliff, Mother. My stepfather — the closest thing I ever had to a father. I loved him. And he loved me, when you never did. But you were both set on taking him from me.'

'But I did love you,' Charlotte cries. She turns from her daughter's anger, a look of shame on her face that says maybe she never did.

'Ryan took Gordon away from me,' Mia yells, spittle flying from her mouth. 'I couldn't prove it, but I saw him, I saw them fighting — shouting — and then Ryan pushed him.' She jolts forward, pins the scissors to her mother's throat. Charlotte lets out a gasp of fear and pain as Mia pushes the scissors deeper into her flesh, piercing her skin, drawing blood. 'The scream I heard when Gordon fell haunts my nightmares.'

* * *

Charlotte

I feel sick, dizzy from Mia's earlier attack, my mind whirring. Had Ryan killed Gordon? Had he gone on to attack those young women, kill Kerry Ann? I think how Mia killed her gran, pushed her down the stairs, how she's set to kill again without remorse. They are twins. The same genetic make-up. Have they both got a twisted gene?

I glance at Riona, see her hands are free, that she's scrambling to untie her ankles. Mia goes to turn.

'Forgive me,' I yell, trying to keep her attention.

She smiles, slowly pulls the scissors away from my throat. 'No can do, I'm afraid.' As she throws her arm into the air, gripping the scissors with force, aiming the point once more at my neck, I close my eyes, accepting my fate. It's no more than I deserve. 'You should have saved me, Mother,' she says, her voice calm. 'And yet you chose to do nothing.'

CHAPTER FIFTY-THREE

Bernie

'Quiet, sweeties,' I say to the cats mewing on the back seat, as I pull up behind a car bumped up on the verge opposite Yew Tree House. 'We're here now.'

There's no sign of the police yet, but they shouldn't be long. My sensible side is saying to wait in the car, but I've never been sensible. Not where the safety of my nieces is concerned.

I climb out of the car. I know this house, recall the red Fiesta parked on the drive when I arrived here in 2009 to tell Colin White his daughter had been murdered. The connection to Kerry Ann White's murder is unsettling. What possible reason could Alene have to come to this monstrosity of a place?

I lock the car and snatch up a gnarled fallen branch from the side of the road. Leaving the cats on the back seat, I head across the road and onto the drive, where I notice the slashed tyres on Riona's car and a yellow Mini.

Someone's lying face down at the edge of the property, and I hurry over, take the man's pulse. He's alive but unconscious. Blood's drying on the back of his head. I race back to my car to get a blanket from the boot, pulling my phone from my pocket as I go. There's one bar, the signal poor, but it's enough to call an ambulance.

The front door stands open, and, once I've covered the man, I go to step forward, but a noise in one of the barns distracts me. A beam of light shines from under the door. I turn and race towards it, conscious I'm not as young as I once was, but somewhere inside me is the determined, fearless Detective Inspector Foley I once was. I grip the stick in a tight fist and approach.

The scream from inside the barn is loud and shrill, and I pick up speed, dashing across the drive and throwing open the barn door. I dart my eyes across the scene in front of me, trying to take everything in.

'Bernie, thank God,' Riona cries. She's sitting on top of a woman with long dark hair, pinning her to the floor, a pair of scissors spread-eagled on the ground beside her.

'The police are on their way,' I say, bending down next to my niece, taking in the woman beneath her. She looks around thirty, is dressed in a blood-spattered hi-vis and seems to be fixed in some sort of trance.

'I've got this,' Riona says, bringing the woman's hands behind her back and wrapping rope around her wrists. 'Help them.'

I rise, and with a creeping dread, turn to see three people huddled together in the shadows, tied up, two with hessian hoods over their heads. I race across the barn, registering a badly battered woman with blonde curly hair who I recognise as Charlotte Carter. I pull the hessian bags from the other two people, my heart beating far too fast, my hands shaking. 'Oh God.' It's Alene and Stacey.

'This is my fault,' Charlotte whispers, as I release the women, taking first Alene's pulse, then Stacey's.

'Are they OK?' Riona cries. 'Is Alene OK?'

'Unconscious, but alive,' I call across the barn, my voice breaking as the sound of distant sirens reaches my ears.

* * *

'Come along, Mia,' an officer says, leading her towards a police car in handcuffs.

'Mia died a long time ago,' she says, narrowing her eyes and turning to look at me. 'I took care of Erika's cats,' she says. 'I'm not a bad person.'

'What?' I say, gulping lungfuls of freezing air, shivering with the cold. But she's gone, being lowered into the police car.

Tom and Charlotte have been taken away in an ambulance, and Stacey and Alene sit on the back of another vehicle, both pale and bewildered, wrapped in foil blankets.

'I need to get home to Minnie,' Stacey says as I approach. 'I can't go to hospital, she'll wonder where I am.' Her eyes are manic with worry. 'She's been alone for far too long.'

'Why not give me your key? I'll check on her,' I say, holding out my hand.

'I haven't got it.' Her voice breaks. 'The back door will be open. Mia attacked me in my garden. I was having a cigarette. Next thing I knew I was banging and screaming to get out of the boot of her car.'

I place my hand on hers. 'Try not to think about it. I'll make sure Minnie is OK. Please don't worry.'

I move my gaze to Alene. She's looking down at her fingers, cracks her knuckles on her left hand then on her right, the sound of her joints popping loud to my ears.

'I just thank God you messaged me to come,' I say.

She lifts her head, narrowing her eyes. 'I didn't.'

'You didn't?' But even as I say it, I realise Mia must have messaged me from my sister's phone to lure me here.

'I arranged to meet Ryan here, but when I arrived the door was open,' she says. 'There was no sign of him, so I hung up my coat, got out my phone to message him, and the next thing I knew I was in the barn, tied up, a bag over my head. Mia must have knocked me out.' She lowers her head once more. 'I now know Mia sent me the letter pretending to be Ryan — she must have sent me all the texts too — must have known I went out with him all those years ago. That's how she knew things I thought only Ryan could know. I can't believe I was such a fool, so gullible to think Ryan was back and wanted to—'

'You're not a fool at all. She was clever, Alene. Driven by revenge and anger.'

Bernie approaches, her face full of anxiety, but I see it's more than that — there's sadness in her eyes. 'There's something you need to know, Riona,' she says, taking hold of my hands and squeezing. 'And it's not going to be easy to hear.'

CHAPTER FIFTY-FOUR

Riona

Monday, 20 December 2021

Mrs Danielsson asked me to sing my father's Irish ballad at Erika's funeral. She knew how much we loved singing it together, and although I said yes, now I can barely keep a limb still. The thought of getting up in front of the congregation feels impossible. But I have to do this. I have to do this for Erika.

The celebrant's words sound fuzzy, inaudible, but when Bernie squeezes my hand I know it's time for me to go to the front. 'You'll be OK,' she says.

'Erika was my amazing friend,' I begin. Somehow I've found my way to the lectern, though now facing the mourners, my vision is blurred. 'She gave so much, wanted to help those who suffered from the devastating effects of grief.' I can't help but see the irony right now.

After two false starts, I begin to sing, imagining Erika beside me, smiling up at me. I can almost hear her Swedish lilt caressing the words my father wrote so many years ago in Ireland. A warm glow descends, and suddenly Erika is here with me, in my head, in my heart, telling me she always will be, just as my parents are. *Life will go on, Riona. However tragic, however terrible today seems, you will find strength — you have to, for me, so that my loss isn't in vain. Keep strong for Alene and Kieran, who need you, and for Bernie too, but most of all for yourself.*

After the service, we move outside, and I drift away from the friends and family who are talking to Erika's mother, offering condolences, and make my way into a clump of trees, where, out of sight of everyone, I sob into my hands. 'I'm so sorry, Erika.' I'm struggling to be strong. The sickness inside me, at the thought of her trapped in the cellar, feels as though it will never go away. All those texts I received, thinking they were from her, I now know were from Mia pretending to be my lovely friend. I wish now, as I pat my eyes with a screwed-up tissue, that I'd demanded to see Erika, not accepted her pleas to be left alone. I will never forgive myself for that.

'I can't be strong yet, Erika,' I say, my voice breaking. I brush the back of my hand across my eyes. 'But I will be.' I look towards the pale blue sky, the patchwork of white fluffy clouds. 'I promise.'

* * *

We're in Ensley Village Hall. Erika's mother hired the premises, normally used for a playgroup, for my friend's wake. The paintings that cover the walls — presumably the work of three-year-olds let loose with powder paint — feel jarring against the sadness.

I sit between Alene and Stacey. Stacey is holding Minnie close; I'm surprised she didn't bring the little dog to the actual funeral. She collected her before we came here, has barely let the pooch out of her sight since that awful day at Yew Tree House.

I feel safe wedged between the two of them, holding a cheese sandwich I really don't want to eat in one hand and glass of Prosecco in the other. The Prosecco feels wrong too. Fizz is for fun times and celebrations, but still Erika's mother poured the sparkling liquid into our tall glasses. 'To celebrate Erika's life,' Mrs Danielsson had said, her eyes red and puffy, her voice cracking with emotion.

'I still can't believe everything that's happened,' Alene says, running her hand across her mouth as though trying to shield her sadness. My sister has been through everything a thousand times, as we all have. I guess this is something we will need to talk about over and over, until we know the words off by heart. And then we will attempt to rub the words out. But by then they will have been so deeply written into our psyche, erasing them will be impossible.

I put my glass on the table in front of us, and Stacey takes hold of my hand, as though sensing where my thoughts have drifted. As though knowing that's where they'll be for a very long time to come.

'We will get through this,' she says, and I try for a smile. Thank God we have each other.

Mia has been charged with the murders of her grandmother, Erika and Colin White, but the death of Kerry Ann White, and the attacks on the other women in 2009, remain unsolved, the police concluding that Mia used the original case to strike more fear into Stacey and me.

Mia shared her story with the police of how Colin White had been at Quarry Lake the night Stacey, Erika and I had been there, the night Ryan and Mia fought, and she fell into the freezing water. She claimed Colin told her, long before he died, that he was there, leaving a bunch of fresh flowers for his daughter. It's thought he may have been watching Stacey, Erika and me, though I guess we'll never know for sure. Mia repeated to the police what she'd told me, that she had been relieved when Colin pulled her out of the lake, but then he'd held her tightly, covered her mouth — *called her Kerry Ann.* She explained how he locked her in Kerry Ann's old room at Yew Tree House as a replacement for his daughter. It's thought that losing his wife, followed by the murder of his only daughter, had irreparably disturbed him.

I've tried so hard to think back to that night when we were knocking back cider, laughing, sharing secrets. I often imagine how scared Mia must have been, trapped in that man's strong arms, fearing for her life. I go over how she was forced to stay in that room with the barred windows, in that ugly, cold house, for twelve years with a man who was convinced he'd got his daughter back. But none of it excuses what she did once she was finally free.

Bernie keeps going over the case, still desperate to know who killed Colin White's daughter, who started the chain of events, and why Mia chose to pretend to be the Ensley Killer when stalking Stacey and me — it's unfathomable.

I told the police how I heard Mia say 'we' when she talked about burying Colin White, but Mia denies ever saying it, insists nobody else was involved in the man's death.

Tom has gone back to Norfolk, to Agatha and Christie and his dog-walking business. I'm not sure I will ever see him again. Time will tell, I suppose. But for now, romantic relationships are so far from my thoughts. I need to find myself again. Try to find a way to cope with the loss of my friend, and everything that's happened.

'He's in Ensley,' Alene says now, taking a sip of her orange juice.

'Who is?' But I know who she means. Stacey pointed him out to me. In fact, I remember him approaching me on the day I met Stacey at Lola's café. He'd asked how Alene was. A nice-looking man, though thin and drawn, as though life had chewed him up and spat him out.

'Ryan Carter.' Alene half smiles, as though his name evoked a tiny jolt of happiness. 'He's moved into Janet Grayson's house, apparently.'

'How do you know?'

'Charlotte came round to see me last night.' She gazes into my eyes. 'You told her, didn't you? About Kieran.'

'I'm so sorry. I was so angry with her at the time, and—'

'It's OK, Riona.' She touches my arm gently. 'Kieran has a right to know who his father is. I should never have kept it from him. No more secrets.'

'No more secrets,' I say with a smile. 'Does Ryan know about Kieran?'

She nods. 'Charlotte warned me he's troubled, takes medication for mental health issues. She blames herself for that.'

'People can get better with help,' I say. 'He's been through so much.'

'She said too that he's been to the police about the death of his stepfather. Apparently they had a fight, and he fell to his death.'

'What will you do? About Ryan, I mean.'

She shrugs. 'Take one day at a time.'

CHAPTER FIFTY-FIVE

Tom

Thursday, 23 December 2021

'Hey Aggie,' Tom says, as a heavy bundle of Staffordshire terrier tears down the frosty path to greet him. Aggie is a rescue dog. She is grateful for Tom's love and returns it unconditionally. Tom crouches and pours his affection onto the animal; it goes some way towards cleansing his troubled soul. 'Where's Christie?' he says, as a white Cavachon appears in the doorway wagging her tail. Tom rises. 'So I guess I'll have to come to you if I want a hello,' he says to the second dog, dragging his case towards the front door.

His mum appears, a small woman, a scarf around her head. Tom believes the cancer was brought on by the trauma she's been through, knows she'll never get over losing Becky.

She smiles a rare smile. 'It's good to see you, Tom,' she says, pulling herself up onto her toes and kissing her son's cheek. 'You were away so much longer than you said you'd be.' She nods down at the dogs. 'We've missed you.'

'I had to stay. Things didn't quite go to plan.'

Her eyes brighten for a moment, and he sees in her face how desperately she wants things to be normal. 'What's her name?'

He shakes his head, steps into his mum's terraced house. 'It wasn't like that.' But it was, it was just like that. He can't get Riona out of his head. Fell for her big time, which wasn't meant to happen. All he'd intended to do was look out for her, after everything he knew, but his feelings for her grew. He knows now it can never work out between them. He's thought of every scenario in his now-tired brain, and it can never be. He told her too many lies that he can never go back on — from the stupid white lie that he was staying with an aunt and uncle, an attempt to make his reasons for being there more plausible, to the huge lies that he can never whisper. She would never understand. Maybe he should have told her everything from the off, but then how could he?

'Something smells good,' he says, leaving his case in the hallway, and, followed by a dancing Aggie, he enters the cosy lounge.

'I've made a casserole,' his mum says. 'When I got your message, I thought you might be hungry after the long journey. You will stay, won't you? Not just collect the dogs and run?'

'Of course I'll stay, Mum. I would never pass up one of your casseroles.'

'Cup of tea?' She's keeping upbeat, despite the last year, and every year for the last twelve. The toing and froing to ICU, the glimmers of hope, the shards of pain. Tom glances at the photo of Becky on the dresser, her smile so bright, her dark hair pulled back in a high ponytail. It was taken just before she was attacked in Ensley in 2009, when there was still sparkle in her blue eyes.

'Let me get the tea,' he says. But she shakes her head, determined, and disappears into the kitchen.

As his mother clatters around filling the kettle, finding mugs, Tom's mind drifts to the moment his sister died — a trigger moment, the very second he decided he had to find out who left Becky bleeding out on the pavement. Her head injury was severe, causing first coma, followed by brain damage.

He hadn't expected his search to end so tragically. If he could go back and do things differently, he would.

It all started with a visit to Colin White.

They had both lost someone to the killer. It would be good to talk to him — someone who understood — or so he thought. Tom believed the man might share something with him that he didn't already know, something that would lead him to the killer.

It was late November when Tom pulled onto the drive of the giant, ugly Yew Tree House in Little Ashley. A cold night when he climbed from the car, crunched across the drive, passing a red Fiesta, and rang the doorbell.

The door was opened by an overweight man of average height, his hairline receding, greying at the temples, and what hair he did have was oiled back from his lined face.

'Colin White?' Tom asked, stepping from foot to foot, glancing about him at the barns, the surrounding trees, the encroaching shadows.

'Yes?' The man's pale grey eyes were steady, as though if he slipped from Tom's gaze he would panic. There was the distinct smell of alcohol on his breath.

'I'm Tom Evans. My sister was Rebecca Evans, a victim of the Ensley Killer.' The words felt painful on his tongue. 'I understand you lost your daughter too.' He paused to take a breath. 'The thing is, I'm going through hell right now, and needed to talk to someone who would understand what I'm going through.'

The man's face morphed into a smile. 'Come in,' he said, beckoning him, and leading the way into the lounge. 'Whisky?'

'Just the one, cheers.' Tom lowered himself into an armchair, his eyes scanning the room: a full bookshelf, a framed photo of a young woman with dark hair standing next to Colin. 'Your daughter,' Tom asked.

Colin picked up the photo. 'Yes, this is my Kerry Ann.'

He put the picture back down and splashed amber liquid into two crystal glasses, handed one to Tom. 'So, your sister was attacked,' he said, sitting down.

Tom nodded. 'She died recently.' His voice cracked. 'A direct result of the assault.'

'I'm sorry to hear that.' Colin took a long gulp of his drink. 'You never get over it. Losing someone you love.'

'No. No you don't.'

Colin tapped the crystal glass against his teeth, keeping his eyes firmly fixed on Tom. 'So, how do you think I can help you?'

Tom fidgeted, suddenly unsure why he was there. 'I just—'

'What? Want to get through this? Want to feel normal again? Want to strip away the agonising pain?'

Tom shifted forward in his seat, put down his drink. 'Maybe I've made a mistake coming here.'

'You're looking for closure, Tom, and there's no such thing. Kerry Ann's been gone twelve years, and it never gets any easier.' He leaned forward, placed a hand on Tom's leg. 'Tell me something — if you found the killer, would you punish them?'

Tom had asked himself that question over and over, through the years. And he'd known, in his darkest moments, if he'd found the person who took Rebecca from him, from his parents, he would kill them without a second thought. *A life for a life.* 'Maybe,' he whispered, not proud of his words.

Colin brushed his hand across his chin, swirling the whisky around in the glass. 'Trouble is, so many get off these days, don't they? When they're caught, some band of do-gooders will start arranging appeals, or making documentaries, and before you know it, they're back out in society on a technicality, ready to kill again.'

Tom started to feel uncomfortable. Colin White was intense. The loss of his beloved daughter had clearly affected his mental health. And Tom understood, but his own well-being was fragile, and chatting with this man was pushing all kinds of buttons. 'I should go,' he said, about to rise. 'I have to get back.'

Colin put down his drink. 'No, stay. Please.' He raised his arm, a chunky gold bracelet slipping down his wrist as he gripped Tom's shoulder. 'I haven't spoken to anyone about Kerry Ann's death for so long.'

'I'm sorry. I shouldn't have come.' Tom pulled away from Colin's grip. 'This was a mistake.' He made his way into the hall, towards the front door.

'Help me, please!' The female voice came from upstairs. Tom stopped, looked up towards the landing.

'Who's up there?' he called.

Colin appeared. 'It's my daughter,' he said, following Tom's gaze.

'You have another daughter?'

Colin was silent for a moment as the cries of help continued.

'For God's sake, who is that?' Tom gripped the banister and ascended the stairs two at a time.

Colin followed, took hold of Tom's arm. 'It's none of your business. You're right, you need to leave — you need to leave right now.'

'Help me!' The sound was coming from behind a pad-locked door, but before Tom could move towards it, Colin seized Tom from behind.

The two men began scrambling across the landing, throwing punches, stumbling into the bathroom and back towards the stairs.

'What the hell's going on?' Tom yelled. 'Who's locked in there?'

'It's nobody. It's the TV. I left it on.'

Tom swung a punch, and Colin staggered backwards towards the top of the stairs.

Tom moved forward, grabbed Colin's wrist, but he was heavy. Colin slipped free, his bracelet coming off in Tom's hand as he toppled backwards.

The sight of Colin's flailing arms as he tried to grip the air, the vision of his head slamming hard against the wall as he seemed to fall in slow motion down the stairs, sent shards of fear through Tom's body — he hadn't meant *this* to happen. He hadn't meant for Colin White to be at the top of the stairs one minute, the next lying motionless at the bottom, a pool of blood crawling out from under his head like an army of red ants.

Tom's heart thudded against his ribs, panic searing through him, as he spun on the landing, pacing, dragging slim fingers through his hair. *He should run. Never come back. Nobody would ever know he was here.* He shoved the bracelet in his pocket. He would get rid of it. And the glass in the lounge, he would need to take that too.

'Who's out there?' It was the voice again, small and helpless. 'Colin, is that you?'

Tom's chest tightened. 'No. No, it's not.'

'Can you help me. Please?'

He looked down at Colin's lifeless body and back to the padlock on the bedroom door. He couldn't let this person behind the door see his face. He'd killed a man. *Oh God, he'd killed a man.*

'Please. Open the door. He keeps me locked in here. Please let me out.'

Tom stepped towards the door, pressed his face against the wood panelling. 'Who are you?'

'Can you help me, please? Let me out?' The voice was so small. His thoughts spun to Becky. He couldn't desert this woman, whoever she was.

'I don't want you to be afraid,' he said. 'I won't hurt you.' He looked about him, found a brass ornament, and knocked off the padlock with one, two, three swipes before turning the handle.

Inside, a tall, slim woman of about thirty stood by a barred window, her dark hair wild down her back, her face waxy pale. She was dressed in a grey, shabby tracksuit, the room a blur of pinks and creams. She didn't move, just stared at Tom.

'Are you OK?'

She moved her head, tilted it, her eyes watery.

'Who are you? What's your name?'

'Mia' She moved, looked past Tom. 'Where's Colin?'

'He's at the foot of the stairs — he fell.' Tom gulped, his voice shaky, heart thudding against his ribs. 'It was an accident. I think he's dead.'

'That's good. He's a bad man.'

Tom's thoughts tangled. 'Did he lock you in here?'

She looked upwards, then back at Tom, thought for a moment. 'I was brought here to replace his daughter when she was murdered.'

Tom shook his head. 'Oh God. That's so sick.'

'Indeed it is.' She stared at him for some moments. 'What's your name?' Her voice was calm, even.

'Tom. Tom Evans.'

She glanced out of the window at the endless country-side. 'I like you, Tom Evans.'

'Listen, I'm going to call an ambulance and the police, Mia, and they will come here and help you.'

'That's good.' She moved from the window, passed Tom with short, thoughtful steps, looking back just once as she left the room.

He followed her onto the landing, gripped hold of her arm. 'How long have you been here?'

'Oh, absolutely ages,' she said, pulling free. 'It must be twelve years now.'

They reached the foot of the stairs where Colin was lying. The man groaned. His fingers twitched.

'He's not dead,' Mia said, heading into the kitchen. 'You told me he was dead.'

'Thank God.' Tom pulled out his phone and pressed the screen.

'What are you doing?' Mia was back, looking up at him with wide, vivid-blue eyes.

'Calling an ambulance, the police.'

The young woman's movement was swift. The scissors seemed to appear from nowhere. She plunged the prongs into Colin's chest once, twice, three times, blood spattering her face, her tracksuit, Tom's shirt.

'Christ. God. Stop, for God's sake, stop.' Tom grappled with her wrist, wrestled the scissors from her hand. Threw them across the hallway, where they bounced against the wall out of reach.

'He's better off dead,' Mia said. And despite the flames of anger in her eyes, her tone was still eerily calm. No hint of emotion. 'He belongs in hell.'

Tom should have run at that moment. Should have yanked his shell-shocked body out through the front door and into his car. He should have driven and driven — got as far away from Yew Tree House as he could — but he didn't. He stayed.

'And now your fingerprints are all over the scissors as well as mine,' Mia said, her mouth curling into a twisted smile. 'And, oh dear, you have Colin's blood all over your nice shirt. It looks like we're in this together now, Tom. You and me. For always.'

He stared at her for some time, poor deranged Mia, his head in turmoil — this woman in front of him had been imprisoned for twelve years by a man who had lost his mind after losing his daughter to a killer. 'What if someone comes looking for him?'

'They won't. Nobody comes here, and he retired from the airport years ago.'

He helped Mia to bury Colin White at the back of the house. He helped her to scrub the blood from the carpet at the foot of the stairs, from the wall where the man had hit his head — all the time telling himself that this man had ruined Mia's life because she was in the wrong place at the wrong time.

Tom and Mia made a pact never to tell a soul what had happened at Yew Tree House that night — to go their own ways. She even destroyed the photograph of Colin with his daughter in a fit of rage.

'What will you do now?' he asked her when it was over. He was standing in the hall, the door open, his body shaking from what they'd done. Knowing the horrific memory of digging a hole and throwing the man into it would stay with him always.

'I'll be OK,' Mia said. 'There's a car on the drive. I'll go to Willow Nook Cottage.'

'Willow Nook Cottage?'

'My gran's house.' She paused, stared into his eyes, and he noticed there was nothing there — no spark, no life. 'Thank you for saving me, Tom,' she said. 'I will always be grateful for that. I will never let you down.'

'Are you sure you'll be OK?'

She shrugged. 'Colin told me my mother and brother thought I drowned all those years ago.'

'They'll be pleased you survived.'

'I doubt it.' She took a long deep breath. 'We'll see what happens when I return to Ensley. I have lots of people to see. My gran, my brother, my mother, and I need to track down Riona Foley and her friends.' She paused for a moment. 'They all need to pay for what they did.'

'Pay?'

'Any of them could have helped me.' She stared for a moment. 'Oh, don't worry, Tom. I'm only going to have it out with them, that's all.'

'Where will you say you've been?'

'I won't need to say anything.' She pulled Colin's hi-vis airport worker's jacket from a cupboard and slipped it on, grabbed a set of car keys from a hook. 'I will simply lie in the shadows and wait.'

Now, Tom shudders at the memory of her words, as the sound of his mother putting mugs on the coffee table in front of him brings him back to the moment.

'Here you go, love.' She drops into the armchair, the dogs pouncing onto her lap. 'Get that down you.'

He leans forward, picks up the steaming mug, and blows on it. He heard on the local news that Colin White had been found in the makeshift grave that awful night that Mia tried to take her revenge. He thought he might get a call from the police after that, that Mia would tell them he'd helped her to bury the man, but it seems she's taken the blame for his death and kept him out of it.

He smiles over at his mum, who is fussing the dogs. 'They love you,' he says. *As do I.* He wishes he could tell the truth about everything that's happened, wants to admit to the police about the part he played in Colin White's death, but the fear of what that revelation would do to his already vulnerable mum is too much — so he'll live with the burden that keeps him awake at night.

His mind drifts to Riona. The mess he made of everything. Could he have done more to protect her? Mia had mentioned her name, mentioned making her pay, so he'd tracked her down in the Fox and tried to make sure she was OK — intending to keep a close eye. He'd even gone to see Charlotte Carter – to warn her – but she hadn't listened.

He hadn't expected the complication of falling for Riona — and yet, even then, he didn't tell her the truth, instead convincing himself Mia would never hurt her. But he'd seen how dangerous Mia could be. He should have done more.

He will never forgive himself for that.

CHAPTER FIFTY-SIX

Ryan

Thursday, 23 December 2021

'Mr Carter.' Chief Inspector Blake reaches out his hand for me to shake. 'You wanted to talk to me about the murder in Ensley in 2009. You said it was urgent?'

'It is, yes.'

The DCI gestures to a younger man following us into the interview room. 'This is DS Brown.'

We sit, a small table between the two officers and me. 'I know you worked on the murder case back in 2009,' I say. 'I should have come in a long time ago.'

'You said you have new information.'

'I do, yes. My sister, Mia Carter, has been arrested for three murders.'

'I know about that, yes.'

'Well, you need to add the murder of Kerry Ann White, and the attacks on Rebecca Evans and Clare Marsden to that charge.'

'You think your sister is the Ensley Killer?' He leans forward, elbows on the table, fingers entwined, his eyes widening as far as they can in their heavy sockets.

'I know she is,' I say with conviction. 'Though she planned for it to look like it was me.'

The officers glance at each other, and I see doubt in their eyes, doubt about me. I panic for a moment that this could blow up in my face, as my mind drifts to seeing Mia yesterday at the prison.

'Did you see the article in the paper?' she'd said, jolting forward in her chair, and I leaned back, distancing myself. 'About Colin White taking me, trapping me in that awful ugly house to replace his daughter?' She laughed, the chair creaking as she moved slowly backwards. 'Of course, as you are aware, it's not true. Colin overheard our conversation that night at Quarry Lake. He was laying flowers for his beloved Kerry Ann when he heard me telling you how I attacked those women. How I made it look like it was you.'

I remembered her words from so long ago. How she'd let rip about me killing Gordon, then lowered her voice to a twisted whisper, to tell me what she'd done. Colin must have been there in the shadows, listening — discovering who killed his daughter.

'Colin heard how I wanted to frame you for the murder of Kerry Ann,' Mia continued, 'how I wanted you to pay for killing Gordon, for taking away the only person I've ever loved, the only man who ever understood me.'

'I never meant for Gordon to die,' I said. 'It was an accident, Mia. He attacked me. I retaliated.'

'You pushed him, Ryan.' Her eyes were fixed on mine, vacant, her face serious. 'I saw you with my own eyes. Of course, I couldn't prove it, still can't, so the only alternative was to frame you for another murder — maybe two or three or four. I had it all on your laptop: everything about those women, screenshots of their profiles and your conversations with them. How you lured them to Ensley. I didn't use a photo of you. Didn't want them to catch you until I was ready. Though I couldn't resist putting on the profile how you liked *Iron Man* and metal music. It gave me quite a thrill.'

'But I didn't attack those woman. You know that, Mia.' I was aware of my throat closing, wanting to choke.

'Of course I know that,' she said, twirling a strand of her hair around her finger for some moments. 'I hid your laptop at Willow Nook Cottage. I used your hi-vis too. I cleaned off the blood, but it would still have been covered in Kerry Ann's DNA. And I'd planned to kill again before I dished you up to the police.' She looked down at her hands, her nails bitten ragged, and her silence made the hairs stand up on my neck. She lifted her head sharply, and there was that vacant stare again. 'When I got to the cottage, freed after twelve years, the laptop was gone. Gran told me how she found it, discovered the contents, and destroyed it. She thought you were the killer, Ryan, and protected you, just like Mother. Well, you can imagine how angry I was.'

'Is that why you killed her?'

She shrugged. 'One of the reasons.' There was silence before she added, 'So, back to Colin White. As I say, he didn't take me to replace his daughter, he took me because he knew I'd killed his daughter, and locked me away *where I couldn't hurt anyone else.*'

My body was trembling at her revelations. 'But why didn't he just turn you over to the police?'

She tilted her head to one side, ran a hand over the base of her neck. Her expression was odd, as though her face had morphed somehow. She looked quite deranged. 'I've wondered about that myself,' she said. 'I guess Colin may have heard that I was about to frame you, and realised it would be his word against mine. Or perhaps he simply wanted to punish me in his own way.' Another shrug. 'Who knows? He was as crazy as a box of frogs.' A beat. 'I guess losing someone you love does that to you.' Her mouth twisted into a distorted half-smile, but her eyes were blank, as though nobody was home. 'He was going to kill me,' she continued after a few moments. 'But when it came to it, he couldn't bring himself to. I bet he wishes he had.'

'I don't even know you,' I said. 'I'm not sure I ever did.'

'Nobody does. Not now Gordon has gone.'

I covered my face with my hands, rubbed hard, trying to erase her — my sister, my twin.

'Nobody will ever know any of that, of course,' she said. 'The public will have far more sympathy for me if they believe he kidnapped me to replace his daughter — poor little Mia, trapped by the big bad man. Hashtag "FreeMia" is already trending on Twitter, did you know? Those idiots may even get me out of here. Next stop Netflix.'

I stared at her for a long moment, before rising to my feet, turning my back and walking away.

As I left the prison, the cold air hitting me like a sharp slap, I went over everything again: How Mia told me that night at the lake, just before she crashed into the water below, how she had lured women to Ensley. How she'd worn my yellow hi-vis jacket when she attacked them, how she had enough 'evidence' to ruin me. I went to pieces that night. Knew she had the power to destroy me, and I couldn't do anything to stop it.

So I let her disappear beneath the water. I let my mother whisk me away to Cornwall, where I've been hiding all these years — a scared little boy in a grown man's body, dosed up on mind-numbing medication.

'And you have proof your sister committed these crimes?' The DS brings me back to the moment, leans back in his chair, arms crossed over his muscular body, his look of doubt now rearranged to one of disbelief.

'I do, yes.' I place the phone I smuggled in when I visited Mia yesterday onto the desk in front of them, and press play on the recording, unafraid that they will suspect I killed my stepfather. 'I don't know how admissible it will be in court,' I tell the inspector over my sister's cocky confession. 'I've seen a lot of crime documentaries. It could be considered entrapment, I guess.'

'How the hell did you get the phone through security?' the inspector asks once he's finished listening to the recording.

I raise my shoulders in a shrug. 'It's amazing what you can find out on the web if you dig deep enough.' I push my phone across the table towards him. 'But the main thing is, you now know, without doubt, who the Ensley Killer is.'

* * *

I've been back from the police station for several hours. The house clearance company are here, taking away endless crap my gran accumulated over the years. Mum is renting a flat in Hitchin. She doesn't want to be here in Willow Nook Cottage, where her mother died — where her daughter committed murder. She's struggling to come to terms with what she believes is her fault, and I can't help thinking that perhaps, in some ways, it was. Mum always thought hiding and keeping secrets was OK, but I've come to learn they will always come out — eventually.

As I sit at the oak table in the window, watching men fill a huge skip on the front garden, snowflakes start to fall, tumbling from a pale sky. It will soon be Christmas. We never celebrated as children. Gordon didn't believe in it, and Mum was too afraid to argue.

A cold tear rolls down my cheek, and I bash it away with the back of my hand. Families can make or break you, and mine has broken me. But, I tell myself every day, broken things can be mended — maybe they won't be quite as they once were, but they can still be whole again.

I have a son out there. His name is Kieran. Eleven years old and just setting out in life, but I'm scared my family history could destroy him. I'm afraid if I enter his life, it will ruin him.

Is being capable of taking another's life hereditary? Are killers born or made? Does a killer gene run in families, or is it simply the experiences we suffer that trigger evil? Maybe it's a bit of both. My sister murdered four people, five if you add the tragic death of Rebecca Evans. Was my sister driven to it, or was there a killer fuse already inside her waiting to be lit?

Is it possible that I'm different? I try to remember the details of the night Gordon died. The fight we had, the way we stumbled across that cliff edge, pushing and shoving. The way I yelled at him — manic — so angry for the years he'd abused my mother and me. I don't recall pushing him over the edge, though I will never forget his bloodcurdling scream. If that gene is part of my make-up too, can I really control it if things get too much?

Maybe I will sell the house, move far away from Ensley. The last thing I want to do is hurt Alene — hurt my son.

But as the clearance men throw old newspapers into the skip, I see her making her way down the path towards the house, wearing a beige coat tied a little too tightly at the waist, her dark hair in a shiny, pretty bob. She moves closer, and I see she looks almost as young as she did when she was eighteen — the same, but different — *Alene*. Her eyes meet mine through the window, and she raises her hand. I wave back, batting down a flutter of something I haven't felt for so long. I wonder if I loved her once. Whether I could love her again.

Perhaps I'll stay in Ensley a while to find out.

CHAPTER FIFTY-SEVEN

Riona

Monday, 25 September 2022

As I jog along the pathway that curves around Quarry Lake, I see the weatherworn bench with no plaque. I know now that Charlotte Carter had arranged for it to be erected anonymously in Mia's memory back in 2009 — perhaps out of some sort of guilt. But she couldn't maintain it from such a distance, and couldn't have her daughter's name put on it for fear of revealing that she thought she was dead, so it's been left for thirteen years to the elements.

I sit down, resting my back against the slatted wood, my eyes taking in the still, shimmering water. I remove my earphones and lay my camera on the bench beside me. I picked up the Canon again in the spring for the first time in years, falling in love with photography once more. Sometimes, as I snap the wildlife around Quarry Lake, I feel my dad close by, smiling and nodding his approval.

The autumn sun is warm on my back, and the lake is a beautiful shade of navy, making it impossible to believe the secrets it once held.

Ensley attracted a lot of attention after news broke about Mia Carter's arrest. Her story triggered interest everywhere. Twitter went crazy, particularly with the ridiculous campaign to release her, which came to nothing.

A salvage team moved in in February and excavated some of the old vehicles and equipment from the original quarry that drowned almost a hundred years ago, the findings donated to a vintage excavator trust in Cumbria.

But the most startling find was the skeletal remains of a body, which turned out to be Janet Grayson's husband, who she said walked out on her when Charlotte was six years old. His skull was cracked in several places — by a hammer, they think. Stacey's convinced Janet killed her husband, and that her killer gene was passed on to Mia, but there's no proof of that, and probably never will be.

Aunt Bernie kept Erika's cats. They're still not the friendliest, but they are content sharing a house with Bernie, who forces affection on them whether they like it or not. She's considering setting up a private detective agency at the moment, once she's finished crocheting classes, and if she has time between growing vegetables and winemaking.

Alene is OK. She's been seeing Ryan, but they're taking it slow, and she hasn't had any beauty treatment since that awful night at Yew Tree House. I'm not sure why, or if she'll ever have any more, but she seems happier in her own skin.

Ryan and Charlotte sold Willow Nook Cottage. Charlotte's still living in Hitchin, seeing a counsellor, and Ryan has bought an apartment in nearby Welwyn. Alene told me he was questioned about the death of his stepfather, but nothing came of it. He's seen Kieran a few times, they're making progress, but there's a long way to go before my nephew would ever consider him his father.

Stacey and I meet every six weeks or so for a drink in the Fox, or a coffee at Lola's. We mainly talk about Erika — old times. She's still sorry she let me down all those years ago, grateful that we're friends again. I've forgiven her. It seems trivial to bear a grudge after everything that's happened.

'Hi there.'

I turn to see Tom, two dogs at his side, and I smile. He messaged me a few days ago, asked if we could meet. I decided, as I hadn't seen him since that night at Yew Tree House, we should meet on neutral ground, and the lake seemed the right place.

'It's good to see you, Tom.' I reach out to fuss the dogs. 'This must be Agatha and Christie.'

He sits down beside me. 'I wanted to contact you before now, Riona, it's just . . .' He pauses, looks out at the water.

'Are you OK?' I ask.

He turns, eyes watery. 'My mum died.'

I place a hand over his. 'Oh Tom, I'm so sorry.'

'And I've been talking to the police.'

'The police?'

'There's so much I never told you, Riona, and I don't even know where to begin. But while Mum was alive, I . . .'

'Why not start at the beginning,' I say, knowing already that this won't be easy to listen to. I've pieced together a lot of things about Tom: his sister, it turned out, was attacked by the Ensley Killer, by Mia; Colin White's bracelet was in his car glove compartment; and I'm sure he never met me by chance that night in the Fox before Christmas.

It will be good to know the whole truth, and I'm ready to hear it. And whatever that truth is, I'll be here for Tom — it's clear by his bloodshot eyes and how thin he is that he desperately needs a friend. Maybe, in time, we can be something more. Who knows? Let's take it one step at a time.

THE END

ACKNOWLEDGEMENTS

Thanks so much to Kate Lyall Grant. It's been an absolute pleasure to work with such an amazing editor on *I'm Watching You*. I'm so grateful for all her support.

Thank you to everyone at Joffe Books, including fantastic copyeditor Matthew Grundy Haigh, excellent proofreader Julia Williams, and fabulous cover designer Nick Castle. And thanks must go to Jasper Joffe for giving me the opportunity to be part of the wonderful Joffe Books team.

Sending big thanks, as always, to my lovely friends Karen Clarke and Joanne Duncan for their brilliant support throughout writing *I'm Watching You*.

Thanks to everyone on Facebook, Twitter, Instagram, and, of course, in real life, for being there and cheering me on. I appreciate every single one of you.

Thank you to everyone who reads and enjoys my books. I still find it amazing that people are reading my words as far away as America and Australia. Thanks too, to the brilliant blogging community and lovely reviewers who take the time to give such wonderful reviews.

Big thanks to Liam, Daniel, Lucy and Amy who tirelessly support me, and to my youngest son Luke who's always there to brainstorm my plot, I'm always amazed by his creativity.

Thank you to my mum for rooting for me, and to Cheryl and my dad, who I miss terribly, and my acknowledgements would never be complete without.

And last but never least, thank you, Kev — *I couldn't do this without you.*

Thank you for reading this book.

If you enjoyed it please leave feedback on Amazon or Goodreads, and if there is anything we missed or you have a question about, then please get in touch. We appreciate you choosing our book.

Founded in 2014 in Shoreditch, London, we at Joffe Books pride ourselves on our history of innovative publishing. We were thrilled to be shortlisted for Independent Publisher of the Year at the British Book Awards.

www.joffebooks.com

We're very grateful to eagle-eyed readers who take the time to contact us. Please send any errors you find to corrections@joffebooks.com. We'll get them fixed ASAP.